Mike Bond is a foreign correspondent for the *Financial Times* Business Information and a consultant to London Oil Reports. With his wife, Peggy Lucas, he has also co-authored the *Insider's Guide to Mexico* and the *Insider's Guide to Kenya*.

Mr Bond has engaged in military operations against elephant poachers with Kenyan rangers, and has travelled and explored many thousands of miles of East Africa. He has been a correspondent in Nairobi, Moscow, Eastern Europe and Paris, and a war and human rights correspondent in the Middle East and Latin America.

*Also by Mike Bond*

Fire Like The Sun

# The Ivory Hunters

Mike Bond

First published in 1992
by HEADLINE BOOK PUBLISHING PLC
First published in paperback in 1992
by HEADLINE BOOK PUBLISHING PLC
A HEADLINE FEATURE paperback

10 9 8 7 6 5 4 3 2

ISBN 0 7472 3757 3

Printed and bound in Great Britain by
HarperCollins Manufacturing, Glasgow

HEADLINE BOOK PUBLISHING PLC
Headline House
79 Great Titchfield Street
London W1P 7FN

For Peggy

What truths can there be,
if there is death?
        – Leo Tolstoy

# Prologue

## I

The eland descended four steps down the grassy hillside and halted. He glanced all the way round the rolling golden hills, then closer, inspecting the long grass rippling in the wind, behind him, on both sides, and down to the sinuous green traverse of acacia, doum palms and strangler trees below him where the stream lay. The wind, from the east over his shoulder, carried the tang of drying murram grass and the scents of bitter, pungent shrubs, of dusty, discarded feathers and glaucous lizard skins, of red earth and brown earth, of old scat and stones heating in the midafternoon sun. He switched at flies with his tail, twitched his ears, descended five more steps, and stopped again.

Thirst had dried his lips and eyes, tightened his throat, hardened his skin. Already the rain was drying out of the grass and soil pockets; here only the stream remained, purling between volcanic stones, rimmed by trees and tall, sharp weeds. He circled a thorn bush and moved closer several steps, his spiral grey horns glinting as he looked up and down the valley from north to west, then south, then up the slope behind him.

The shoulder-high thorn bushes grew thicker near the stream. The downslope breeze twirled their strong, dusty scents among their gnarled trunks; the sour smell of *siafu*, warrior ants, prickled his nose. He waited for the comforting twitter of sunbirds in the streamside acacias, the muffled snuffling of warthogs, or the swish of vervet monkeys in the branches, but there were none.

Licking his dry nose with a black tongue he raised his head and again sniffed round the wind, batting at flies with his ears, dropped his jaw and panted. There was truly no bad smell, no danger smell, but the wind was coming down the valley behind him and to get upwind he'd have to cross the stream and there was no way except through the thorn and *commiphora* scrub, which was where the greatest danger lay. He glanced back over his shoulder, gauging the climb necessary to regain the ridge and travel into the wind till he could descend the slope at a curve in the stream and keep the wind in his face. The sun glinting on the bleached grass, bright stones and red earth hurt his eyes; he sniffed once more, inhaled deeply, expanding the drum of thin flesh over his ribs, and shoved into the thorn scrub.

A widowbird exploded into flight from a branch on the far side of the stream and the eland jumped back, trembling. The sound of the stream pealing and chuckling coolly over its rocks made his throat ache. The heat seemed to buzz like cicadas, dimming his eyes. Shaking flies from his muzzle, he trotted through the scrub and

2

bent his head to suck the water flashing and bubbling over the black stones.

The old lioness switched her tail, rose from her crouch and surveyed the eland's back over the top of the thorn scrub. She had lain motionless watching his approach and now her body ached to move; the eland's rutty smell made her stomach clench and legs quiver. She ducked her head below the scrub and padded silently to the stream, picked her way across its rocks without wetting her paws and, slower now, slipped a step at a time through the bush and crouched behind a fallen doum palm part-way up the slope behind the eland, only her ears visible above it.

Far overhead a bearded vulture wavered in its flight, tipping on one wing, and turned in a wide circle. The eland raised his head, swallowing, glanced round; water dripping from his lips spattered into the stream. He shivered the flies from his back, bent to drink, raised his head, water rumbling in his belly. He turned and scanned the slope behind and above him; this was where he'd descended and now the wind was in his face and there was still no danger smell. His legs felt stronger; he licked his lower lip that already seemed less rough from the water filling his body. He trotted back through the thorn scrub past the fallen doum palm, bolting at the sudden yellow flash of terror that impaled him on its fierce claws, the lioness' wide jaws crushing the nape of his neck as he screamed crashing through the bush. With one paw the lioness slapped him to the ground but he lurched up and she smashed him down again, her fangs ripping his throat, choking off the air as his hooves slashed wildly, and the horror of it he knew now and understood, dust clouding his eye, the other torn by thorns; the flailing of his feet slackened as the sky went red, the lioness' hard body embracing him, the world and all he had ever known sliding into darkness.

The lioness sighed and dropped her head, the stony soil hurting her jaw. After a few moments she began to lick the blood seeping from the eland's throat and mouth and the shoulder where her claws had torn it, then turned and licked her left rear leg where one of the eland's hooves had made a deep gash. Settling herself more comfortably among the thorn bushes, she stripped back the skin along the eland's shoulder, licking and gnawing at the blood and warm flesh beneath.

Crackling in the brush made her lay back her ears; she rumbled softly, deep in her throat. Heavy footsteps splashed through the stream and she growled louder, her rope tail switching. The male lion came up to the eland, lifted his lip and snarled.

Still growling she backed away slightly, lowering her head to grip the eland's foreleg. The male sniffed the eland's shoulder, crouched, ears back, and began to chew it. Then, gripping the shoulder in his jaw, he dragged the animal sideways, the lioness crawling after it, still holding the leg. Baring his teeth, the male leaned across the eland's shoulder, bit down on the foreleg and pulled the eland over to get at its belly and flanks. Carefully the lioness edged round the carcass, reaching tentatively for a rear leg. With a roar the male flicked out a huge, flat paw that caught the side of her head. Her neck snapped loudly and the lioness tumbled back into the thorn brush, one rear paw trembling briefly.

The Samburu warrior rose from his hiding place among the rocks high up the slope, stretched his stiff legs and picked up his spear. From the shade he watched the lion's thick, black-maned head burrow into the eland's belly. Since dawn, when the Samburu had begun watching the two lions, the young male and old female, they had mated nearly three times ten, but now he had killed her, giving the Samburu a possible solution to the problem that had been bothering him all day.

## II

The Samburu climbed to the ridge, keeping out of sight of the lion a half mile below, his bare, thick-soled feet silent on the ravelled, stony earth, his goatskin cloak soundless against his slender limbs. Once over the ridge he broke into a run, down a long, wide valley with a *laga*, a dry, sandy stream-bed, against a line of umber cliffs bloodied by the afternoon sun. Where the cliffs became a scrubby talus slope he ascended to a large, spindly desert rose bush with red flowers. He waited till he'd caught his breath, unsheathed his *simi* and began to draw its blade up and down the head of his spear, till both edges glittered and easily shaved the few hairs on the back of his wrist. He sheathed the *simi* and knelt beside the desert rose, cut a downward slash in its stem with his spear, and waited.

Soon a bubble of white sap had collected on the slash. He fitted together the two halves of his spear, thunking the shaft against the earth to seat the top section firmly in the steel haft of the lower one. Then very carefully he drew both edges and the tip of the spearhead along the bubble of sap. He went back down the slope, careful not to touch the spearhead against the brush or bring it near himself.

A gerenuk standing on hind legs to munch at the twigs of an umbrella acacia dropped to all fours and scampered away, halting to look back over her shoulder, but the Samburu ignored her. He reached the *laga* and turned north, walking fast but not running, stepping once over the groove in the sand where a puff adder had crossed his earlier tracks, and he reminded himself to be watchful among the bare rocks warmed by the afternoon sun.

He climbed out of the valley to the ridge and down part-way, smiling when he saw the lion was still there, far below. The lion had dragged the eland's intestines, stomach, and lungs to one side, eaten the liver and both rear legs and flanks, and was now lying belly down and holding the eland's head and chest with his paws as he ripped strips of muscle from its neck.

The Samburu checked the sun now a forearm's length above the western hills. He sniffed the wind, which had scurried round and now came upstream from the lion, towards the thick scrub below him. But once the sunlight had climbed above the stream-bed this would reverse, and the cooling air further upstream would begin to descend from him towards the lion.

Again he estimated the distance from the lion and the eland carcass to a single doum palm standing upstream of them, whose first fork could be reached quickly and whose trunk was strong enough to withstand the lion's lunge and too vertical for him to climb. And again the Samburu felt doubt and fear and once more estimated the distance between the lion and the tree.

Keeping the spearpoint well ahead of him, he crept on hands and knees down the slope, into the failing wind. Thorns caught on his skin and sank into his palms and he extracted them noiselessly, breathing as quietly as possible, holding the spear free of the ground so it would not clink on stones, always conscious of the pressure of the wind against his face.

With a crunch of bones the lion severed the eland's foreleg from the shoulder. The Samburu moved closer, fearing the pounding of his heart, hearing the rip of connective tissue as the lion pulled muscle from the eland's ribcage and, muttering contentedly, gulped it down. Ahead of him the Samburu could see the doum palm rising above the scrub; the wind in his face died, his pulse thudding in his ears.

On hands and knees, weaving the spearpoint ahead of him through the thick and tangled thorn scrub, holding down one by one the blades of pale bunchgrass as he moved across them, detaching each finger-length thorn that sank into his skin or cloak, keeping as much as he could to the fiery but quieter stones that seemed to whisper into the soil when he placed his weight upon them, he reached the doum palm as sunlight left the valley floor and began to climb the slope.

A touch of wind ran up his back and he tensed to run, but the lion did not snarl or charge, must not have caught his smell. More insistently the breeze returned, flowing down the stream as the sun dropped it into shadow. The Samburu stood, spear drawn back, the sap-coated point beside his eye. Twenty paces ahead, the lion's shoulders rippled huge and tawny as he stripped connective tissue from the eland's ribs, his back muscles flexing down into his thick back legs, his triangular ears kittenish above the mass of black mane. The Samburu darted forward, hurled the spear, and dashed back to the palm, his cloak sailing as he scrambled up the scaly trunk to the first fork and the lion crashed roaring against the trunk and leaped up it, a bough above the Samburu's head snapping with the lion's impact on the trunk and spinning outwards and splashing into the stream. All this the Samburu saw clearly, slowly, as if it took no time, was timeless, the lion's huge white teeth, red tongue, yellow furious eyes, the impossibly broad square jaws framed in its colossal black mane nearing as the lion thrust himself up the trunk, his front paws the size of a man's belly, their yellow curved claws shattering bark as they dug into the wood. The Samburu snatched his *simi* and leaned downwards, as if to cut this forepaw wider than his thigh, seeing now the spear hanging from the lion's side, its head sunk between his ribs.

Unable to hold his weight the lion slid back down, wood chunks showering him. He growled, deep and disconsolate, turned and snapped off the spear with his teeth, padded back to the eland and darted a few steps after two black-backed jackals that fled through the bush. He glared at the Samburu, sniffed the eland, and streaked through the scrub to collide again against the doum palm. The Samburu lost his grip as the trunk snapped down then whipped back, his *simi* flying, bark slipping through his fingers, but he clenched his ankles round his branch, a huge paw whistling past his head as he twisted back up, grabbed the trunk and stood on the branch. The lion slid back to the ground.

Again he chased the jackals from the eland. He seemed to trip, righted himself, jerked his head round and began to lick at his wound. This did not satisfy him and he squirmed to lick beneath his tail, plodded to the stream, drank, fell down climbing the bank, returned to the eland and resumed eating. After a few moments he stood as if hearing something from afar, jerked spasmodically, and fell. He dragged himself on forelegs towards the stream, wavered to his feet, turned his wide-maned, bitter face in a roar of rage at the Samburu, toppled over the lioness, and lay still.

Sunlight had fled to the upper eastern slopes. To the north, across the vast, empty Suguta Valley, the sky shifted steadily from cobalt to blood and lavender; doves called from the candelabra euphorbias, 'And you too? And you too?' A honeyguide fluttered past the doum palm, alit on a higher branch, and cocked its head expectantly down at the Samburu. 'Come with me!' it twittered. 'Honey! Honey! Come with me!' A string of puffball cumulus trooped across the eastern sky, nose to tail like elephants, sunset reddening their flanks, as if they'd been rolling, as elephants once did, in the ochre desert dust of the Dida Galgalu.

Furtive, then more assured, the jackals returned, barking their alarm calls at each bird's flutter or whisper in the wind, glancing often at the motionless lions while they chewed hurriedly on the eland.

The Samburu slipped down the doum palm, found his *simi* and edged closer to the lions. He threw a large rock that thumped against the male's head, making the jackals bark, but the lion did not move. The jackals did not back away, one standing proprietorially atop the eland's ribs. An owl called from the downstream darkness.

The Samburu threw several more rocks but the lion seemed truly dead. Gathering up his cloak and holding his *simi* before him, he moved closer, the lions now a single fawn-coloured mass in the gathering gloom. He poked the *simi*'s point into the lion's eye: yes, he was dead.

It took all his strength to roll the lion on to his back. With the *simi* he slit down the centre of the lion's lower jaw, down his neck, the centre of his chest and belly and back to his testicles and the root of his tail, and started to free the skin on both sides from the stomach and ribs.

The moon rose yellow as maize, deformed like a melon that has lain too long on one side. On the ridge beneath the moon a clan of hyaenas yodelled like demon children; the Samburu paused to wipe his *simi*, looked up but could not see them. He dragged the male lion's carcass free of his pelt, went to the dead eland and sliced long strips of skin and sinew from the two unchewed legs, folded the lion's pelt, lashed it with the sinew, and carried it on his back to the palm. With a long strap of sinew sections he pulled the pelt up into the fork of the tree, returned and began to skin the lioness.

The hyaenas had circled from the east around the southern upper end of the valley, crossing his trail. Now they were coming fast along the west side, halfway up that slope. Soon they would pick up his scent again, and the eland's, and begin to close in.

Hurriedly he gathered dry leaves from the base of a thorn bush, and with his *simi* cut thin strips of bark from a small tamarind tree. These he piled near the lioness; then he ran to an umbrella acacia and snapped twigs from the edge of its canopy where giraffes had browsed the leaves and killed the branches. Something black moved through the grey scrub silvered by moonlight – a low, hunchbacked scurrying silhouette, the lead hyaena, scouting him. They were silent now, smelling his fear.

He ran back to his pile of leaves and tamarind bark, but the wind had scattered it. Brush whispered as the hyaenas drew closer, a moon-pale eye blinking. He scuffed together the leaves and bark as best he could, crunching down the acacia thorns with his hands. Wiping the blood on his shins he unwrapped a small flint from a fold of his cloak and struck it hard against the edge of his *simi*, the hyaenas whining appreciatively as the smell of his blood reached them.

Like a small planet flung from its orbit, the spark flared across the darkness and ebbed against its bed of leaves. The wind fanned it; it burned a hole in its leaf and dropped through, went out. Claws ticked on rocks; more than lion, leopard, even more than buffalo he feared and hated hyaenas – skulking, elusive, afraid of man until he's alone, at night, without fire, when they attack in hordes and tear him apart alive, crush his still-living limbs in their jaws, as they had his cousin Oaulguu's father-in-law, caught alone in the desert near Ilaut. The Samburu knew now that they would have him too, not just his lion skin; faster and faster he struck the flint, a hyaena snickering at its flash, the sparks dying on the wrinkled leaves. He flung a boulder at the closest hyaena, who barked sharply and retreated, the others clacking their teeth in anticipation. With his *simi* he dug more rocks from the soil and threw them till there was only one hyaena between him and the doum palm and he charged it, screaming, swinging his *simi*; the hyaena backed away, snarling, then pounced at his heels as he clambered up the palm tree and crouched, breathless, on the limb beside his lion pelt.

In the clear blue moonlight he watched the hyaenas circle the eland and lioness, draw closer, then suddenly swarm them, yipping and snarling, crunching bones and ripping flesh. For a while they clustered round the eland, fighting and dragging it first one way then the other, till more hyaenas appeared one by one out of the dark scrub, deposing several of the first group who then, growling and whimpering, turned their attention to the lioness. With regret the Samburu watched them, his hand descending often to check the sinew binding the male lion's pelt to the branch beneath his feet. He who takes more than his share, *N'gai* says, ends with nothing. This big, black-maned lion was *N'gai*'s gift, to pay the year's school fees for his sons. He would not spurn or squander *N'gai*'s gift.

### III

Long before the stars died the birds began to sing – cool rippling doves, loud cheery starlings, the long lilting trills of warblers and thrushes. The hyaenas had ceased snarling and yipping around the eland; against the paling stars the Samburu could see the tiny gliding spots of the vultures that had come before dusk and circled all night.

Dawn raced like fire across the savannah. Three hyaenas still lay with their heads inside the eland's bared ribcage; another was chewing fleas at the base of his tail; the lioness' pelt was shredded, her head severed and half-gnawed in the scrub. The first vulture skated down on wide, whistling wings and landed near the eland, cocking its rubbery red head; a hyaena ran barking at it and it lumbered off, flapped above the hyaena and circled back. A second drifted down and roosted in a thorn bush; another hyaena raised its muzzle from the eland's belly and growled.

The Samburu lowered the lion's pelt on its sinew and slid to the ground. He steadied the pelt on his head, grasped his spear and trotted eastwards up the slope into the full raiment of the sun.

The lion pelt was still heavy with fat and blood and the lion's heavy fur, heavier than the stone-heavy *podocarpus* boughs he had carried often from the banks of the Ewaso N'giro to his mother's *manyatta* when he was still a boy and the desert had not yet come. He should stop and skin the pelt cleaner so he could carry it with less exhaustion, but as he crested the ridge he realized the hyaenas had left the eland and, yowling, had taken

13

up his trail. Further north, along the stream, the others answered. Glancing back as he ran, the Samburu tried to unsheath his *simi*; a stone shifted underfoot and his ankle snapped loud as a dry stick in the bright morning air, and he fell face down among the rocks. He lurched to his feet, raised up the pelt, and hobbled forward on the spear; the pelt tumbled from his head, skipped and rolled, spinning awkwardly, downhill. The four hyaenas checked their lope to watch it slam into a thorn bush, knocking loose a weaver's nest that bounced over the rocks and vanished in the scrub.

The Samburu cut a strip from his cloak and wrapped his ankle but could put no weight on it. Using the spear as a cane he sidestepped down the slope; below, the hyaenas drew together round the pelt and halted on their haunches, watching him descend. He drew his *simi* and waved it, yelling, but they did not retreat.

Single file the other hyaenas had cleared the scrub along the stream and were hurrying upslope. The Samburu reached the pelt, shaking with pain; the four hyaenas glanced back at the rest of the pack and trotted towards him, haunches down, ears back, jaws grinning. His back to the pelt and thorn bush, he fitted his spear together and held it in his right hand, the *simi* in his left. The pack of hyaenas joined the first four, now numbering the fingers of three hands. Whining, eyes darting side to side, long jaws gaping with delight, as if imploring him not to fear, this would all end quickly, they circled him, sniffing the bloody pelt, his fear.

He backed tighter into the bush, its thorns pricking his back and thighs, blood trickling down his spine. The hyaenas split up; he sensed some coming up behind, their claws rattling the loose soil, the branches twanging in their wiry fur, their anxious panting. As the three before him darted in, low and fast, he caught the first in the shoulder with the spear, the second across the skull with the *simi* but the third gashed his calf and, leaping past the *simi*'s swing, ran to the others and sat licking the blood that spotted its muzzle. Whining, the speared hyaena backed away; the second, slashed across the head, crouched beyond reach, ears back. A big female sniffed his bleeding head and, turning her curious, affronted eyes on the Samburu, bolted at him. She leaped back from the *simi*, then tore his knee and bounded aside as he spun to spear another from the left. He swung the *simi* at three more coming straight, one leaping for his throat, the massive female soaring at him with jaws outstretched, her breath hot in his face as he drove the spear shaft down her open jaws, ducking, flung her past him, the spearhead going with her. He chopped another's spine with the *simi* as it tore into his ankle, jerking the blade upward to slice another's throat as it snapped for his face, lashing sideways to bare another's shoulder before it screamed and dove away.

In this moment of death he felt a great calm. Panting, tongues hanging, the hyaenas gathered to watch him bleed. He glanced behind the bush, but the spearhead was out of reach. One darted in but sprang back when he raised the *simi*. With his good foot he rolled one dead hyaena towards them, then the other. The big female, bleeding from the mouth, eyes ablaze, slunk nearer, sniffed the first body and as she turned to the second the

Samburu jumped forward and cleaved her neck halfway through. But he could not pull the *simi* free as the others charged him, howling, his *simi* jammed in her vertebrae by the angle of her neck. He flailed at the others with the broken spear till he could yank the *simi* free, and the others fell back, watchful, angry.

His feet slipped on the soil muddied by his blood. Sun drummed on his head; the land spun round and round before his eyes. Attentive and eager, the hyaenas crouched cheerfully on their haunches, nostrils and jaws wide, as if it were a game, he thought, about to begin again. He glanced at the blood sliding down his shins: staunch it soon, he thought, or die. Again he saw his bones crunched by them, and he bared his teeth.

The huge sun slid overhead, whitening the desiccated sky and searing the sulphurous soil, the tortured barren scrub. Flies buzzed at his blood; a hyaena stood, stretched, sniffed the changing wind, and trotted swiftly northwards, angling downslope. One by one the others rose and followed. Unbelieving, the Samburu waited by his bush, but they were gone, gone away, a new wind raising dust devils and scuttling dead leaves like vipers under the thorn scrub, drying the blood on his lacerated legs and sucking the last moisture from his throat.

He gathered up and reshafted his spear, looked across the undulant, afternoon-hazed bitter brush wavering with heat, but could not see the hyaenas. Baffled, he tore apart the rest of his cloak and tried to wrap his legs; it was difficult to walk with this flesh and muscle hanging in strips down the narrow white bones, with his broken ankle lurching sideways at each step, driving impossible

pain up what was left of his legs. But *N'gai* had favoured
him still with life, this magnificent life with its aromas
of bush, soil and wind, its bird songs and buzzard cries,
its hum of flies and ants and butterflies and all that
composes the cosmos in perfect synchronization. And
because his youngest sons needed their school fees *N'gai*
had willed that he should live to carry back this lion pelt
and it must be done as *N'gai* willed, to find a way to
raise this pelt, steady it atop the head, to lean forward,
take a step with these legs baring their bone beneath
flags of muddy flesh, to raise this bandaged foot and
place it on the crumbly soil, then bear the weight so
evenly on the spear shaft, bringing forward the other
foot, and all that mattered was to make each step possible, carry it through, then another, then another. He
must cross the dead savannah of Lailasai, but if *N'gai*
had spared him the hyaenas it would not be to kill him
in Lailasai, but to lead him home, where at the *duka* of
Mohammed Amin Sala he would receive four hundred
shillings for such a pelt, enough to send the boys to
school, and with each step he repeated this thought,
under the weight of the pelt and the heat of the sun.

Each time he fell the sun's heat woke him, and he
dragged himself to the pelt and, kneeling, raised it to
his head then forced himself up, steadying his stagger
till he could again step, then step again, then step again,
towards the ridges of the Ol Doinyo Lailasai hovering
before him in the late afternoon heat.

Again the sun had died. How cool the land, how soft
the violet light, as he crested the last rise and Ol Doinyo
Lailasai towered before him like the entrance to an

immense mystery he was beginning to understand, in the clarity of pain and early starlight, when the birds are silenced by the sudden wall that falls between day and night, and in the very far distance the rock mountain where *N'gai* was born guarded his *manyatta*. If the hyaenas did not come he'd reach it before the sun grew hot tomorrow, if he walked all night, and yes, *N'gai* was good to him and his sons for he would reach it now, and taking a deep breath of this dry, chill sunset air he did not understand nor realize the shocking, crushing force that suddenly separated him from the earth and hurled him in scattered awareness among the bushes whose thorns no longer hurt, the pelt's weight no longer bearing him down, and he tried to remember why he was carrying it, then could not remember what *it* was, remembering then, only, *N'gai* has been good, *N'gai* has been so good.

Finger still on the trigger of his AK47, the young Somali slipped from his cover in the euphorbias and, hugging the dark places between the brush, crept to the Samburu lying gape-mouthed on the tousled sand. He was truly dead, this barbarian; the Somali wondered at the power of the rifle, seeing how the bullet had entered the Samburu's chest just above the heart, and had come out the left eye, which dangled down his cheek on a trace of tissue; the impact of the bullet had forced brains like the insides of snails out the Samburu's ears; a pool of near-black was spreading round his head.

An uneven clump, clump-clump of hooves approached; shouldering his rifle the Somali turned to another leading a camel. 'Ho, brother! Did I not shoot well?'

The other smiled. 'Yes, Warwar, it was well done. Now let's load your pelt quickly. The shot was loud.'

'It's a shame to share this with the others.'

'You would live alone?' The other dragged the lion pelt from the bushes where it had tumbled. 'Check there's no money on him.'

'Him?' the young Somali scoffed. 'It's a barbarian in rags – an old *simi* and a worn spear.'

They lashed the pelt atop the camel and continued leading it south as the last rays of sun receded across the lilac sands. Just before dark they crossed a furrowed trail coming from the northwest. Warwar knelt, fingering a round, deep print. 'It can't be!'

His brother walked alongside the tracks, noting the different sizes and strides. 'Three females, one old. Plus a calf.' He scanned the back trail, the rough scar in the earth's reddish eroded crust shadowed by the fading horizontal light. 'The last of the northern herds. Driven by thirst down out of the mountains, headed for the Ewaso N'giro.'

'How many days?'

'Weeks. We won't catch them till the river.'

'Perhaps they'll find us a bull.'

'Hush, you dreamer! Don't bring bad luck.'

'Since when would it be bad luck,' Warwar laughed, 'to come home loaded down with ivory?'

# Chapter 1

By reading, MacAdam realized, he had enlarged his awareness but impaired his vision. Now to see the world clearly he was forced to look at it through a wall of glass.

He unbuttoned his shirt and wiped dust from his spectacles, watched the camels milling in the paddock where the Rendille woman had driven them. Not even eight o'clock and already the sun hot on the back of your neck. The grass underfoot not too brittle for December: so far the short rains had been good.

Under a thorn tree by the paddock the dismounted cab of a Land Rover served as a shed from which he took two bottles of hydrogen peroxide and a large tube of biosulphate. This probably would not work but was better than that mixture the Rendille woman used that killed four camels last year.

A string of Samburu kids lined the stockade, their fuzzy hair paled with dust kicked up by the camels shuffling nervously and swinging their heads to snap at flies along their haunches.

The Rendille woman climbed the stockade and jumped in, her head barely to the camels' bellies. With a switch she drove one into the chute; Isau, the Samburu foreman, dropped the gate behind it. MacAdam slipped a noose of sisal round the camel's knee and as it lurched forward against the front gate of the chute he yanked the noose tight, jerking up its knee. It brayed and tried to pull back, tautening the noose that he then tied off against the stockade. He threw a halter rope around its head, tossed the end to Isau who looped it once around a beam and held it tight.

With the camel neighing and jerking at the halter MacAdam washed a large boil on its neck with hydrogen peroxide, took a knife from his pocket and sliced the boil open. The camel screamed, craning its neck, green grass spittle frothing its yellow teeth and pale gums. MacAdam squeezed the boil, blood and pus running down the camel's rough, dusty fur. Wiping pus from his fingers on to its neck, he screwed a syringe top on to the biosulphate tube and squeezed some into the wound. He slipped the noose from its knee; Isau tossed free the halter; MacAdam opened the front chute gate and the camel trotted, swinging its head angrily, into the pasture. The Rendille woman drove another camel into the chute.

It was nearly noon when he finished. Dust and sweat caked his face; blood and pus streaked his shorts and knees. He thanked Isau and the Rendille woman, who nodded, her eyes on the savannah, as if he had not meant his thanks and therefore to accept them would further demean her, or that neither his thanks nor he were significant. For an instant he saw himself as they must see him, an easy-smiling, hearty man with a booming voice and nothing to say, with a fine home and wife and possessions that inoculated him against others' joys and sufferings and his own. A gregarious fake. *Oi meni-nisho k'kiri nememe*: flesh that is not painful does not feel.

He put the last half-bottle of hydrogen peroxide back in the Land Rover shed, rubbed his hands clean with dust and walked past the thatch-roofed sheds where several ancient Land Rovers rusted calmly on blocks in the tall grass, past the long stone barn with its galvanized roof, towards the slate-roofed house under flame trees, frangipani, bougainvillea and jacarandas, a candlestick euphorbia towering cactus-like on either side.

Dorothy was not downstairs. He entered the parlour cool and dark after the blast of the sun, poured gin and tonic water into a glass and wandered into the kitchen for ice, then out on the veranda, sipping gin and watching the heat seethe over the wide golden savannah; behind it, blocking the horizon, the blunt, vast bulk of Mount Kenya was cloaked in clouds.

On the equator the days pass one like the next. You come here young, marry, raise a family, die, and leave no tracks. Occasionally you go 'home', to London and the Cotswold mists, the old streets of Cirencester, the city's bookshops, movies, pubs, museums, the facile English conversations. After a few weeks you wake up one day and decide to go back to Africa – the rest is just a game.

Like malaria, Africa. Once bitten you can never shake it. They used to call acacias 'fever trees', thinking malaria came from them. Now they 'know' malaria comes from mosquitoes. Some day they'll realize malaria comes from the continent itself: Africa is a fever. For Africa there's no chloroquin. No matter if you leave it, it's engraved in your blood.

Yet Africa is dying, taking the fever with it. Have no attachments, MacAdam knew the Maasai said: see the world as it passes, not siding with lion or gazelle. A century ago the whites came, ploughed and fenced the savannah, cut the forests, grazed their ignorant cattle where the wildebeest had roamed. They killed the warriors and made the docile ones clerks, told them we nailed God to a tree because He threatened to free us of our sins. 'What are sins?' the Maasai answered. 'God is the land, the trees, the mountains, the animals, the sky, the rivers and the rain. How do you nail this to a tree?'

Now the land, the trees, the animals are gone; the whites were right – God's not so hard to kill. And most of the whites had gone, too, leaving behind them a plague to finish off what they began. This plague, MacAdam had reflected so many bitter times, was medicine without birth control. It allowed the weak to live, populations to explode, the limitless savannahs and jungles cut into tiny *shambas* where swollen families burnt and hacked the vegetation, then clung to the malnourished soil till it eroded to bedrock. Without the grass and trees the soil dried, the rains died, and you could see a man coming miles away by the dust he raised.

'But you don't see a lion's killing a waterbuck from either side,' he reminded himself. He should not try to attribute 'good'. Learn not to care, again and again he had told himself, about the death of Africa.

Dorothy's footsteps upstairs. Africa, that still enslaved the black woman, in MacAdam's experience wore the white one down, made her either passive or hard. In the first years of their marriage there'd been friends, other ranchers, with a common longing for an England whose mirage grew ever more entrancing as the reality was forgotten. But now the neighbours and her own children were gone, Dorothy couldn't stop talking about going 'home'.

The Samburu distinguished between house and home. A house was what the Europeans had, here in Africa. It was not their home. Home was where the family lived, generations, the familiar soil. A place which had no written history because it was in their bones, as their bones were in the soil. The Mau Mau had come because the Africans got tired of waiting for the white man to go home.

When MacAdam and Dorothy went down to Nairobi she perked up, but said she hated it. As the other white ranchers left the Lerochi plateau, Kikuyu politicians had bought their ranches and resold them in tiny parcels whose buyers could not make enough from them to live. Their goats tore up the last grass; the rains scoured the broken topsoil into dirtied streams that gnawed gullies through parched valleys. Now MacAdam and Dorothy were the last whites on the plateau. When the rains were good their cattle prospered. When there were no rains he cut the herd to two hundred heifers and a few bulls, and wandered northern Kenya with them like a Samburu nomad.

Dorothy's tread was listless on the stairs. When they were young there'd been so much passion, joy in each other. Now they were old friends and passion a trick of memory. He felt himself turning into sinew. 'Take a second wife,' Aiyam the Samburu elder had counselled. 'Look at me – at more than seventy years I have four wives – I keep them happy!'

He'd take no other wife. Once yes, with a joy that bordered on abandon. But those days were dead. Dead and buried. The other wife had never been his own, and they'd been right to kill it. But when he dared to think honestly about her, he saw that only then had he lived down to the bottom of his soul, with a joy so hot and bright it cut him to the bone. He'd acted like a fool, he would tell himself, a teenager lost in visions of himself. It never would have lasted; he would have ended just as badly off as he was now.

In the kitchen he took three ice cubes from the fridge and plunked them into his glass. How soon they start to melt, he thought. Have I reached the age when nothing is enough? What else *is* there? When you're young it's so easy – you love danger. Look for it. But once you test yourself, face fire, you never have to doubt again. Then you see that courage is so little. In any case I've got no danger now. No risk means no joy.

'Hullo,' he smiled, hating his smile and the timbre of his voice, tucking the gin bottle away and hiding his glass in a corner of the sink as Dorothy slippered into the kitchen. 'Another lovely day.'

# Chapter 2

The trail of red dust rose diagonally into the bright late afternoon sky, its thickness attesting to the speed of the approaching vehicle. MacAdam glanced at it from time to time as he moved along the fence between his out-buildings and the weaning pasture, loosening the staples on the wooden posts, pulling the barbed wires tight one by one against a bracing post with a cable stretcher, then hammering the staples home, so that this section of the fence now stood tight and true.

You don't do what you don't want to, he'd always told himself, unless you have to to preserve yourself. If you avoid what you don't want to do, you've more time to do what you want. But what if there's nothing you want to do?

Now he could see the vehicle, a dark blue Police Land Rover: probably come to arrest someone in the *manyattas* behind the ranch – it annoyed him, making the steel grips of the cable stretcher feel slick in his hands.

The Land Rover slowed as it reached the white-fenced lawn; it stopped at the back door. MacAdam tossed the cable stretcher on to his shoulder and walked angrily towards the house. A tall man in a camouflage uniform and blue beret stepped out of the Land Rover, waved, and strode towards him.

He felt a sudden surge of pleasure and dismay. Tipping the cable stretcher against a post he took the other's hands, grinning. '*Jambo*, Nehemiah!'

'*Mzuri*!' the man smiled: All's well. '*Jambo*?'

'*Mzuri sana*,' MacAdam answered automatically – all's very well – as if what he'd just been thinking was but a fantasy and now he'd awakened to the intercourse of men, where doubt and despair had no place. 'Something to drink? Let's get out of this sun.'

Nehemiah took off his beret, stooping to enter the kitchen. 'Coffee?' MacAdam said. 'Tea? Beer?'

'Hey, coffee! You don't remember?'

They sat at a sun-faded white wrought-iron table beneath the jacarandas whose petals littered the mown grass like purple snow. 'Seeing you, right now,' MacAdam laughed, 'I think I can remember everything we ever did. Where did it go, all that time?'

'And the ranch – you're happy?' Nehemiah asked.

MacAdam gazed out at the tawny grass brilliant with sun, the pale stone buildings, their rusted roofs and riotous bougainvillea, the white backs of distant cattle reminding him of the Samburu and antelope whose land this, a hundred years ago, had been. 'We've made it through some bad seasons – raised our kids—'

'Tom's still at LSE?'

'Graduates in June. Seth's started at Edinburgh, a degree in journalism.'

'Great. Great.'

A moment's pause as MacAdam sought not to think of Nehemiah's wife and three daughters killed seven years ago in a flaming crash of their car with an out-of-control *matatu*. He faced it head on. 'How are you and the world of women?'

'No time. No time.' Nehemiah tucked up the crease of trousers, sliding back one heavy black boot as he leaned forward. 'It's war, Mac.'

MacAdam sloshed the remnants of his coffee round the cup, trying to dredge up the sugar. 'So Christ, what's new? The Rwandans massacring each other again, the northern Sudan Moslems killing the southern Christians, the CIA spreading war between the Ethiopians, the Ugandans back to disembowelling one another—' He shrugged. 'Fuck them all.'

Nehemiah sat back, great black hands folded on the worn white metal table. How strange, MacAdam thought, to have black skin. All these years it's taken me to see what a great gulf it is between us.

'So what you plan to do?' Nehemiah prompted.

MacAdam felt irritation rise in him. 'The Somalis have been moving southwest into Kenya for two hundred years. I can remember when there were none in Wajir – now they own the place and are taking over Isiolo . . .'

Nehemiah raised his eyebrows. 'Here's next.'

'I'll be dead and gone. I was just the previous tribe; my kind have already moved on. Just like your people did three centuries ago, coming down from Ethiopia and Sudan – now you're on the Mara, and from Athi back to Serengeti – so what?'

'Your people crossed the land bridge from France to England thousands of years ago – your history's this endless wandering, peace and war, to and fro across the Channel – we're all nomads. But the stronger keep their territory. The weak give theirs up.'

'A lot of good that did you and me.' He saw the understanding strike Nehemia like a slap, the gap-toothed smile that could not hide it. He drove it home. 'We turned *our* backs on our dead, our friends, didn't we?'

He knew what Nehemia was thinking: the loss of Aden was British. Britain deserved to lose, propping up its dirty oil sheiks, then not having the resolve to carry through – leaving her SAS men to die under the blistering Omani sun.

'It's the elephants this time, Mac. In three more years they'll all be gone. Just like the rhino is now.'

Lost in his previous thought, MacAdam had a sense of supreme regret for what could have been – a true empire, the world united under common rule of law and civilization, focused on the benefit of humankind, each person, now and for the future. But they'd spoiled it with their arrogance, with the weakness and shame that came from strength. 'Screw the elephants,' he said. Again Nehemiah's gap-toothed smile, his eyes laughing. 'They break down my fences and tear up the savannah – they've uprooted every goddamn umbrella acacia on this whole end of the Lerochi – my cattle have nowhere for shade – the land gets drier . . .'

'Ten years ago Kenya had three hundred thousand elephants. Now we have five thousand. We *had* five thousand rhino. Now we have thirty, in chain-link enclosures protected by guards. Last year we had eight hundred thousand tourists. They won't come when there's no elephant; they won't come to see rhino behind chain-link fence – they can do that in zoos at home. And when they hear about the poaching they get scared and stay away – this year's figures're way down – only the wars in west Africa are diverting tourists here; otherwise half our places'd be folding their tents.'

'Fuck them! Why turn Kenya into Disneyland for fat pale people to wander round in four-wheel drives?'

Nehemiah shrugged. 'No tourists means no foreign exchange, no hard currency to buy petrol and medicines and computers and telephones and educational materials and everything else that separates us from the Stone Age.'

Back to the same question again, thought MacAdam – do we move forward, towards a united world, or does Kenya slide with so much of post-colonial Africa back into the chaos, tyranny and superstition of the past, as if this last century were only an aberration? The Kenyans didn't want that – not Nehemiah nor anyone who'd seen both sides. Yet it *was* sinking back, even Kenya; even Nehemiah knew they were fighting a rearguard action.

'Then there's the issue of the animals themselves,' Nehemiah continued. 'Do we allow them to be wiped out—'

But wasn't that progress too, that the elephants were killed off like the mastodon and giant rhino before them,

31

like all other wildlife and wild places? 'We can't stop time,' MacAdam said.

'But you can change the way it goes,' Nehemiah insisted.

'Shit!' MacAdam rose, knees and ankles stiff, went into the kitchen, stony-cool after the hot shade of the jacarandas, and came back with the coffee thermos. Nehemiah was standing, beret in hand, looking southwest towards the Aberdares, his boots set wide apart as at parade rest. A natural stance it becomes, MacAdam thought. A natural way of becoming protector, defender. But of what? The trouble with war's that what you defend soon doesn't matter, you always end up killing what you wanted to protect. 'More coffee?' he offered.

Nehemiah shook his head, slapped his beret against his fist. 'You and me are dinosaurs too,' he said, echoing MacAdam's mind in that particular way he'd always had. 'Of a time when you respected what you wanted for the world and were willing to fight for it. Are you losing that?'

Across the savannah MacAdam watched the trail of dust announcing Dottie's return from town. 'You're barking up the wrong tree.'

Nehemiah ignored him. 'The President's created a special unit. Anti-poaching, anti-guerrilla – it's become the same thing. A hundred men, full support, partial use of a plane, G–3's, the President's backing—'

MacAdam laughed. 'You can't stop the bloody Somalis with a hundred men.'

'We *pick* the men we want. The materiel. Very few strings.'

'He'll tie you all *up* in strings! Too afraid of a coup.'

'He fears that from the Kikuyu, not the Maasai. The Kalenjin have never had to worry about us.'

'And you?'

'I'm Deputy. Under M'Bole.'

'Great!'

'He's not that bad, Mac.'

'Not if you want to buy a few tusks . . .'

'He's straight, now. And I'll be on the first ops. We've picked up reports of a new band of Somalis coming down from the Kaisut Desert, headed for the Ewaso N'giro—'

'Going after the last herds—'

'If we can catch them in a firefight—'

'Who've you got?'

'Luos, Kikuyus, some very tough Maasai—'

MacAdam laughed. 'You guys're all tough, Nehemiah. But tough ain't enough.'

'That's where you come in.'

'I'm the whitewash? To please all the European wild-life organizations worried about the elephants?'

Nehemiah chuckled. 'The President wants you. You're in the middle, you're the balance . . .'

'He doesn't give a shit about me.'

'You're a "good Kenyan". Never taken advantage, never cut and ran. You give more than you get.' Nehemiah paused, glanced at Dottie's approaching Range Rover as if timing his request. 'So he needs you to give some more.'

Chickens squawked and scattered as the maroon Range Rover crossed the yard and parked under the galvanized shed roof. 'I'm through giving,' MacAdam said. 'From now on, I'm going to learn how to *take*.'

Hair flashing red, squinting as she pushed up her sunglasses, Dottie came towards them, bundles in her arms. 'Well hu*llo*, Nehemiah!' she said as if he were an everyday visitor, leaning round her packages to kiss his cheek. 'We've missed you lately.'

'Life on the Lerochi's too tranquil to miss anything.'

She carried her packages towards the kitchen. 'Come *on*! It's quiet as a tomb up here!'

Nehemiah winked at MacAdam. 'Will you?'

MacAdam felt uncomfortable, the chagrin of refusing a kindly offer, of not wanting to be used. 'You've got plenty of young bucks with fire in their bellies who can follow a track through the bush day or night, sleep with the snakes . . .'

'*Any*body can do that. What I want's someone with experience. These aren't just poachers, Mac, they're well-armed guerrillas with infiltration routes from Somalia, and a network of safe houses among the Somalis in Kenya. You remember the Somali President's letter to his generals – to spread economic chaos in Kenya, prepare for war . . .' Nehemiah stood to pull out a chair for Dorothy. 'You don't throw recruits at that.'

Dorothy set her gin and tonic carefully on the table. 'You're not trying to take back my husband?'

'Says he's too old, Dottie.'

'He still wants to die with his boots on.' She laughed

her deep, high, drinker's laugh, as if every joke were, finally, about herself.

MacAdam felt shame for her, for himself before Nehemiah, and for Nehemiah, being exposed to it. But *my shame's why she drinks*, he realized. He saw her, years back, kissing the kids into bed, their little round pink faces above the sill of covers, her rough, loving voice. Her drinking was the wall between her and herself, he'd thought then. Her way of limiting yet accentuating the beauty of life, a governor. But now she was governed by it.

'You can't go off like that,' she halted the glass before her lips, 'just leave the ranch.'

He looked at her. 'There's nothing I do that Isau can't.' Then he looked at Nehemiah. 'And there's nothing I could do, out there, that some young officer can't do better.'

'No young officer I know has fought in Dhofar, faced that kind of Moslem insurgency. Like the Somalis.'

'Dhofar was *wrong*, Nehemiah! You know that. I shouldn't've been in Oman – none of us should.'

Nehemiah watched him. 'OK. I agree. But Kenya's not wrong now. And we need you.'

'I don't give a damn about being needed. That's the oldest con in the book. Nobody's needed, nobody's irreplaceable.'

Nehemiah wiped his mouth with a large black hand, thumb and forefinger sliding down the opposite sides of his lower lip and meeting in the centre. He seemed to be concentrating on a point far out on the savannah. 'Then what are you here for?'

'Here, the ranch?'

'*Here*!' Nehemiah brought his hand down and slapped his thigh. 'Here, anywhere!'

'That's what I've been wondering.'

'And what's the answer?'

'Ian's better at asking questions,' Dottie interposed, 'than finding answers.'

'That's true.' MacAdam felt himself judged by them both, that she saw him, forgave him, in a way he could not himself, but that this weakened him. 'I've had a sense, lately, that my life's been going nowhere, that somewhere long ago I made a wrong turn.' He faced her. 'Maybe leaving England, but I can't think that's true.'

She exhaled roughly, denying it. 'You – without Africa?'

'So give it a chance, Mac.' Nehemiah turned away, anxious not to push.

MacAdam looked down, a jacaranda petal lying loosely in his lap, his upper lip indrawn within the lower, an affectation of Nehemiah's. 'There's too much to sort out here . . . I've no time for rules of engagement, channels, all that shit.'

'There *are* no rules of engagement any more,' Nehemiah said, pushing his cup away as if suddenly it contained a piece of dung. He got up, formal in his uniform, boot heels bowing him forward. 'You find them, you shoot them. Simple as that.'

'You're not leaving already?' Dottie's voice was harsh, anxious and relieved.

'I've done all I came to do,' he answered.

MacAdam walked beside him to the blue Land Rover. 'Remember M'kele?' Nehemiah said.

'Your uncle, or something, a hunter. That the one?'

'The best tracker in the tribe. Can follow the trail of the butterfly, simply by the shadow it has cast on the ground.'

'Would you *stop* that tribal shit!'

Nehemiah laughed. 'He was an elephant poacher once. When there were elephants by the hundreds of thousands. He'll be with us on the Ewaso N'giro.'

'Us?'

'If you come.'

MacAdam paused. 'Give me a day or so, to think. I'll go into Rumuruti and call you.'

Nehemiah took his arm, drawing closer. 'I didn't think she'd like it.'

'She's bored. Lonely. I'm trying to get her to go back for Christmas, see the kids.'

'You too?'

Nehemiah's arm in his resuscitated the old closeness; he felt connected. 'It breaks your heart to have no country,' he said.

'You're the latest of our wandering tribes, Mac. Don't fall into thinking black and white.'

A troop of ostriches – three tan females, a black-and-white male and a string of chicks – were crossing rump-high through the field beyond the fence. 'We almost lost them,' Nehemiah said, 'till we banned the trade in feathers. Think of a world – Kenya – without ostriches!'

MacAdam watched the solemn, self-possessed birds hop a low link in his fence, the young ones scuttling under. 'Reminds me of the one in Nyahururu who hated cars. When tourists stopped to take his picture he'd kick their tyres flat, then wouldn't let them out to fix them. I can see him now, trotting furiously, round and round the car, waiting for someone to hop out.'

'Remember the Tana River, below Kiboko Camp – where the valley's two miles wide or more – remember how we used to see elephants, solid elephants, all the way across? Or when the trail of elephants from Marsabit down to Losai was a mile wide and fifty miles long . . .' Nehemiah unlocked the rear hatch of the Land Rover and opened a long pine box. Inside it lay five silver-black automatic rifles separated by canvas sheets. He lifted one out and handed it to MacAdam. 'HK G–3 – you know it?'

'By reputation.' It felt very solid yet not heavy, as if with a will and soul of its own, self-balanced. He politely checked it over, hating it somehow, yet when he tossed it up to his shoulder it fitted perfectly between his arm and cheekbone. 'Nice.' He handed it back.

'No, no – it's *for* you. It's what the President has ordered for the squad.' Nehemiah slipped a carton of cartridges from the pine box into MacAdam's hand. 'It's what you and your men'll be using—'

When Nemehiah'd gone he walked back feeling light-headed and sluggish under the sun, as if he'd given away nothing yet too much, into the cool house, and locked the rifle and cartridges away in the dark den, whose books were ranked like instructions to a rite whose meaning he'd forgotten, primal wall paintings of animals who no longer existed – newer paperbacks with haughty titles, as if they offered truths to unveil the mystery, older stuffy hardbacks sitting on their dusty reputations. Why did they scribble? What did they imagine they were giving to the world, themselves? Didn't they know that a life without action, a life not lived out deeply in the unreasoned essence of itself, is worthless?

Now Nehemiah would have him take up the gun again to defend the world of scribblers from chaos and destruction. Who'd be such a fool?

From the kitchen came the voices of Dottie and Felista the cook discussing dinner. Shall it be curry sauce on the lamb, or mint? Broccoli or cauliflower? Afterwards shall we sit in the parlour and read or read in bed? The wooden clock over the dry fireplace loudened, as it always did, the last few strokes before six, then hammered its echoing chimes round the room as though within a tomb. He had a sudden pang for what would come after he was gone, for things he would never know.

Once life had been the land unending, hills of fields and trees curving out of sight to unknown places. Why'd he stopped seeking, seeing? Anodyne – that was the word for it though he'd forgotten what it meant. Or atonement? It was tied, somehow, to sex. When the love between you dims, you blame the woman. When the life within you dies, you blame life.

You *know*, you blind bastard, he told himself, what kills life. It's the death of joy that kills life, the renunciation of the heart. Like tearing out your eyes because you don't like what you see. Sure, you can give up love, the kind of love that tears you all apart with need, then fills you up with completion. Till you're so dull and numbed you never even think of her, have forgotten even the feel of her hair against your cheek. Gossamer, that was the fucking word for it. The perfume of her. Bitch. With her you couldn't lie, not only the major untruths, but the little exaggerated details, the inexact anecdotes that destroyed the truth. 'No,' you used to tell her, 'that's not exactly right,' and you'd say it till you said it right. Bitch.

An hour never used to pass that you didn't think of her. Now you're all dried up, and wonder why.

A lavender, crimson sunset drained from the savannah, staining the long gold grass that rippled in the wind like lions running. Why in the morning is there so much hope? And in the evening only a fatigued desperation? To the west the flat-bottomed cumulus trailed south, their bellies the colour of a desert rose, as though even in beauty there is poison.

Seeing the far crests of Ol Doinyo Lossos backlit purple by the vanished sun, MacAdam felt today would be a good day to die. Not in this impervious house but out on the savannah, bones crunched by hyaenas, like a warrior's, melting into the dust.

If he went with Nehemiah it would be for the thrill. Not for Nehemiah or Kenya or the elephants or any sense of duty. Not to get away from the ranch or Dottie. He would do it for the desert, and to hunt the only animal worth hunting. The only decent prey.

# Chapter 3

He was walking with Dorothy along the road that parallels the railroad tracks north of Naro Moru. There was a single tree out on the plain where they'd once sheltered in a thunderstorm, fearing the lightning. Now they turned north at the fork past the tree, hurrying home because a rogue lion was supposed to be near, then they saw the lion going along the palisade fence towards the neighbour's, and MacAdam thought, we're safe, he'll eat the neighbour and his daughter, and not us.

Then in the dream they were sleeping and he woke with a sense of danger and saw from the bed that a door in another room was opened, one he had closed when locking the house against the lion. To be safe he decided to check it, got up and walked round the foot of the bed, in the darkness stepping on something huge, rough-furred and warm – the lion. He backed around the bed to wake Dottie, then thought why do I always ask *her* advice – shall we try to move or stay in bed, hoping that he's eaten, won't be hungry?

Still in the dream he heard himself snorting, choking, as he tried to force himself from sleep, be awake to face the lion, and waking realized there was no lion, only he and Dottie and the night.

He lay listening to the house and grounds; the dogs weren't barking; once from the pens a calf called for its mother; only the moon came slanting through the open window.

As the dream retreated and the security of house and bed seeped back he remembered the fear he had felt hurrying home from the lion, then stepping on the large warm furry thing at the foot of the bed and knowing it was the lion. He thought of the night outside and of those who lived in fear, of his estrangement from it. His sense of danger persisted. Maybe, he wondered, I'm not supposed to go with Nehemiah?

Two days after Nehemiah's visit MacAdam had gone into Rumuruti and called him. 'Didn't think you'd want to miss it,' Nehemiah'd said. There'd been no bad omens. Then a week to organize the ranch for Isau to take over, but that too had gone smoothly, with no sense of angered spirits, of actions out of step with fate.

He rolled from the covers, took a *simi* from the floor beside the bed, unsheathed it. The hall floor, then the stairs creaked beneath his feet. The kitchen flagstones chilled his toes; the den smelled of old coals and mouldering books, the dining-room floor was slick, scented with beeswax. Something scuttled up the wall; he smiled, lowering the *simi* – gecko.

Bone-white, the moon had drained the night of light. The wind tasted of dry grass, cattle, distant smouldering fires, bougainvillea. Brutus, one of his Maasai dogs, came and licked his hand, sniffing him to ascertain the reason for this unusual appearance in the middle of the night. MacAdam knelt beside him, rubbing the dog's soft short coat along his rangy, thin shoulders and narrow, sharp ribs. Brutus sniffed, licked his eyebrow, the dog's loud, wet tongue for a moment in MacAdam's eye making him laugh, and he hugged him, and felt at once the dog's urgency to be free, to guard, not be constrained. 'You're a fine boy,' he said, scratching behind Brutus's ears, and the dog trotted back to protect the calving pens. A star fell westwards across the sky; how bitter and cold, MacAdam thought, out there dying in fire. Naked and barefoot on the savannah, knife in hand, the dog near, he felt safe and free.

He returned to the veranda, not understanding a continuing unease centred beneath his lungs as if he'd been punched there. Waiting to go into battle. He climbed the stairs, sheathed the *simi* and lay back with hands beneath his head, watching the reflection of moonlight on the ceiling. Dorothy's breathing was nearly soundless; he turned on one elbow to watch her face half-revealed by the sheet and the nodding shadows of rose boughs beyond the window. Her finely arched brows and forehead beneath the tousled, slightly curled hair, the eyes shielded by darkness, the faint line down each cheek to the corners of her mouth, the slender lips with the furrow under her short nose – all seemed so familiar, older and more familiar than this room, the moonlight, himself.

'Can't sleep?' Her eyes watched him.

'Thought I heard something outside. Sorry – did I wake you?'

She smacked her lips, rising. 'Got to pee,' she said, shuffling her nightgown round her, and padded to the bathroom, the sound of her urination loud through the open door. The toilet rushed, hissed, subsided; she slipped back into bed. He reached to pull her into his arms; she kissed him quickly on the cheek, 'G'night.' He brought his hand down her back, slowing at the curve of her waist, down her hip and thigh and beneath her nightgown, sliding it up past her pants. 'Go to sleep,' she murmured, taking his hand, but he moved it down inside her pants. 'Ian!' He lay back, one hand loose on her shoulder. 'Now you're angry,' she said.

'No.'

She caressed his brow quickly. 'It's time for sleep. You have to leave early.'

He restrained a desire to sit up, leave right now. 'It's good I'm going.'

'Lie down, darling.' She nestled into her pillows, squeezed his arm. 'Get some sleep.'

He lay facing upwards till grey began to fill the room, then took his clothes downstairs and dressed, the kitchen light harsh in his eyes. He made a cup of instant coffee, and went to the den. From the desk he took a key and unlocked the closet, inside it was a tall steel cupboard with a combination lock which he opened and removed the G–3 from a rack of sombrely glistening rifles.

He slipped the web sling over his shoulder, the rifle feeling good there, as if healing some ancient want, its weight balancing him, its odour as intoxicatingly familiar as the breath of a woman one has never stopped loving. A can of oil, solvent, and a cleaning rod in his hands, he elbowed shut the closet and returned to the kitchen, sipping his coffee as he wiped pine sawdust from the barrel, breech and stock with an old undershirt. He removed the bolt and placed his thumb inside the breech, held it to the light and looked up the barrel, its rifling sharply outlined against the whiteness of his thumbnail.

Dottie came down, tugging back her hair, not looking at him. 'I suppose you expect I'll run the ranch?' She poured out the teapot and set new water to boil. 'If you leave with Nehemiah you can get Isau to run the bloody ranch. I'm going away to London.'

He put down the cleaning rod, the rifle across his knees, feeling angry at her turning on him again, as she always did, when it was already done, decided. He was angry at her dishevelledness, her having grown old, but sensed the root of his annoyance lay in the dream: he'd wanted to *ask* her what to do about the lion. 'Maybe you should. After this I think we should sell the cattle and lease the land. Go back and try to live in England.'

She sat down fast opposite him. 'You'd never survive.'

'I'm not surviving here.'

'You get along.'

'Is that what living *is*, to you?'

'You'll never be happy no matter where you are. I'm just your latest reason.'

He bit his lip, wanting to strike the table, her, everything. 'I was happy, for a while. I *need* something . . .'

'I'm tired of your needs. If you had any sense you would be too.'

He wanted to stroke the softness beneath her chin, the tawdry fall of hair past her jaw. 'I've never felt so defeated,' he said.

'You're a warrior, darling. You always strike back.' With both hands she pushed the hair back from her cheekbones, tightening her face. 'I can't handle it any more, Ian. For good. You and Africa.'

'And every breath I take I blame myself for bringing you here.'

'You don't have to leave this morning, darling. When Nehemiah comes why don't you just tell him you've changed your mind?' Her fingers were like tendrils against his cheek. 'Let's try going back? Right away?'

'I can't drop out now, at the last minute. There's Somalis drifting into the Ewaso N'giro, west of Buffalo Springs – that's the last elephants in northern Kenya.' He held her hand; it was like a tiny white flag of surrender. 'Once this's over I'll go up there, join you, try it for six months. Leave some young heifers and build up the herd again when we get back.'

She sat up and pulled away her hand. 'I don't want to *come* back! Ever!'

Daybreak through the four square mullioned panes of the kitchen window was like a plains fire out of control.

'And I'm not sure I'll want to stay. So we try it, then decide . . .'

Her face flushed. 'You're really doing this, aren't you – pushing *me* to go back so you and Nehemiah can have your fun!'

'It's not fun, Dottie. It's survival. For the elephants. For Kenya. But most of all for me.'

She looked at him dry-eyed. 'You'll never leave Africa.'

'I said I'd go up there with you, try that.'

'And all the time mooning over Africa – I've *seen* you, Ian, when the newness of London wears off and you get bored with your bloody dull Cotswolds, start wanting to come back. You draw all down inside yourself and you're unpleasant to my friends and snarl at perfect strangers! If we go back we sell the farm and make a complete break.'

'I won't do that. Not yet. But I'll try my best to stay there.'

'Your best, my dear, isn't good enough. Not any more. Not for me.'

Her face was set. He felt a weight slowly slipping from the back of his neck, replaced by pain. 'So what do you suggest?'

'Just leave, chase around the desert with your friends. Playing soldier. You're too old, dearie – your hair's going grey. Already the men call you "*Mzee*"!'

He smiled to hide the hurt. 'Maybe you should stay a while with the kids. Let me do my soldier thing, then I'll come up. After that we'll decide if we want to stay up there or come back here.'

'Even the way you say it! "Up there"! It's not part of your life.'

'It never has been.'

'It was mine, once! *You're* the one who dragged me down here. "You'll love it, darling"! Your tales of

47

safaris – "wait till you see the sunsets"!'

'Nehemiah's my oldest friend. He needs help. He would never speak or even think of it, but twice he's saved my life, when he was detailed to the SAS in Aden. In Africa, the way we think, I don't even have the right to refuse him.'

'You! You men! "The way we think",' her teeth flashed as she mimicked him. 'With your wars and noble vows and blood debts and all that other Kipling rot! Can't you grow up, see beyond it?'

'Without Nehemiah I wouldn't even be here! You want me to see beyond that?'

'Would you be here without me?'

He watched the coffee cup he turned in circles on the table. It was one of those moments begging for the truth. That changes things. 'Yes, I'd be here,' he replied.

'*I* wouldn't. I'd be in London and spending weekends in Kent, with friends and family, not in an alien world, a *primitive* world, with a man who doesn't love me!'

He stood up and gently tucked in his chair. 'As usual, this is going nowhere. If you don't think by now I love you, you never will.'

'I never will.'

He put the cleaning rod, oil, solvent and cloths into their kit and laid them on the table beside the rifle. 'Nehemiah'll be here any minute. But when I come back from this patrol, we'll do what you want, Dot. As long as you lay off the bottle. You quit drinking and we'll sell out and go to England.'

'Bastard!' She pushed herself up with her hands. He shrugged and turned towards the den, the teacup she had hurled shattering against the jamb, but he continued to the den, gathered up his backpack, bush hat and canteen, and returned to the kitchen for the gun and cleaning kit. He wanted to kiss her goodbye, sensing as with every campaign that this might be the last one, that he'd never see her again, that it was not wrong to die but wrong to leave her. But he didn't, stepping past her into the morning scent of jacarandas, fuchsia and bougainvillea, into the rising sun glinting off the thatched roofs of the Rendille rondavels beyond the camel pens. There was no peace, no joy – only duty to be done, day after day, life after life, long after its reason was obscured by time.

Suddenly the entire fabric of their lives grew clear to him, how it had been woven day by day on an adulterated pattern, one that had not contained all of him, nor all of her, and now the garment didn't fit, had worn in the wrong places, constrained them by day but no longer kept them warm at night.

Oh poor Dottie, he whispered, not out of condolence but of sorrow, that her human trace had gone astray, that he had failed her, that they'd ended up too close and far too far apart. If one could unravel the false strands, back to the beginning . . . but the pattern had been lost – they'd killed it by dying separately inside it. And it was too late to disassemble both their lives; even a poorly fitting fabric clung to the soul and could not be renounced.

Was he really leaving this farmhouse, this savannah, for the final time, never again to cross the yard in twilit dawn after feeding the bum calves, never again to see the stone house rising tall and square before him, having once again defeated the night, its familiar windows bright with family, food and love, making him feel, 'I've made this, it's mine'? Already it grew alien, awaiting other lives, he and his loved ones so soon forgotten – where was the echo of what they'd been, in this house?

Dorothy's still there, inside. But even when he *was* there, he wasn't. She was right, he'd left long ago. When? Was it his leaving that had made her drink? Where had he gone?

A camel brayed with anger out on the savannah; smoke rose in indolent columns from the rondavels; new sunlight struck the savage earth. He sensed suddenly how women have emptied men through submission and fidelity, stolen their power by demanding that they not wander, not war, not hunt, not fertilize other women. What weaklings, how feeble we've become. I too. To call this life.

# Chapter 4

The softest, sweetest leaves of the baobab tree are high in the top branches, and she was determined to get them. She stretched her trunk as high as it would reach, coiled the tip round a branch and bent it down. But even standing on her rear legs she could not pull the branch low enough to reach her mouth.

Annoyed, she dropped to four feet and ripped away mouthfuls of lower, bitter stems, grunting at their dusty, rough taste. Without listening she heard ripping soil behind her as her sister pulled up chunks of murram grass, the crackling of boughs from a neighbouring tree as old aunt yanked them down, the squeal of baby bull calf as he waited for the tasty leaves.

The young elephant tried a desert date bush, but it was sour with ants and she spat half out. She moved back to the baobab, rose up again on her back feet and snatched the high branch. Swaying back and forth, she used her weight against the branch; it was limber, would bend down but would not snap. She stripped bark and leaves with her trunk, angry at the sting of flesh.

Mother would just reach up and yank the bough

down, or put her shoulder against the baobab's massive trunk and shove it over. Then the young elephant would rush to the topmost, sweetest branches and chew them down, sheltered in her mother's rumbling shadow. The young elephant whinnied with sorrow and glanced behind her.

The others were moving towards the water, and she ran to catch up. In the shade of the tall bankside trees the hot skin of her back shivered with anticipation. The branches and leaves in her stomach still tasted sour and she thought of the cool water soothing them.

There was no human smell on the wind. Old aunt moved first out of the brush to the water's edge. When no thunder and death came, the others moved out behind old aunt and the young elephant felt the delicious water rise up her legs into the dry skin of her belly and up her sides to her shoulders, and she poured it down her throat, washing the dust away, the twigs and leaves and dirt and root scraps; all was pure in the coolness of this moment. She sucked in more water and cascaded it down her back, shivering with delight as it chilled the hot skin.

She was sleepy now as they tramped single file back under the tall trees, stopping to snatch at vines, their earthy taste good in her wet throat. Old aunt led them through the thinner scrub beyond the trees and out on to the warm savannah; the grass crackled pleasantly underfoot, the sun a comfortable weight on her shoulders.

A sharp smell made her jump with fear; she raised her trunk to taste it on the wind, spun round to face it, ears wide. It came from the north, upriver; she could hear nothing but the birds and the song of bees and butterflies, the rasping wind on the murram grass, the distant murmur of the river that reminded her suddenly of her mother. The odour was rough, strong, yet exciting. She peered towards it, seeing only the flow of heat and sunshine over the earth.

Old aunt trumpeted angrily; the young elephant raised her own trunk and ran towards her, calling, spun on her heels and faced the smell again. The baby bull calf ran past her, towards old aunt. The young elephant's sister came and nudged her with her trunk, sniffed the breeze, blew it out her trunk.

Again old aunt trumpeted and sister ran to her. Old aunt turned away from the smell, along the edge of the river brush. The young elephant dropped her head and snatched at the grass, not tasting it, waiting for the smell. Slowly she began to follow the herd.

A distant but louder trumpet startled her, out of the river brush to the north, from the smell. Old aunt waved her trunk angrily, pushing bull calf and little sister ahead. The young elephant halted, looked back.

A huge bull elephant broke through the riverside brush and walked steadily towards them, his head above the baobabs. Letting the others go, the young elephant stood till the bull came near and circled to get her smell, nickered, drew close and reached down his long trunk to touch her shoulder. His odour was acrid, intoxicating, frightening, strange yet suddenly familiar, like a place where she had been a long time ago and just now remembered. Nervously she trotted towards the others; the bull huffed and followed, swinging his massive head to keep his tusks above the scrub.

But as they neared the others he turned her aside, back towards the river. She squealed and old aunt rumbled back; the bull was beside her now and she wanted to go to the herd and get away from him. Suddenly the bull screamed with rage and pain as guns roared all around them and a vicious agony struck her stomach, making her legs fold, and she crashed to the earth, the agony ripping through her chest. The guns crackled from the riverside trees, louder, more awful, and over the wails of old aunt and the terror of her sister she heard the bull's furious trumpet and the thunder of the earth as he charged the guns and they seemed to concentrate, grow louder, fuse into one permanent roar, as if the world had split apart.

She heard little sister squealing and dragged herself to her feet, the agony spreading like fire inside her; she could not see her sister, could see nothing, hearing only this storm of guns and the bubbling squeal of her sister and the moans of old aunt and a weird humming like angry bees. Another pain struck her head, knocking her down. The grass and earth before her face were near and far away, full of odours and empty; she rolled on to her knees and pulled herself up, her belly tearing as if rooted to earth. The poor land itself was struck, twisting and spinning, blood-red. She stumbled towards the cries of her sister, another horrible pain striking her hip, the guns banging closer now, and she could smell humans coming through the grass, their metallic, sweaty, hyaena stink, and here was bull calf lying covered with gore, that which had been his life moments ago now spread over him and the grass.

Little sister would not move nor was there breath coming from her mouth; the young elephant dug her tusks under little sister and pushed her up but she fell down and an awful explosion thudded into the young elephant's brain, knocking her back on her haunches, but she stood and ran wildly screaming at the guns as the blows struck everywhere and all at once the earth was with her and anything was better than this pain.

In the smell of cordite and powder and blood, and in the sudden silence after the shooting, Warwar felt nauseous but empty, as if he had already thrown up everything. He stood and stared out over the long grass at the young elephant's flank rising like a grey lava outcrop; his rifle barrel touched his cheek, searing the skin.

'Dead!' someone screamed. 'He's dead!'

It was Suli, screaming. He must have killed the big bull, Warwar thought, wanting to walk out across the savannah and never live with humans again.

Parting the long grass with his rifle, he neared the young elephant. Her skull was cratered and splintered by bullets, her head and ears a roseate pulp. He tried to remember how afraid he'd been when she charged. She was nearly dead even then, he told himself.

Suli was still carrying on, his voice tilting like a woman's in mourning. So he killed the bull. Now let him carry his tusks. Warwar leaned his rifle against the young elephant's flank, pulled out his *simi*, and began to chop at the thick flesh from the base of one upraised tusk. Her tongue lay half out of her mouth, coated with wet grass. He shoved the tip of the *simi* between the grey flesh and the tusk and drove it upwards, twisting the blade to slit the tough skin.

He finished slicing away the skin on the outside and, down on his knees, leaned in to pry the root of the tusk with the *simi*. As he did her eye moved.

He dropped the *simi* and jumped away. Her eye followed him. Weirdly the words of the Prophet came to him: 'Even when you do not know it, Allah watches you.'

Ibrahim was calling. 'Ho!' Warwar answered. 'I'm here – the young cow.'

Ibrahim's voice neared, panting. 'He's killed your brother!'

The sky leaned over and crashed into the earth. Warwar righted himself, holding the elephant's ear, the skin grainy as stone.

'The big bull,' Ibrahim gasped, running. 'Threw him in the air and stamped him.' Ibrahim took Warwar's shoulders. 'We could do nothing. We kept shooting. Nothing would stop him.' Warwar shoved Ibrahim away, ran towards the sound of Suli wailing like a loose cloth in the wind.

Ahmed lay in bloody grass by a thorn tree, head crushed, one arm torn off. His leg was jerking as if he would run away. Warwar lay down with his face on his brother's chest.

'Hurry!' It was Rashid, whispering to Suli. 'We have to hurry!'

Warwar stared up at him. 'We're never going to leave here!'

Rashid's hand over his heart was an open lie. 'We must rush. Rangers will come.' He looked across the grass tops. 'The bull can charge again.'

'Where is he?'

'He ran into the trees, there, along the river. We'll take the other tusks quickly, and your brother, bury him later.'

This was not Ahmed, but a body covered in its own blood and the blood of elephants. Already the flies were at it. A single hawk flew high over the savannah. Now it is just me. You have died and now you live inside me and nowhere else.

In the crushing silence of sorrow he walked through the tawny tall grass and took his rifle that leaned against the young cow elephant. Ibrahim was chopping away her second tusk. 'She's not dead,' Warwar said.

'Dead enough. We have to move quickly.'

'We'll go nowhere till I kill the bull.'

Ibrahim's head jerked up. 'You are the youngest here, and give no commands. I regret your brother's dead, but keep your tongue, as Allah wills.'

'Go as you like, all of you.' From the sheath inside his cloak Warwar took a leather sack filled with bullets. He dismounted the clip of his AK47, and reloaded it. 'I will bury my brother, and kill the bull. That is what Allah wills.'

# Chapter 5

The bull's blood-spattered path was wide through the crushed brush. You will never grieve, Warwar told himself. When you were young you thought love was important. Now you see it, too, is illusion. You will learn to live without sorrow. To be free, of everything. As you covered Ahmed with stones so the jackals cannot eat him, so you will cover his death inside your heart. The whooshing burst of a francolin from a bush made him jump back, jerk up the rifle. No, he told himself, follow the path straight, Allah says, no need to fear.

The bull had run with his head to the wind, and now the wind stayed in Warwar's face and the bull would not smell him. Unless he circled. His blood thick on the grass, splashed over the splintered thorn trees and chunks of volcanic rock like disinterred skulls, filling up cracks in the earth like a river overflowing. It stuck leaves and broken grass to the soles of Warwar's feet. There were huge clumps of dung mixed with orange blood: gut-shot. The fury of such pain. The fury of being plucked from life, for no reason. He will not want to die, until he's killed me.

The breeze blew hot in Warwar's face, smelling of hot grass and hot blood and stones breaking under the sun.

With an explosive whirr of wings a flock of sunbirds scattered in shattered golden shards before him. Again he loosened his grip on the rifle. Over against the trees an old man baboon watched from a red termite mound; Warwar imagined him laughing, and pointed the rifle at him; the baboon ducked into the grass. Pinned to the top of the sky, a single eagle circled, alone and complete.

What you never learned, old bull, is don't get trapped by love. For two days didn't we follow the old cow with her bull calf and the two young cows? We could have had their ivory, but we waited, hoping you would come. The young cow, the one I shot, was in season; foolish as any man in love you came to her. Now you have paid. In agony, your body torn to pieces by bullets. Fool, didn't you understand? As long as you don't need, you can't be trapped.

The bull's path cut suddenly across the wind, towards the river. Gut-shot and thirsty. Or seeking cover in the riverside jungle, a perfect ambush for one last charge. No time to raise the gun, the tusks shearing, slicing, snatching me up, the spinning sky, over the bull's great back like a mountain, the mountain's great feet smashing me down, crushing, crushing. What Ahmed knew.

He thought of Ahmed bringing in the goats at night. Ahmed's sinewy hand on Warwar's shoulder, counselling wisdom, patience: you and I are outcasts, little brother. We are in the clan but not of it. We must not expect too much, must do more than our share. It's not our fault our family's dead, yet we must pay. We are alone, but we have each other.

Nearer the river the grass came up to his shoulders. The wind touched his right cheek, a warning. Now the bull will circle upriver and turn back, wait till I cross his scent.

A clash of branches overhead and Warwar leaped back, screaming up at the bull's huge crushing mass, but it was only blue monkeys in the doum palms. Nothing but the somnolent chant of birds, wail of an ibis, bees bumbling in the brush, scree of a shrike over the savannah, seeking love or prey. A mamba greener than the grass watched him out of pit-black eyes. God split your tongue for lying, and you kill us for revenge. It is people who pay for God's deeds. We and his animals, created to expiate His sins. Do you feel less guilty, Lord, now Ahmed's dead?

Into the riverside jungle, sudden shadow cool as a knife blade on the back of his neck. Old leopard scat on a fallen trunk, trail of *siafu*, already feeding on the bull's blood. We may live for years; our carcasses last only hours. I won't be alone if Soraya is with me. But she'll go to an old man with a drooping gut and many goats to give her father. And I'll hunt pasture in the desert.

Leaves caressed his arm, softness of shaded soil against his soles, smell of cedar bark shredded by a tusk. I regret your pain, he told the bull. I would be you if I could. I did not shoot you. Yes, I did shoot your young mistress. But without many tusks I could never have a young mistress of my own. Dark thick knots of blood now underfoot – choking on your heart!

That – moving in the trees! Grey like a cliff, taller, vanished. Warwar backed away, could not soothe his trembling wrists, the metal stock slippery, sweat in his eyes but he did not dare raise a hand from the gun to wipe them. When he comes it will be a mountain falling, unstoppable.

Sweet chirp of birds, insect murmurs, sough of branch on stem and leaf to leaf, steady susurration of the river like a woman sleeping, drum of his pulse, tick of sweat falling on the breech, whistle of a frond bent backwards. On the twisting wind the ravaged angry bull smell, blood and iron hatred.

Ahead a grey glimmer through spiring black trunks, green submerged light. Warwar aimed – no shot. He ran to the next tree, the next, lungs choked, arms shivering. Everywhere a cage of stems, vines, boughs, branches, towering trunks. Can't see *him*. He was *there*, just beyond the camphor tree with the broken crotch, there, its bark scabby as old elephant hide – if he's not a bull but a devil he can vanish, come up behind. Warwar shoved apart a faceful of broad blood- smeared leaves, twisting sideways through tangled creepers snatching at the rifle, the bull's footprint deep in the soggy soil infilled with blood, wide round as a tree, wider than Warwar's body this one foot, and he was trembling now but would not halt, wanted to climb this *podocarpus* with its comforting wide branches up to safety, taller than *his* head, to *see* him, his furious odour thick as metal on the breeze, the shifting breeze, and why was it changed? He turned his face to feel the breeze but it had not shifted, and as he realized this and understood what it meant, with a scream of roots the *podocarpus* behind him was wrenched from the earth, struck by the bull's great raging chest as trumpeting he bore down on Warwar, shutting out the sun, tusks flashing, his mad red eyes and tortured mouth and savaged head and every detail of his monstrous flesh visible and clear, his great legs like trees reaching to smash Warwar down, and Warwar was empty and dead already, his soul fled the body that raised the hammering gun whose bullets beat like wasps up the bull's chest and up the great tower of his neck and under the jaw and the sky was blocked as the vast tusks came swinging down shearing the rifle he raised to guard himself, and the weight of the world struck him and he was not there, was nowhere, did not care.

# Chapter 6

For a moment the Ewaso N'giro, an arisen moon deepening its roiled, unrolling surface, was a vision to which MacAdam held the key, then the vision was gone and he could not understand it.

He could hear his men's voices, softened by the jungle and the night, from the circle where they sat round a fire that he could smell but could not see. There was the wake of a croc nosing for the far dark shore like an arrow pointing him to somewhere, as though he might rise up from his lookout here beside this fallen *podocarpus* and follow the arrow back into the vision. A spoonbill cried, frightened maybe by a snake; he turned back to the rippling moonlit river but could not grasp the vision, could only remember that he *had* grasped it and the moment had been lost.

With a light whistle Kuria signalled his approach, his rifle clinking as he swung his leg over MacAdam's *podocarpus* and crouched down. 'Anything?' he whispered.

'Leopard hunting the other bank – half hour ago. Croc just crossed, down there – watch out another doesn't jump you. Vervets in the trees upstream, but they're quiet now.' What he'd told all the men earlier he repeated now to Kuria, 'If the Somalis turn back to hit us they may circle camp and come from this side, so watch the jungle.'

For a moment Kuria said nothing, then, 'I hope they do, Captain.'

Getting up he squeezed Kuria's shoulder. 'Never hope for a fight till *you* start it.' He threaded his way silently towards camp, changed his mind and, averting his eyes from the glow of the fire, slipped upriver along the bank some hundred yards past camp to a second sentry, then circled behind camp to check two others in the jungle. When he returned to camp the men were talking quietly in groups near the fire, the Maasai in one cluster, the Kikuyus and one Meru in another, three Luo, tall and heavy-boned, in a tight clump on the edge of darkness. Nehemiah was crossing back and forth between them, checking, questioning – a mother hen, MacAdam thought, trying to link disparate tribes with the awkward artificiality of Swahili, dreaming that an Africa of warring clans can unite into the countries drawn once on a white man's map.

Yet the squad *was* becoming one. In the week since he and Nehemiah had taken them into the jungle the men had grown quieter and faster, working now as a single body of which each was a member. Yet, MacAdam realized, he still felt an interloper, for his white skin, and for his always keeping something in reserve the whiteman way, something even he could never touch.

A log in the flames crackled with termite eggs, sending up sparks, and again he felt irritation because of the fire. The poachers were too careful, too close to the land to show their presence like this. Woodsmoke lingers on a man's clothes and hair for days, can be smelled half a mile away. 'We should avoid the fire,' he'd told Nehemiah. 'Lions won't come in on so many of us.'

'The men don't feel right without one.'

Everybody changes, even Nehemiah. The Kenyan *askari* is no longer ready to run ninety miles in a day across the desert without water. Too much easy food and Coca Cola and motor vehicles have slowed even the Maasai. Every strength sows the seeds of future weakness: material advances destroy our defences against the primitive.

If you love your culture, he'd always argued, defend it or it will vanish. Hadn't Toynbee counted twenty-six major civilizations in the history of humanity – and said of them only western Latin Christendom still survives? Fifty years ago it dominated Africa. Now only shreds of it remained in Kenya and South Africa; everywhere else the continent was turning back to tribalism, chaos, constant warfare, ignorance and superstition, just as the roads, schools, railroads, hospitals and homes the Europeans once built fell into disrepair and were abandoned. But how many times had he broken his heart over this, and to what good?

Nehemiah's huge bulk settled beside him. 'All quiet on the western front?'

'Not if you're leopard prey . . .'

A chuckle. 'I know this isn't how you'd do it—'

'It's not my say.'

'Sure – that's why you're here.'

'We've been tracking these guys for two days. We gain on them in the day and lose them at night.'

'Even M'kele can't follow tracks at night, Mac.'

'Now that they've split up, we should too. Some of us to follow the three with the camels carrying the tusks and the one M'kele says was hurt, and the rest of the squad to follow the seven on foot.'

'We're on foot, too. We can't catch camels. We'll be lucky to catch the ones on foot – in any case, *they're* the ones looking for more elephants.'

MacAdam reminded himself to stop biting his lip, to breathe. 'There's something about the others – the one who killed the big bull. I want them.'

'We can't catch camels, Mac,' Nehemiah repeated.

MacAdam shifted his knee from a sharp rock. 'By tomorrow night we'll be east of Wamba and into the Matthews Range—'

'If these guys leave the river, the jungle, go north—'

'They will, and that's where they'll lose us.'

MacAdam felt, rather than saw, Nehemiah nod, the admission of what they'd known all along. 'The men're tired,' Nehemiah said.

'So let's take a chance, leave the jungle and cut north into the mountains, spread out and see if they run into us? Maybe they're planning to meet up with the camels there, somewhere up in the Kaisut Desert.'

Nehemiah's fear for his men was like a current in the air. No commander can be good who doesn't dare to sacrifice some men, MacAdam thought. That's why I've never been good. The fire crackled, spat, subsided. A pair of owls was hunting the river's edge, calling to each other. Love, he thought. What else is there? He could hear Nehemiah's stomach rumble. Three days of shit food, a hundred and fifty miles with a pack and rifle in the unbreathable heat, beating through the wall of whipcord vines and creepers of the jungle's midday night, snakes waiting in ambush, or a lion following silently till one man drops a little too far back, the quicksand and mosquitoes and crocs along the river. And now we'll lose them – three of the Somalis have fled with the camels, and the others will turn north for a run across the desert slopes of Naingamkama and into the bamboo jungles of the mountains where we'll have to slow down to avoid ambushes, where they can split up and vanish.

'The men're too green,' Nehemiah said. 'I can't deploy them out there alone, armed with Enfields, against seven experienced poachers with automatic rifles. Any guy who ran into the poachers wouldn't last five minutes.'

'It's *your* fucking elephants.'

'As if you didn't care.' Nehemiah's eyes twinkled in the fire's light.

'So let's split up – let me take two or three men and cut them off; you and the squad keep on their tracks till we link up again?' MacAdam watched a strip of bark curl into the flames, imagined what was going on in Nehemiah's mind, how he'd balance the need to kill the poachers with his wariness of dividing the squad, his knowledge of the dangers of jungle versus open desert, balancing his hatred of the poachers with his desire not to lose any men, particularly now when the campaign was beginning and losses could slow it substantially. He shouldn't push him. 'When we all get G–3s . . .' He brushed his unshaven jaw against the cool barrel of the rifle Nehemiah had given him that stood loosely in the curve between his neck and shoulder.

Nehemiah gathered his legs beneath him. 'The men don't need to wait on automatic rifles.'

'I didn't mean it like that.'

'Of course you did. Generosity is your ultimate weapon.' Nehemiah stood. 'Take M'kele and three others. We'll meet you at the upper end of the N'geng valley—'

'Below Musawa?'

'At dusk, three days from tomorrow. You'll be on dry rations.'

'We'll kill something if we're hungry.'

'Don't light a fire,' Nehemiah chided.

MacAdam grinned. 'We may just eat your poachers. Alive.'

Nehemiah rose and stepped to the cluster of Maasai, bent to speak. He and a smaller, slender, stooping man returned. 'Are you tired, Uncle?' Nehemiah said, respectfully, in Maasai.

'*Hapana kabisa*,' M'kele answered in Swahili to include MacAdam. 'Never.'

'Don't mind, Uncle, this whiteman understands Maasai tongue. Do you think we'll catch them?'

'Not soon.'

'Ian thinks they'll head into the Matthews Range,

wants to head straight north and cut them off.'

M'kele said nothing.

'What do you think?' MacAdam said.

'We are not catching them like this.'

'Who would you take?'

M'kele turned towards the fire. 'Gideon and Joseph from the Kikuyus, the Meru Kuria, the Maasai Benjamin and Darius.'

'Would you go also?' MacAdam said.

'I would go happily. These poachers are not Maasai, they are not even Kikuyu. They are Somali people.'

'Then we take Gideon, Kuria and Darius,' MacAdam said. 'With you and me, M'kele, that makes five. Have someone replace Kuria on forward sentry. Tell the three of them to sleep. We leave at 2400.'

He lay awake beneath his blanket, the thunder of his pulse drowning the whine of mosquitoes, the chirr of crickets, the dissatisfied roars of lions impatient beyond the firelight, the rustle of men settling into sleep. Strangely he felt like praying, closer to the universe and farther from man. He thought of Dorothy soon to be in distant London and reached out of his blanket to knock on wood, a stick by his head, that she was not fearing, in danger, too alone.

For an instant his vision watching the moonlit Ewaso N'giro returned, but again he could not grasp it. Life seemed so full of chances for love yet so empty of love itself. What do I do, he wondered, to keep it at bay? With a sudden surge of peace he felt that love's best found in doing what you need to do, to be free. But freedom, underneath it all, is death.

As the fire dimmed the lions crept nearer, the mosquitoes redoubled their efforts; between the high, thick leaves the stars glittered with the cold mockery of space.

# Chapter 7

The lions were silent; hyaenas wailed on the distant barren slopes of Louwa Warikoi. A blanket over his face to deter mosquitoes, his breath wet-hot inside it, MacAdam lay thinking of the elephants the poachers had slaughtered: the old matriarch and her bull calf, the two young cows, less than ten years old, one in heat, an old bull courting her. The poachers had stalked them upwind – so easy – had opened fire as the elephants grazed a deep grassy slope above the Ewaso N'giro; the bull and one young cow, the one in heat, had charged the poachers, face into the vicious penetrating hail of AK47s – maybe only a soldier could imagine what it was like to charge into those guns. It doesn't help to think about it, he told himself, but it would not go away, would not let him sleep. If we get those guys, then I was right to go with Nehemiah. No matter what.

He saw the poachers laughing, already counting the money as they chopped away the tusks, their teeth and lips frothy green with the leafy *miraa* they chew to give them endurance. Now three had split off and taken the camels and tusks, and it was *they* he wanted most, the young one who killed the bull. At least the bull had killed one Somali; MacAdam smiled thinking how his men had removed the stones covering the dead man so the scavengers could have him. 'You will be the shit of hyaenas,' they had laughed. 'The shit of jackals.'

And now the seven on foot were only two days ahead. He saw how he might corner them among the steep peaks and rugged defiles of Ol Doinyo Lenkiyio, the Matthews Range, how the poachers, desert men from Somalia, forced now into the mountains, exhausted by pursuit, might make the elemental mistake of sticking to the valleys rather than climb the slopes. He would lose one man, he sensed. Jesus, let it be me. Of all of them I'm the oldest but M'kele, have the least to live for, except for what I can teach them. The feeling came back he'd had weeks before, gazing on the sunset savannah from his house on the Lerochi: a good day to die. No, he told himself, as if to make it so by willing it, I will not lose a man.

23:52. The three-quarter moon clear, no clouds, thirty degrees above the horizon. He stretched, checked his rifle, folded his blanket. Something was wrong in this silence. He watched the sleeping men, bent to wake M'kele, but instead took his rifle and went upriver to the first sentry, who stood to check his approach.

'Your ears are strong, brother,' MacAdam whispered.

'I heard you leave camp.'

'What's new?'

'Hippos breathing – middle of the river – noisy as trucks. I keep watching the jungle.'

'Good. There's one chance in a hundred the Somalis'll attack, but any time you stop watching is when they do it.'

The man wiped mosquitoes from his face, saying nothing, as if MacAdam had insulted him with this simple truism. 'Guard well,' MacAdam added, squeezing his shoulder. 'M'kele and I and the three others will come this way when we leave – don't shoot us.'

Hiss of a chuckle under the man's breath. 'What good would that do?'

He checked the other sentries, all alert, then woke M'kele and his three men. They ate a handful of cold *ugali* each, shouldered their packs and rifles. He led them east along the river, on the poachers' tracks, among branches, vines, creepers, stolid huge trunks, and saplings, then left the tracks and turned north, picking up speed as the moon climbed and the land rose and slowly the jungle gave way to brushland, then rolling savannah, and they could run steadily till the hills grew steeper and the soil sandy and soft, burying their steps. With a fire in his heart he drove himself uphill, gasping for breath but not slowing, seeing the dead elephants and the poachers' laughing, *miraa*-smeared lips, hearing his own men breathing behind him, as if this were a race and he trying to extend his lead.

The hills crested onto the cindery flat savannah south of Ouarges, 'the place where the people gather to go raiding' in Samburu language, and again MacAdam broke into a run, the light pack with its sloshing canteens chafing his shoulders, the heavy rifle off-balancing his stride.

Before dawn he called a halt, head spinning, legs sloppy with exhaustion. 'You guys – too young for me.'

'Shit,' Kuria bent over, holding his knees. 'I'm beat.'

Darius rubbed sweat from his eyes. 'You run like a fuckin' black man.'

Dizzy, MacAdam hugged him, Darius' sweaty temple hot against his own. 'I *am* a fuckin' black man. I just have white skin.'

The men's grins were like stars. MacAdam felt an incredible burst of love. Sun poured over the edge of the world inflaming the tan earth, grey thorn scrub and brittle grass. The lava rocks sharpened and glowed; birdsong and desert ambrosia rose from the soil, radiated from the air. He unscrewed his canteen and handed it around, drank last and sparingly, sweat trickling into his mouth.

As the huge orange sun cleared the horizon its heat blasted across the savannah, inflaming the humped spines of Ouarges mountain and the taller Matthews Range behind it. 'If they turned north. . .' MacAdam panted.

M'kele took up the thought. 'Not in the mountains, yet.'

Exhaustion pooled grey circles under M'kele's eyes, the thin shoulders of his camo shirt wet under the pack straps. 'If they turned north,' MacAdam repeated, 'soon we cross tracks.' M'kele raised his head slightly, meaning maybe.

MacAdam wiped the sweat from his glasses, resettled the pack on his blistered shoulders, picked up the rifle heavy as concrete and walked fast towards the humped spines of Ouarges already dancing in the heat, the men in a tight string behind him. Despite the heat he felt good from the halt, for the taste of water and the new songs of birds and the morning breeze whispering over warming rocks whose trace of night's moisture brought to his nostrils the drying fragrances of sand and parched lava, the earth's crust hardening over its core.

The sun rose, its white wrath bearing down on his head and shoulders, searing his skin through the cotton shirt and his scalp through the perforated bush hat and his dusty, sweat-caked hair. By noon he was forced to halt them every hour, wild heat writhing round them like devils. In the illusory shade of a blistered thorn tree they sat, stunned and silent, the labour of opening a ration can almost beyond them. 'Water,' MacAdam rasped. 'How much?'

'Two canteens,' Gideon said.

'Sip each.' He forced himself to his feet. See, it's not so bad, he told himself. I'll walk up this hill, show them not to be tired. Officer's job – shame them into what no sensible man would do.

The hill was too steep; he turned round to scan the countryside as if this had been his intent. The men below did not look up, inanimate, a feature of the bristly lava savannah but for the weird collision of their jungle camouflage against the burnt soil. The rifle on his shoulder seemed the only thing linking him to earth; half-hating himself, he turned and climbed the hill.

From its summit the land appeared bereft of life but for his men under the scraggy thorn tree, like four ants hunting shelter among the crags of a blistered moon.

Beyond the earth's eastern edge, almost beyond space itself, the stark red tree-crested abutments of Ol Doinyo Sabichi, the *inselberg* of God, home of *N'gai*, towered over the razor-edged land as though imposed from above.

To the southeast lay the Shaba's endless plateau of black coals beneath the sun, beyond it the vast baked Merti plateau tilting down into the boundless miasmic marshes of Lorian Swamp where even the great Ewaso N'giro dies in sand. To the northeast the Woyamdero Plain unrolled across countless gorges and inaccessible chasms and dust-choked steppes into the lost regions of Gora Kudi and Bokhol, till somewhere, in the land of mirage and imagination, rose the purple-black Ethiopian escarpment.

And northwards, as if implanted from a different universe, were the muscular heights of the Matthews Range, a green Ararat above the rising desert. But closer, where the savannah vanished suddenly into the dry forests of the mountain's first slopes, why that tiny shifting clump of bush? MacAdam put down his rifle, snatched off his pack, tore it open and yanked out his binoculars.

Heat and mirages danced in the lenses. One eyepiece had been knocked; he couldn't focus it. There – not brush, but figures, moving. He dashed to the edge of the summit, whistled down, waving his hand. Like a sleepwalker M'kele arose, adjusted his bush hat. MacAdam beckoned wildly. M'kele grabbed his pack and gun, ran upslope, the others after him. Huffing, they burst over the top, eyes wide with effort. 'It's them!'

MacAdam shoved the binoculars at M'kele.

M'kele did not take them, turning to peer across the rippling canyons of heat where MacAdam pointed. 'It's them.' With the back of his hand he wiped sweat from his lips. 'Seven men with rifles. Moving very slowly.'

# Chapter 8

Is it all dreams and loneliness, with no purpose? Ahmed would never have admitted this. How awful to die never having scratched the surface of your soul.

Warwar watched the truncated, bloody-stumped tusks of the dead bull rise and fall with the jerking stride of the camel before him. This bull, who wanted so much to live, instead perished ignobly, in horrible pain, so that squat two-footed animals could carve his great tusks into trinkets: I don't believe you, Lord, that man is king. Man's a scorpion, dangerous, solitary and unloved. Only a God could care about man.

The dawn desert savannah was bereft of life but for the wind-hunched *commiphora*, a distant hyaena cringing out of rifle range. Step after step, the camel's rump up and down before you, his hemp tail twisting aside to deposit dung on your path: freedom is a lie.

Judge not, Ahmed would say. And Allah would say I was chosen to succeed Ahmed because he was wrong. I must not succumb to the weakness of understanding.

Warwar swung the AK47 to the other shoulder, liking how it tightened the sore chest muscles where the dying bull's tusk had knocked him. Opening his mouth, he slid his jaw from side to side to feel the pain snake up his face and into the skull; anyone could be pretty, but to have such a scar made a man.

The wind swung, bringing the stench of rotting flesh from the tusks. Eat well, flies; lay your maggots, like the vermin that will buy these tusks and wear pretty bracelets and think they carry the spirit of the king.

If I want I can leave them, Ibrahim and Rashid. Just as the three of us split from Suli and the others, after the killing of the elephants. They have gone north to seek more elephants, leaving us the duty of returning home with these tusks – but who is to order that I stay with Ibrahim and Rashid?

As Ahmed said, I am in the clan but not of it. If I left now, they would have to give me my share. I who killed the big bull. Then I could follow my own path west across the great Chalbi, the maneater desert, not northwest with Ibrahim and Rashid into Somalia. Warwar let his mind wander like a hawk over the vast Chalbi, being *there*. But if I separate the paths, I will not have a camel to carry my share. And what will happen to Soraya?

He stopped short, his eye caught by a trace of something across the distant western sands – elephants? 'Cousin!' he called. 'Wisdom must be blind – you have not seen those tracks?'

Nearing, they saw it was two sets of parallel wide lines cutting evenly into the desert crust. Painfully Warwar knelt to fondle the sand. 'Whitemen?'

'Two Land Rovers, lightly loaded,' Ibrahim answered.

'Rangers!' Rashid said.

'It is not the right footprint for soldiers.' Ibrahim pointed his toe at the tread marks. He followed them fifty paces or so, returned. 'They passed yesterday; there's not much dust in the ruts.' He scuffed sand over a track. 'But why go north, across the Kaisut, when they could pass around it?'

Where Warwar knelt a cobra had crossed, its own track more recent. 'If Allah has favoured us with fortune, how can we refuse it?' He rose carefully to his feet. 'Follow them, and they will tell us what they do, and what they have to offer.'

The sun rising behind him threw his huge shadow far ahead on the reddened, sparkling sand, to the right a more massive outline formed by his two companions and the three camels. The tracks vanished in the tan, elaborately rippled land, its grey bushes and *jirme* cactus caught out here and there on tiny pedestals of crust, its distant stony outcrops that seemed always to be waiting, and which he had come to think of as *marabouts*, places where mullahs, holy men, lay.

The others had removed prayer cloths from a camel saddle; he knelt near them on the sand facing northeast, waited a moment for his mind to clear, noting a *siafu* that was attempting to climb a ridge of crumbly sand at the edge of his cloth. The ant scrambled up the loose, tiny slope that gave way as it neared the top, and it tumbled to the bottom again, immediately renewing its ascent. Why did it not shift to the right, and climb the easier, lower edge? Why did it always return to the most difficult point? Why did it strive? He let his eyes drift shut, seeing and not seeing the desert, mountains and arid sky, letting the Prophet's thoughts, like rain, nourish his heart.

When his mind was free he returned to the camels, stepping round the stocky, thick-bearded Ibrahim, who was bent checking a front hoof. 'I've seen what they're doing, these whitemen!' He touched Ibrahim's shoulder. 'Like the *siafu*, they're trying to take the most difficult route, to North Horr.'

'What *siafu*? Speak sensibly!'

'Allah has shown me, how they are doing things!'

'This is not the way to North Horr.' Shading his eyes, Ibrahim studied the tyre tracks converging ahead into a single shimmering line.

'Why else do they cross the Kaisut, only to turn north into the Chalbi? Why run from one desert into another?'

'They are blind, or fools.'

'Or like the *siafu*, they think they must always go straight ahead.'

'Then we'd cut them off by turning north, where their vehicles cannot travel.'

'Precisely.'

Ibrahim reflected. 'We'll do it, then. Otherwise we've lost them.'

'Exactly!' Warwar felt a rush of joy, as he always did when he had shown his elders how well he thought. The feeling built into a steady elation as he followed them north, contented to be last, no longer fearing as the youngest to be scorned, but perceiving all with a brightness precise as this sapphire sky and flawless desert.

At midday they halted in a dry, sandy *laga*. While the

others rested, Warwar untied an empty water gourd from a saddle and walked up the *laga* till he found a vertical sheet of basalt. He dug with his hands at the base of the rock. At first the sand burned his fingers; further down it was cooler and compact as he scooped it by handfuls from the hole.

The sand stuck to his fingers; he raised them to his lips and felt their momentary salve against the blistered skin. He lowered himself into the hole and dug deeper, dry sand at the top tumbling back in. A shadow crossed the pit. 'Nothing?' said Ibrahim.

'Not yet.'

'You're wasting time. Come!'

'Pull me out!' Warwar called, but Ibrahim had gone. He pushed himself up from the pit, brushed damp sand from his hands and clothes, and returned to the camels. The sun weighed dizzyingly on his scalp; the air was torpid, too hot to breathe; he thought of herding goats in the shade of doum palms and fig trees on the cool banks of the oasis at El God God.

Beyond the *laga* the black land stretched infinitely westwards to a line of magenta buttes that were certainly a mirage, for nothing could be so far away and yet so clear. The soil was rubbled with volcanic detritus, a sea of bituminous lava sucking in the sun, as if they rode across the still-live cinders of the earth's last conflagration.

Warwar's wounded head was pounded by the sun, his shoulder aching unconsciously from his AK47 with which only days ago he had killed the elephant king who had murdered Ahmed. The sharp lava sliced through

85

his sandals and they stuck with dried blood to his soles. The lion skin did not matter, nor the dung of the camels he stepped on because it was cooler than the rock, nor the rifle he longed to throw away but would not, for the others would then kill him. He stumbled into the back of camel and it kicked quickly, splitting his shin. He fell down holding his leg. Laughing, Ibrahim offered a hand. 'Come, nestling, and get a drink. We've stopped till night.'

'There's still light!'

'We're at the Chalbi's edge. If we've planned well, the Land Rovers'll be below – we don't want them to see us coming down.'

Warwar followed Ibrahim to where the third man, Rashid, held a nervous camel. With his *simi* Rashid sliced open a neck vein, the camel jerking back its head, the blood spraying into a leather jug till it was half full. Rashid pinched shut the vein, blood trickling up his arm, the camel's breath hot on Warwar's cheek.

From a camel heifer whose unweaned calf had been left behind they squeezed milk into the jug and shook it with the blood, each one then holding the jug above his lips and pouring his share into his mouth without touching the rim, Ibrahim first, Warwar last. The hot tang of the blood mixed with the sweet, creamy milk made his body shiver with delight; exhaustion and dizziness falling away like a *djellabah* discarded in the coolness of night.

The first star, the shepherd's, flamed above the eastern hills. After prayers the others rested and Warwar wandered with the camels as they nibbled at scraps of thorn bush and occasional blades of bitter grass. His mind drifted to Soraya's face as she had glanced up at him before her father's door, how her black eyes had taken him in. Unless she loved him she'd never look at him that way.

He could see her now, even from a distance, as she walks proudly home from market after sunset, her black cloak rippling with the movement of her body underneath, her eyes above the veil full of mirth and understanding, the bundle of corn or firewood balanced so easily on her erect, elegant head – never in El God God or all the Marrehan had he imagined anyone like her. But soon an elder would give her father thirty goats, five cows and ten sheep, and Warwar would lose her for ever.

If so, he would not marry. As in the story of a desert spring with water so sweet once men have tasted it they never can forget it, nor want any other, after he had seen into Soraya's eyes no other girl enticed him. His temples hammered; his palms sweated, wasting precious moisture. The camel heifer they had milked was straying; he whistled and ran after her, tossing stones to turn her back. The sun had fled; timid stars had sneaked in from the darkness.

The camels followed him, their hoofbeats loud and uneven on the stony soil. Ibrahim rose, stroking his beard. 'Let's go.'

Leaning his gun against a euphorbia, Warwar quickly loaded the camels, Rashid holding each one by its halter down on its front knees. Again Warwar was last as they turned west towards the last orange flare of sunset on the ancient hills where man was born, the stars which had seen him born still staring down tonight. True, he reflected, I'm young and have no money, but my share of the tusks and the black-maned lion's skin will bring a cow or twenty goats; it was I who first saw the twin Land Rover tracks. If there's bounty to be found among these whites, half of it should be mine.

Warwar led the male camel with the bull's tusks and the lion skin. The others moved faster; holding the AK47 sling away from his sore shoulder, Warwar trotted after them, tugging the male camel's halter. Before him the star-splintered bowl of night sank suddenly into unfillable depth, as though they'd reached the earth's end and stood facing dark space. 'The Chalbi!' he murmured; the male camel whinnied its assent and Warwar clapped a hand over its muzzle. Far below on the desert floor glinted the spark of a single campfire.

# Chapter 9

He led the male camel down, its front hooves dislodging chunks of hardened sand that pounced against his calves, its head jerking up the halter. For hours they descended bare slopes whose stones still held the day's heat, whose sand burned his soles and rasped round his ankles, the dark forms of the other camels weaving back and forth below him, their grunts, the creaking of their saddles, and the slither of their hooves loud against the silence of the stars.

The Lion had risen high above the moon when they reached the gentler slopes stretching to the desert floor. The distant campfire was hidden now by intervening dunes, but like the others Warwar had fixed its location against the stars. They halted to tighten the camels' saddles after the long downslope, mounted, and rode fast northwest, as if to flee the Scorpion's tail arching up out of the desert behind them.

Before dawn he could smell woodsmoke; they tied up the camels in a low *laga* and checked their rifles. 'The youngster,' Ibrahim whispered, 'is to stay with the camels. If he hears three rapid even shots he's to bring them quickly. Despite any other shooting he's to stay here.'

Warwar fidgeted with the AK47 sling against his sore shoulder. 'It's not honourable to ask this of him who first found these car tracks.'

'You're not a man, yet.'

'Enough to kill that Samburu and the great bull. Enough to cross the Chalbi without fear.'

Ibrahim turned his back, his voice moving towards Rashid. 'No, not yet without fear.'

Their footsteps sifted into the darkness. The breeze quickened, strengthening the woodsmoke smell. A lion roared to the north; jackals keened; doves began their pre-dawn cooing, *jug-jug, jug, jug*, like a purling spring. Alone, Warwar fiddled with the mode selector of his rifle. Ibrahim must have a motive to exclude him so dishonourably. No man would accept this. He checked the camels' tethers, patted each one's nose to calm it. Feeling with his feet the depressions Ibrahim's and Rashid's steps had made in the sand, he followed them. After a long sandy slope he saw the fire directly ahead. It blinked as someone moved before it. They were up already, the whites – soon they'd leave.

He cut south of the others' tracks into the cover of a shallow gully and ran towards the fire. When its flicker danced on the dune tops he climbed to the gully edge, keeping his gun down, and peered over the top.

The flames were leaping, freshly fed. Two black shapes moved to and fro before them. Behind it, to one side, were two blue tents, their open flaps facing the fire. To the other side were two Land Rovers, a strange white tent stretched between them. The smell of coffee narrowed his nostrils; there was a gasoline odour too, and another sour, acid smell he remembered now as the black material of the wheels the Land Rovers travelled on. He peered behind and to his right but could not see Ibrahim or Rashid.

The two shapes were dismantling one tent. They shined sharp lights into the other tent and into the strange white one; he could hear their voices, modulated and respectful, blacks speaking to whites. He slid forward on his belly, not knowing what he would do, pulling the AK47 alongside him.

A whitewoman in a white jacket stepped from the tent. With both hands she fluffed back her pale hair, stretched languidly and crouched beside the fire. A moment later she stood and raised a cup to her lips, put it down. She moved around the fire, silhouetted, towards the clump of cactus where Warwar lay.

A tall whiteman came out of the same tent and stood uncertainly, glanced towards the Land Rovers and back to the fire. He straightened his clothes and bent to speak into the strange white tent. The two dark shapes whom Warwar had identified as Africans entered the same tent the whitewoman and whiteman had left, and carried out two canvas cots which they folded and stacked inside a Land Rover. They brought out two of the weird sacks which Warwar had seen whites carry on their backs, much more difficult than on the head – indicative, he thought, of the whites' always finding a complicated way to do simple things. The Africans leaned the sacks against a Land Rover and began to dismantle the second tent. Two younger men, one white, one black, stepped from the white tent, which Warwar recognized now as not a tent at all, merely the netting which the whites used out of fear of mosquitoes.

The whitewoman came towards Warwar, stepping round the thorn scrub, once looking back to the fire. He hugged the earth, slid his rifle forward and sighted down the barrel at the approaching glimmer of her hair. Glancing back hurriedly, he could not locate Rashid or Ibrahim – had they decided there were too many and left? Or were they back now with the camels, awaiting him, angry and determined to take away his tusks and lion pelt? With the woman coming closer he could not retreat. If she saw him he would shoot her, then run, but on the sandy soil the Land Rovers would easily catch him.

The woman's shoe scuffed a rock. She skirted a termite mound tinged golden with predawn and halted. He lay breathless, sure she had seen him, his finger tightening against the trigger, his eye following the dark glint of the barrel to the centre of her white chest. Now, in the moment before her death, he suddenly liked her bright hair and easy, open walk, so different from his own kind. She acts like a man, he thought, steadying the barrel, exhaling slowly as he squeezed the trigger. Why won't she speak?

Abruptly she unpopped the trousers she wore and slid them down, squatted beside the termite mound and with a loud, diminishing hiss made water, sighing with relaxation. He held his breath against the smell, sweeter yet greasier than his own. It's the forbidden things they eat, he told himself, feeling his penis harden against the ground.

She stood, rearranged her clothes and returned to the fire. He still could not see Ibrahim or Rashid. He sensed they had left, but could not think why. They're women, he told himself, knowing it wasn't true.

He imagined himself offering ten cows, twenty sheep and fifty goats to Soraya's father. More than a legitimate bride price, it was testimony of his love for her, acknowledgement of his wealth and her uniqueness. Most of the girls in his tribe had to marry older men – how joyous she would be to have him, young and full of love! He who had killed the elephant king!

The stars had thinned, the hills sharp against the paling sky. The woman, two whitemen and three blacks sat eating round the fire. Six, Warwar told himself, is not auspicious. Still not knowing exactly what he would do, he snapped the mode selector of his rifle to automatic and crawled forward, shoulder nagging painfully, through the thorn scrub.

They had finished eating; one of the blacks was scrubbing the dishes with sand while another loaded the Land Rovers. The whiteman and woman bent over a large sheet of paper on one Land Rover's hood, the two younger men peering over their shoulders. When the two blacks had finished their tasks, the whiteman laid the large paper on the ground and pointed things out on it to them. They nodded at the paper, one making a line on it with his finger.

These are fools, Warwar reminded himself. They worship paper and metal, not God. The Africans work for them, drive them probably, instead of being proud to be African and refusing to speak with whites. These Africans are not loved by God.

He rose from behind his bush and walked towards them. The desert glowed with poor man's gold, the majestic moments before sunrise when every grain of sand and blade of rock is fired with expectant light, the long thorns of the crouched acacia glitter like sharpened needles, the sky flashes like mica. The time, Warwar remembered, God wishes us to die.

His footsteps startled the six crouched over the large paper and they looked round suddenly, one of the blacks leaping up with anger. Warwar shot him, two bullets into his stomach spraying blood out his back as he rose into the air like a leaf smacked by the wind, the woman screaming, the tall man shoving her back, the others raising their hands. 'Go!' Warwar said to the two other blacks. 'Go – I don't need you!' But they did not understand Somali or were too frightened till he strode forward and waved his hand sharply, and unhappily they edged away. 'Go!' he yelled in Swahili. 'I don't want you.'

One glanced at the tall whiteman who motioned with his head. The two blacks began to back up, their hands still raised, so that when he shot them they were for a moment like puppets he had seen once in El Wak bazaar – jerky arms held high till the bullets struck and the arms flapped down over the writhing torsos that then flopped lifeless to the ground, as if the puppet master had dropped their strings.

Watching the two die was a mistake, he realized, in

the instant that the young white dashed at him. But he fired in time, a long burst that recoiled the rifle sharply into his ribs, the white halting in midair and catapulting backwards, the woman screaming and covering his body with her own, wailing 'No! Stop! No!' in Swahili. She looked up at him, her face contorted and spattered with blood. So quickly he could not react she leaped, her claws ripping his face, knocking him backwards, but the tall man grabbed her and yanked her back.

'Fool!' Warwar tried not to hunch over his injured ribs; his arm shook. He fired at her, hip-high, but the shot was wide, spurting sand.

'Kill us all!' she yelled back at him, her fists beating away the tall man's hands. 'Carrion, motherless bastard – murderer!' She spat, choking, weeping; it ran down her chin.

Warwar felt embarrassed and thrilled by her. Keep control, he told himself. He aimed the rifle more carefully, seeing how the bullets would rend her belly, rip her apart. He wanted to check his magazine, tried to remember how many shots he'd fired, be sure there were enough, imagined shooting into the dark place between her legs.

'We've got money,' the tall man said. 'Cameras, binoculars . . .'

'What's that?' Warwar took his eyes from the woman. He could kill her later, naked.

The tall man hesitated. His Swahili was not good, or he was very frightened. 'To see far – closer.'

'How many guns?'

'You're a *shifta*, aren't you? Please, don't kill us –

take everything – we have no guns, it's against the law.'

'You,' he pointed his rifle at the woman, 'bring me this far-seeing thing.'

He kept the gun on her as she walked unsteadily to a Land Rover, reached between the seats, returned with a glossy thing like two small black bottles joined, set it on the sand, and backed away.

'You look through it,' the man said, seeming not to see Warwar.

He knelt to pick it up. It was heavy. Aiming the gun at them he tried to look though it but lights and colours danced inside it. He threw it down, hearing with satisfaction its glass crack against a rock. 'How much money do you have?'

The woman was wiping her face. 'We'll give you what we have. Just go!'

'We have twelve thousand shillings,' the man said.

Warwar felt the sun's warmth strike his back, the wild exhilaration of twelve thousand shillings. Be clear, he warned himself, joy leads to sorrow.

'Scum of the universe,' said a voice behind him. 'You are unfit to eat the Prophet's shit or speak with men. You are not your mother's son.'

Warwar kept his eyes on the whites. 'Be not angry, cousin Ibrahim, because you tarried and I did not. Don't fear, I'll give you part of this.'

'It is not right to speak to your elders this way.' Ibrahim moved into Warwar's sight, his gun pointing between Warwar and the captives.

'Where were you, then? Did you run when you heard my shots?' Warwar smiled at the whitewoman, who stared back in fury and confusion.

'You've killed too many,' Rashid said.

'These weren't humans but slaves to the whites.'

'You've killed a white. That brings trouble.'

Warwar pushed the dead whiteman's face with his foot; it was heavy and did not move. 'He tried to kill me.'

'No arguments,' said Ibrahim. 'Let's take what we can and go.'

'What about these ones?' Warwar countered.

'We'll destroy their vehicles. They have many days' walk out of the desert. If they survive, we'll be far away, and safe.'

'Where's the money?' Warwar said in Swahili to the woman.

'In that car.' The tall man pointed to the second Land Rover, dark green and seeming older than the first.

'Watch them.' Warwar pulled tents and bags from the back of the Land Rover.

'It's in the front – I'll show you!' The tall man came forward tentatively, as if walking barefoot on hot sand. He stank of coffee, food, sweat, and fear as he bent into the vehicle and opened a metal box that was part of the front. 'Here.' He held out a white-wrapped bundle.

'Throw it.'

It landed at Warwar's feet, shilling notes bound with rubber strings spilling on the sand.

'That gets shared three ways,' Ibrahim said, close behind him.

'The money's mine! *I* found the tracks, hunted them

down and captured the camp. *You* ran away. I'll give you the cameras and other things, the far-seeing thing.'

'Binoculars, they're called, foolish child. We did not run away, we organized an ambush where their vehicles would have stuck in sand – ahead, in the ravine. When we heard your silly shooting we ran back. With your killing you've ruined everything.'

'If I were not a young man speaking to his elder I would say you talk like a woman – full of fear and foreboding. I have won you booty – be wise enough to accept it.'

The jab of Ibrahim's rifle in his back almost knocked him down. His crushed ribs could not breathe. He calmed the urge to turn and shoot, knowing he would fire too late. 'Don't speak like a man till you've grown the hair to prove it,' Ibrahim said evenly.

'You know full well I have. What do you wish, some of the money?'

'We share everything. You're lucky we include you, after you disobeyed.' Ibrahim stepped past him to the others, scornfully exposing his back.

'I obey only God,' Warwar said, but Ibrahim did not seem to hear.

They unloaded the Land Rovers and threw everything on the ground. Most of it was useless – tents, bedding, clothes, many strange digging tools and tiny brushes, heavy bags of white powder that was sour to the taste and sucked the water from his mouth. There was a large rock surrounded in a strange white shell similar to the powder in taste; it broke nicely on a boulder when he dropped it; inside, horribly, were a jaw and teeth, seeming carved from stone. 'You rob the dead,' Warwar hissed.

There was nothing to take but the money, cameras, a small radio. Warwar thought of killing Rashid and Ibrahim now, but they were closest to his family's clan. Ibrahim had taught him to track, brought him this gun, had taken Ahmed into the manhood ceremony last year. Besides, there was no way he could surprise them both; their guns were always ready.

It was a lovely morning. High, white, lacy clouds striated the blue depths of the sky; lower, puffy, flat-bottomed ones promised partial shade; the breeze was cool from the Ethiopian escarpments to the north, perfumed with desert honey and loud with the mating songs of waxbills, weavers, bush larks and thrushes. But separated three ways, even with his share of the tusks and lion skin, the money would not bring Soraya's bride price. 'We can share evenly,' Warwar said. 'But why leave the biggest prize here?'

Ibrahim looked up. 'What's that?'

'When the Ezrael clan captured that European near the Sudan, they kept him till they received a ransom of a million shillings. We will do the same.'

Rashid snickered. 'With them?'

'We kill the man and take the woman. Someone pays to get her back.'

'It's not wise to kill the man,' Ibrahim said. 'Better he walks back, tells them she's to be ransomed. It will take him days to reach others. By then we'll be far. No, we cannot do this. There is no way to receive the money.'

'We'll do as the Ezraels, by sending an emissary to Buna with the demand. When the emissary receives the money he returns to Somalia and the woman is set free.'

'Or killed,' Ibrahim said.

'There's no point in looking too far into time.' Warwar felt his leadership of the situation return. He shouldered his rifle, spoke to the woman in Swahili. 'I don't wish to disappoint you, but you will come with us. We'll go carefully and not too quickly and soon you are exchanged for money.'

'I have no money!' Wild-eyed, she bit her lip. 'No one I know *has* any money!'

'What's no money to you is very much money to us.'

She laughed or sobbed; he couldn't tell. She spoke in her strange deep language to the man, who scowled at her then glanced at Ibrahim.

'What about him?' she said to Warwar.

'He finds his way alone. He says you are with us and we wait for a million shillings. That we will send a message. Tell him you will be safe.'

'With you?'

Warwar smiled at the bodies already coated with flies, ants and wasps. 'They were Africans who worked for whites. The young white was foolish – he would have lived.'

'We should burn the vehicles,' Rashid said.

'Too much smoke.' Warwar took a magazine from his *djellabah* and exchanged it with the nearly empty one in his rifle, walked to the vehicles and fired two bullets into each tyre, reloading to finish the spares, then fired several shots into each engine, the ricochets howling away through the hot, still air, one windshield collapsing like a waterfall of glass. 'Tell him,' he said to the woman, 'to carry water and follow the tracks of the vehicles back to Kenya.'

'This *is* Kenya,' she said fiercely.

'No, this is the Chalbi.'

The tall man watched them tie her wrists and lead her eastwards towards the valley wall. Whey they had gone some distance he found a canteen and followed, keeping as low as he could, to where they untied three camels loaded with tusks, one carrying also what seemed to be a large lion pelt. They made her climb on to the second camel and set off quickly; soon he could not see them in the shimmering haze, and was forced to hunt for their tracks across a stretch of exposed lava. Finally, stumbling over its baked, burning ripples he halted, surrounded by black light. 'Rebecca!' he screamed. 'Rebecca!' With a sob he returned to camp, filled a backpack with canteens, food and a blanket, strung the damaged binoculars round his neck, and plodded through the sand back along the tracks the two Land Rovers had made the previous day.

# Chapter 10

A human footprint, wide in the pad, muscular in the arch, pinched at the heel. Five sharp toes driven deep into the mud of a Cape buffalo trail up a green bamboo valley at the edge of the cloud forest.

M'kele's elongated finger tested the underside of a grass blade bent down into the mud by the poacher's instep. The dew on the grass blade was smudged, and crumbs of mud from its underside adhered damply to the whorls of M'kele's fingertip. A tiny spider rebuilding her web on a twig shaken by the poachers' passage was just now spinning a second cable. 'Ten minutes,' MacAdam whispered.

M'kele shook his head. 'Just now.'

Cold bamboo fronds slipped down MacAdam's neck; mosquitoes gathered, rapacious in the chill. Don't lose a man. The trail ahead vanished up a slope of silvery dark bamboo undulating in downrolling waves of mist. Bamboos blocked either side of the path and closed in on their back trail like predators slinking up behind. Gideon's spare, spectacled face half-emerged from their leaves; MacAdam hand-signalled him: move back and deploy.

In between the bamboos the heavy-hoofed trails of Cape buffalo were skeins of a web where the poachers could creep silently, invisibly, shoot from anywhere. With a hand on M'kele's shoulder MacAdam pushed him down. The air tasted like bullets; he imagined their hot, sour steel smashing the nape of his neck. 'Go back. Climb the ridge and follow it north to the top of this valley, up there where the trees end. It's 14:50. In exactly half an hour, at 15:20, I'll meet you there. Watch both sides of the ridge. But the poachers should be below you, inside this valley, and if you get a chance to shoot don't worry about me because I'll be ahead of you.'

M'kele swung his jaw, motioning MacAdam back also. A stonechat's raspy alarm made him tuck his head; MacAdam saw the bird spring from the top of a lichen-clad cycad fifty yards upslope, the wide soft flap of its wings echoing off the treetops, then silenced by the mist. 'Go!' he shoved M'kele. 'Don't shoot at sounds.'

M'kele was gone. Drops fell from the trees down MacAdam's neck; sweat trickled down his underarm and off his wrist where mosquitoes fumbled in the reddish hairs fringing his sleeve. Mist ovalled the crenelations of his rifle's barrel shroud and beaded on the bright hard plastic of its stock. A grass blade sprang back up from the poachers' track. The chatter of mosquitoes at his ears shut out the faint waterfall roar of the mist cascading downhill.

Softly he crawled upslope, rifle cradled against his

chest, his elbows and knees sucking into the mossy, rooty, tendrilled soil and dung-spattered, hoof-punctured mud as he moved, pushing aside the thick growth of bamboo stalks with the muzzle, holding his breath to slow the loud panting in his throat, saplings scratching his pack and slapping at his ankles and shutting off his sight as though he crawled blind across the bottom of a sea.

Any moment the poachers would shoot, he could feel it; every second his body awaited the hail of hot steel biting through it. You always expect that, he told himself. But this time it's true.

Here the buffalo trail forked, then splintered among mucky bamboo stalks ripped by horns. The poachers' tracks separated, then rejoined, the ridge less steep now as it neared the top of the valley. The poachers have gone on, he told himself, the distance growing again between us, and we almost walked right up their backs. Three white colobus monkeys in the high side boughs of a *podocarpus* at the valley's topmost edge were peering anxiously downhill – no, there were four – no, five of them – what are they seeing? Could my men be there already? That's too early to climb the whole ridge and then all the way up this valley.

Something was wrong and, like all wrong things when you first sense them, he could not place it. He crept ten yards upslope and raised his head to look again, but now the *podocarpus* with the five colobus was blocked by intervening trees, and when he finally could see it again the colobus were gone. There was nothing to do but creep down and cross the valley and back up the other hill to where the colobus had seen something, and find out what it was.

As he moved forward his rifle caught on creepers. Bending to detach it he lost his hat and knelt to retrieve it when with a great crash of bamboo a buffalo jumped up from its bed ten feet away, smashed the bamboos aside with a swing of its huge ebony horns, lowered its head and charged. In its black thundering chest wide as a truck and its white-red enraged eyes and squat, ugly snout, MacAdam recognized Death, Death this instant, with no time to shoot as he stood frozen ankle-deep in bamboo muck, then dived aside, too late for the buffalo to swerve, his chest raked by one sharp broken-tipped horn as the buffalo swung round its wide black rack and came for him again. Now MacAdam could shoot but dared not, fearing to warn the poachers, saw if he did not shoot he'd die, raised the rifle but the rifle wasn't there – knocked away in the buffalo's first charge – and he ran crazily through barred walls of bamboo, the buffalo's infuriated huff smacking his neck. He dived, knowing he'd be trampled, this is *death*, he thought, but the buffalo overran him, a hoof whacking his ribs, the buffalo's body tilting like a race pony's as it turned again, broad blocky head with its outreaching gnarled crown of jagged horns meeting across the shaggy brow, its angry white breath and slobber-speckled chest smashing down bamboos as it galloped at him. He jumped round a tree making the buffalo veer round it also, and then he ducked to the other side; the buffalo pivoted again and he leaped up the first few branches; the animal halted, tearing boulders and stumps from the earth with the side-to-side jerk of its horns.

Crouched into a crotch of the tree, MacAdam tried to present the smallest possible rifle target from the ground. The mist was clearing; the bamboo canopy at his feet glowed with renewed emerald precision; under every stalk he saw a poacher's upraised rifle. The tree cracked and shuddered as the buffalo thrust against it, backed away, looked up, and thrust again. MacAdam wrapped his legs around the trunk and wedged his arms among its branches. He could not see his rifle in the trampled muddy brush below.

The buffalo roared dismally, protruding its glossy lower lip in rage. Then, tossing a bamboo clump off its horn and over its shoulder, it trotted uphill and vanished into the foliage.

MacAdam slid part-way down, still not able to see his gun. The mud reeked of buffalo dung and urine; black water was seeping into the gouges and craters made by the buffalo's horns and hooves; broken bamboo shafts thrust up like half-buried swords. He dropped to the ground, waited, ran a few steps and spun round but the buffalo did not come. A crackle of brush made him jump but it was just a broken branch falling from the tree he had climbed, and here was his gun on the ground before him, as if dropped there from another world.

He switched it to auto, off safety, and scrambled to the tree. Beyond the roar of his breath the jungle was silent, as if the buffalo had never been. Mosquitoes began to hover. Like a slender enchanted leaf, a night adder gracefully descended a bamboo stalk and slid away.

Feeling an awful pain he looked down, astonished to see his chest painted with blood. He crept back downhill, waited in silence, then angled up the valley side towards one ridge, the rank odour of buffalo coming down new shoals of silent mist. He cut sideways and back down to the main trail, crossing new buffalo prints, then on the trail the barefoot tracks of several men scrambling fast.

He left the trail, moving quietly, halted on one knee among cabbage-smelling plants, watching round and round through leafy walls of barred bamboo, wanting to stay here because it seemed safer, but again he moved upslope, on his stomach now, one elbow forward at a time, paralleling the trail. Near the crest he slowed, circled instinctively to the left, where his men might already be. Parrying a wide bamboo frond with his rifle muzzle, he saw crouched twenty yards away a near-naked black man with an AK47.

From this angle MacAdam could not fire except uphill towards where his men should be. When he was sure this Somali had not heard or seen him he turned to check behind him, where ten yards away stood a second Somali, near-naked as the first, this one pointing his rifle at the centre of MacAdam's chest.

# Chapter 11

There was no time to raise and swing round his rifle; bullets from the other man's hard black muzzle would smash him down. MacAdam lifted his hands, knowing this too was useless, this baring of his chest in a trusting plea for mercy. I'm a killer; you're a killer; let's get it over with. But with a sense of grace the instant widened: I mean no harm, I'm not afraid of you – knowing also that the man would shoot. With the tip of his rifle the man motioned MacAdam closer.

Across ten green yards of stems and downcast branches, through the wavering air somnolent with rotting vegetation and the exhalations of a billion leaves, MacAdam conveyed the totality of his life to this young man with his sideways scarred face and thin, wide, hungry mouth, his large eyes rounded by danger and compassion. I need time, MacAdam told him. I haven't been good to my wife. I've been superficial with life – I'm not ready for death – want years, a few seconds, to understand, see the desert sunset – please let me. But MacAdam knew the compassion in the Somali's eyes was not reprieve but only pity for the doomed.

When the rifle fired he clutched himself against the bullets, thinking this is death, you do not feel it, as he fell among the bamboo saplings and could not find the pain. He scrambled for his gun as guns were firing everywhere and he churned round to shoot but the Somali was not there and another ran ducking up the trail. MacAdam fired and the man tumbled horribly, the air too hot and stinking of bullets. A scream rose like a call to heaven then died down, an ant ran over his wrist, his belly wet in mud, air like a train in his ears.

A yellow butterfly crawled, trembling crushed wings, up a red stem before his eye. The heartbeat in his brain was like a fast-moving clock. Unbelieving he looked down at his body but could see no bullet wound, only the buffalo's gash across his chest, and could not understand how the man had missed him at such close range. Then he realized the shots had been Enfields, *his* men shooting.

Something hustled over the leaves, masked by foliage – a quiet breath, a flutter of brush. Not seeing well enough to shoot, he crept forward, finding blood and tracks of bare feet. Three men. He fell to his stomach as bullets whistled and whacked among the trees, the crack of Enfields burst out behind him, and a Kalashnikov rattled harshly ahead.

A bullet struck, catapulting dirt and twigs into his face. He felt fear, then fury with himself for being here, rage at his own men for shooting down at him. Squirming to the left, he began to ascend the last slope, on his belly, one knee or arm forward at a time, the rifle heavy as a log in front of him, sweat and mud and leaves and tendrils and mosquitoes in his eyes, a new staccato of guns erratic behind him. In an instant's clarity he saw he had condemned himself to this purposeless horror because he did not value life, his own life. The slope eased; he ducked over the ridge where the forest opened, and ran up the far side of the ridge through knee-deep tussocks, boots splashing in the muck between them, then breathless out of the mist into the astonishing gold glare of the sun and back over the ridge into the sun-bright glade of forest at the top of the valley.

The clouds of mist spread out beneath him like an incandescent sea in which the crowns of a few tall trees floated like islands. Wraiths of mist clung like *usnea* lichen to the nearer scrub through which the path snaked upwards the last two hundred metres to the valley top; up from this, from the grey ambivalence of cloud forest into the grilling brightness of the sun, ran three men with rifles. MacAdam jumped back over the ridge and darted downhill, then back over the ridge again just above where the three would cross this saddle and probably drop into the mists of the valley on the other side. Remembering how many bullets he'd already used and gauging the point at which the three poachers would cross the saddle, and where he'd best find cover yet could control an open field of fire, he twisted and ducked down to a clump of *senecio* overlooking the saddle and dived down among its rocks. Wiping sweat from his eyes, he laid the white point of his rifle's front sight into the cradle of the rear, against the nearest man's chest.

The men's heads bobbed as they ran uphill. They

were gasping and kept looking back. There was a dip in the trail and their heads vanished, then came up again as from the trough of a wave. The lead one grabbed the next one's arm, pulling him upwards; MacAdam centred his front sight on the lead one's chest and softly touched the trigger; the lead one neared, dodging side to side with pain and exhaustion; it was the tall, scar-faced man who'd held MacAdam in his sights and had not fired.

MacAdam felt nausea, disgust. Blood covered the scarred man's chest and shoulder. He slowed and turned to urge the others on, his mouth round with agony. His heaving chest filled MacAdam's iron sights and for a flash it was to MacAdam ridiculously like a school experiment in which he had once attempted and failed to draw his own blood. He stood silently covering them as the men came up out of the last fog, then saw him, staggered and stopped.

The back two dropped their rifles and raised their hands; the first stared wildly at him, unable to decide between death now and death a little later – MacAdam waved his rifle tip, trying to hide the trembling in his wrists, and very reluctantly the man put down his Kalashnikov. He stared at MacAdam; I've put down my gun, his eyes said. Now are you going to shoot me?

'Over here,' MacAdam yelled. His voice seemed garbled and he could not remember the words, realized these men would not understand Swahili and waved one hand to show they should move uphill from their guns. A figure far below coalesced out of the fog, a grim, sharp, dark point that became a man and rifle, then seventy yards behind it another, both climbing fast. In an instant MacAdam realized he'd have to shoot the men he had if he were to deal with the two now coming. Then he saw the first was M'kele, with Darius behind him, and MacAdam wondered at M'kele's courage, in the open, tracking an unseen enemy who at any moment could turn and shoot him down.

'We got them all!' M'kele yelled.

'You got four?'

'We got four.'

'What about us?'

'Kuria—'

'Kuria!' MacAdam screamed.

'—his leg. He's OK.'

On MacAdam's right perimeter there was a flash of movement as the scar-faced poacher broke and ran for the ridge, his naked blackness darting side to side in the waist-high scrub, angling for a fringe of trees. MacAdam's first shot seemed to go to his right, the rifle kicking back MacAdam's shoulder, deafening, the second shot wide and to the left, above the man's head. Shocked, MacAdam fired again, low and to the left, then high to the right and to the right again. The man hit the crest and was over, then was knocked feet-forwards, flat above the ground, by M'kele's first bullets, as if he were a high jumper on his back crossing the bar. He collapsed in an uphill slog of dust, rolled on his belly and scrambled for the trees, dragging one leg like a wounded hyaena until another bullet hit him and he went down, arching up his belly like a broken-backed snake, and M'kele walked slowly uphill to him and fired a last shot into his brain.

Darius ran up panting, sorrow straining his face. M'kele came down and they gathered up the Kalashnikovs. 'Why you be missing that man, Captain?' M'kele said, stern-faced.

MacAdam felt branded, like a criminal. 'He had a chance to shoot me, and he didn't.'

'They Somali like hyaena sinew. They always kill you in the end.' M'kele and Darius tied up the two remaining prisoners and MacAdam followed them back down into the fog, past the man MacAdam had killed, to where Gideon guarded two other men and Kuria sat clutching a splint bandaged round his thigh. One of Gideon's prisoners called out and the man in front of MacAdam answered, then Gideon's prisoner began to wail like an antelope caught by lions. MacAdam knew they were talking about the dead man up the hill, the tall scar-faced Somali who had looked into his eyes and not shot him.

One of Gideon's thick lenses was cracked like a star blocking his eye. Kuria's left thigh was broken; the bullet had taken out an inch of bone and a fistful of muscle behind it. MacAdam saw Kuria was crippled for life but that he couldn't tell him, not now, that he had to get him down the mountain. His mind was racing for chopper sites, then remembered there was no chopper, but there were only three hours till dark and a hundred different ways to die going down. He had promised himself he wouldn't lose a man and already he'd lost one. But of course, the one he'd lost was the scar-face Somali, not one of his own. With M'kele holding Kuria down, MacAdam jerked the broken thighbone straight, picked chunks of loose marrow and bone chips from the back of the wound, filled it with gauze and *podocarpus* leaves, compressed and rewrapped it. 'Where's the seventh guy?' MacAdam said.

'Dead back there,' Kuria answered. His lips were grey with pain and MacAdam felt somehow he'd wronged him. One of Gideon's prisoners was weeping, head jerking back and forth. 'The guy up the hill was his brother,' Darius said.

'It doesn't m-matter,' M'kele answered. 'We got to kill them all.'

Darius raised his rifle, snapped the bolt. The weeping man looked up, and in his eyes MacAdam recognized the woe of all the world distilled, the collective fear since life began, the fear of death – our own death and that of those we love. And MacAdam felt cold in his own heart from Darius' simple killer's gesture of making the metal sound with his gun, the *reminding* sound: in a few instants this gun is going to kill you.

In the doomed Somali's eyes MacAdam saw himself. It was he, MacAdam, who knelt there tied beside his brothers, facing these hardened soldiers and this whiteman officer who raise their guns to shoot him down.

'We don't shoot captives,' he said.

Darius shook his head. 'President's orders, sir.'

MacAdam quelled an urge to smile at Darius, force him to *feel* this realization – how crucial, essential, life was. But that wasn't the way. 'And then who's going to carry this lazy Kuria man all the way downhill?' he said instead.

'It's the Ministry, sir.' M'kele's voice was a teacher's

coaxing a slow student. 'Our superior . . .'

'If it's Nehemiah I'll deal with him,' MacAdam answered brusquely. He imagined Nehemiah nodding as he told him about this spark of life that must not be snuffed. 'Darius, get bamboo poles for a stretcher,' he ordered, 'and M'kele, get out the ponchos, and Gideon, hustle those prisoners together over there—' He sensed the chaos and danger pass, his men quick and angry as they built the stretcher, placing Kuria on it and wrapping him in the second poncho.

He followed them downhill, with M'kele in the lead and Darius on point, and as he came down it was to a new life, for he knew he had truly died and been reborn, with the horror and beauty of every little thing made clear, every leaf and web and petal and crumb of soil. With remorse he looked into the scarred Somali's eyes and knew he could not live enough for him. 'I'm done,' he said, not knowing what he meant. 'It's over.' But there was not time now to think about it, calling at M'kele to pick up the pace as they dropped out of the mists and back into the world.

# Chapter 12

Rebecca was barely aware of the stiff camel saddle abrading her knees, of the rawhide lashing her wrists to the pommel, of her back arched so unnaturally by the high cantle and the camel's uneven lurching stride, made worse by a terrain so rough it was as if rocks had been scattered infinitely deep across the land, broken and shoved aside to form near-vertical basaltic gullies or random, jagged, unclimbable hills. Her jeans and the skin of her outer legs and her arms were torn by two-inch thorns of umbrella trees and acacia scrub which the camels and Somalis seemed to saunter through unscathed; her neck was numbed by the constant whiplash of the camel's ungainly gait, the way it loped up hills and jerked stiff-legged downslope while she snapped back and forth helpless on its back.

All this was nothing to the sun which bore down like a molten weight dropped from a great height, always, every millisecond, crushing her, flaying her shoulders through the white cotton shirt, as if the fabric were not even there, or worse, as if it magnified the heat. Sun lacerated her neck and the inside of her throat with each intaken breath; it was an oven from which she could not withdraw her face, her hair so hot it burned her skull.

Was it this morning she'd yelled at Milton, and ten minutes later he was dead? She'd yelled because the expedition wasn't going well. Because the outcrops of earlier sedimentary rock she'd seen on the aerials had been less impressive on the ground. Because the normal *mésalliance* with Klaus had been even more arid than usual. Because she'd finally accepted that the officious knowledge and unadmitted insecurity which made Klaus a tolerable scholar made him intolerable as a husband.

Because she'd been so proud on this trip that, seeing him for the first time objectively, like another woman's husband, she could finally find the light between them. Ashamed, but seeing nonetheless, and taking note for the future.

Now Klaus was wandering the desert, trying to retrace two sets of tyre tracks in drifting sand and shifting *lagas*, the sun beating down on *his* head, blinding *him* too, begging him to stop, lie down anywhere on the sand and rest for ever, let his body turn to clear white bone. And at night where would he hide, when the hyaenas strip the flesh from you in seconds and crunch your bones like paper? With wild dogs calling for him to appease their hunger? And she'd snapped at him too this morning, because there was water in a fuel line – 'How can that be when there's no water for a thousand square miles!' she'd spat.

Again she saw Milton's ebony chest being crushed by the boy killer's bullets. She could see every split second of his death, the others' writhing bodies – the awful blood everywhere – the metal coming out of the black barrel so hard, so vicious. Horrible, concentrated death in horrible pain, life wrenched away, all life's loves, all our loves. Inside her head or out in the desert was the same, and the air inside her throat was very dry to keep from crying and her neck sore from forcing herself not to look down, not to look back.

If I'd left Klaus this wouldn't have happened, she told herself. He'd have stayed at Koobi Fora, garnering international acclaim for his students' finds which he so painstakingly disinters before the cameras, working out alternative theories of human evolution with visiting professors who all bring a bottle of his favourite *eau de vie* in tribute, and are careful to cite him in their papers. Is love just *this*? Does it always fade to this too-coherent awareness of the falseness in each other? Once love wasn't this. But that wasn't love, that was an irresponsible dream. Child's play. I shouldn't have done it. Maybe I'd have stayed closer to Klaus if I hadn't had that other. Now what will happen to my sons?

'*Mama!*' A voice shrilled the word for woman in Swahili. 'Hey *Mama*, don't sleep – you fall off camel!'

Shaking herself, she looked down, dazed. Foreshortened by her height, Warwar seemed an emaciated dwarf in his dumpy tan burnoose, a burnt-down candle with a toadying, uneven smile and cheery black eyes full of death. 'Need anything, *Mama*?'

She faced away from Warwar to the cobalt, raw horizon, its far-flung, blazing peaks, its torrid waves of sand and inconsolable mirages, the sedately rocking camel making the scene rise and fall as if seen from a boat upon a softly choppy sea. *Mal de mer. Mal de mère.* She'd been a *mauvaise mère* and now her sons would go back to Klaus' parents in Lucerne and grow up in a sterile Swiss school.

She heard a little girl's sob, then realized it was she, the *mauvaise mère* weeping for her orphaned sons. I will *not* let them see me do this, she told herself. She tried to efface the tears but her wrists were bound to the pommel and she had to lean forward to wipe her cheek on her sleeve.

She must remember that whatever was happening to her was meaningless against any African woman bent beneath her daily hundred pounds of firewood, her two-hour walk every morning from the water hole with a fifty-litre barrel on her head, her rows of corn and beans and squash and her mud hut needing patching and her belly full of children coming out one by one to clutch hungrily at her single, tattered skirt. Remember that.

'Wake up, *Mama*!' Warwar called, swatting the camel with his stick so it jerked forward and swung its head and snapped at her foot. 'It's just me, baby,' she said in English to the camel. 'I didn't do it.'

Moving closer, Warwar again jabbed his stick into the camel's vulva; it whinnied and darted forward, waking the whitewoman. What good is she, he worried, if she falls and breaks her neck? More trouble than a child. Again he puzzled that these whites, so infirm and distanced from the world, should have been capable of overrunning Africa, worse than the locusts who eat the grain that makes the children's bread. They've made a pact with the Devil, he decided, and the Devil's given them use of his tools in return for their souls. But why does he want *their* souls, weak and divided and maggot-like as their bodies?

The Prophet was right, the world finds unity through opposites. Thus did he, Warwar, maintain the life of this strange half-woman in man's trousers – her colour-less face and hair uncovered, the outline of her udders plain for every man to see, her look and manner dis-respectful – so he might win and own the beautiful Soraya, as pure as this one was defiled.

Evening approached, the time he loved the most, when the day's heat faded as if the traveller had stepped down from his camel into the gentlest of streams, where a damp wind rustled the doum palms and the scent of tamarind forgave the day. As he would walk there with his Soraya, along the banks of the spring at El Jurta, where there will be only the sound of the new kids *baaing* for their mothers, and the joy of her tranquillity behind him.

Readjusting the rifle on his aching shoulder, he tied the reins of the whitewoman's camel to the tail of the one led by Rashid. He ran forward and, as required, walked wordlessly beside Rashid and Ibrahim for a few minutes.

'How goes thy beloved?' Rashid smiled.

Barely breaking stride, Warwar removed his sandal. Continuing barefoot, he pulled a long thorn from the sole, then removed the other sandal; the cooling rocks with their strong, sure edges felt good against his feet.

'He's so enamoured he can't answer,' Ibrahim offered.

'He should go back to her,' Rashid said. 'His place, is it not with the women?'

'She's weary,' Warwar answered. 'Perhaps we might halt.'

'He changes the subject.' Ibrahim reshouldered his rifle, letting the barrel droop until it pointed at Warwar's face. 'Speaking of his whitewoman, whom he knows, without our saying, is impure . . .'

'He forgets, perhaps, that without his clan he's nothing.'

'He does not see that.'

'His place then is truly with his whitewoman.'

'What kind of lover is he who disavows his beloved?' Ibrahim's dark, craggy, bearded visage, outlined by the sun-bleached *djellabah* and deepening blue sky, seemed like a mountain Warwar could never climb. 'What kind of man will he be who ignores the word of his elders and moves to attack alone, perhaps endangering his clan, so he can *appear* to have led the attack, can have first choice of the spoils?'

'He does not deserve to become a man,' Rashid said.

Warwar noticed how Ibrahim's beard trembled in the wind, his eyes rubied by the sunset's reflection on the sand. Ibrahim's cloak smelt of goat grease and his rifle of oil softened by the sun's dispersing heat; the sky behind his broad head was clogged with colour – each tint contains all the others, Warwar thought – sensing that something *else* lay behind Ibrahim's anger, that they could kill him now and invent a story for the clan, and have the spoils and woman's ransom to themselves, saying he, Warwar, had died attacking the Land Rovers. His own rifle felt small and hard against his back, as a stone when one turns in sleep and lies upon it. The evening air tasted of a thousand dangers.

'Friend of my family,' he looked directly into Ibrahim's mealy, harsh face, 'when you put my blood upon the sand, don't you lose your own? Am I not in the same clan? Have I not shared the same years with your own sons? Forgive me if my desire to please you has made me too bold.'

'When we're young,' said Ibrahim, 'we play at many lives. We're great warriors with our friends, battling among the palm trunks, with fronds for swords and shields and palm nuts for bullets. As we grow older these dream lives fall from us as skins from the cobra; year by year they dry and blow away in the desert wind. Until we die we're always shedding skins.'

'I don't understand.'

'As you know the elders teach, don't take the dream you live for life.'

'I regret I've angered you, when all I wished was your respect.' He permitted himself a quick look back at the whitewoman. 'But how is he worth respect who threatens another who has not time to unshoulder his own gun?'

'You wish me to give you time?'

'No, my cousin. I am just trying to understand how one's behaviour should be.'

Ibrahim's eyes softened. 'You must decide if you are of this clan.'

'If not?'

'You are an enemy.'

'I am of this clan.'

'Then act as we say.'

'Yet by attacking the whites as I did, when I thought you all had fled,' Warwar spoke directly into Ibrahim's face, 'did I not capture them easily, without our blood being shed?'

'After he changes his skin,' Rashid laughed, 'the young snake foolishly sleeps in the sun, and thinks the eagle won't find him. He won't grow old this way.'

'Return to the whitewoman,' Ibrahim said.

Through half-shut eyes Rebecca watched the boy-killer return and untie her camel's halter from the next one's tail. She tried to find a reason why the heavy one had pointed his rifle at the boy, and could not. But where there is dissension there is hope, she thought, before days of no food and too much sun have weakened me. From here it was only two hundred kilometres west to Koobi Fora, or two hundred east to Moyale, on the border. In her mind she lifted up each of her sons and held him.

The depth of Ibrahim's anger perplexed Warwar – too great for the occasion, it hid something beneath. When Ibrahim's brother Yusuf had died, Ibrahim had been forced to take Yusuf's two wives, both older than he and already with children. Ibrahim had been a good father to these children, the 'sons' of whom Warwar had spoken. With many cows and goats of his own, Ibrahim now might be ready to buy a new wife, a younger one more to his taste and growing reputation. He sat on the council with Shor, the father of Soraya.

When, Warwar wondered, have I ever spoken of Soraya? Could Ibrahim know? If we sell this white-woman, would he use his share as a bride price for Soraya?

His feet were tired; he halted to don his sandals, letting the distance grow between him and the others. He was thirsty; the rifle bothered his shoulder. Is Soraya just a dream I soon will shed? he wondered. Ibrahim has poisoned my mind, made me think like him. He could make his claim to Soraya and mine would be displaced.

# Chapter 13

They untied her wrists and let her walk about for a few minutes, the heavy bearded one always following, his rifle ready. She ached to fall on the welcoming warm sand, but forced herself to keep moving, or her legs would stiffen and be useless later. The youngest Somali, the killer, was wandering the volcanic hills with the camels in search of forage. The heavy bearded one made her sit under a lava overhang and tied her ankles to a saddle. 'I'm so thirsty!' she said in Swahili; he did not seem to understand. '*Maji*,' she cried, '*tilia maji. Sikia kiu*!' She pointed to her mouth, tried to catch his sleeve. He nodded gently, speaking in Somali as he retied her hands.

The breeze across the desert as the light died was so sweet she could almost drink it. To the west the dunes rose and fell with the cadence of the sea, crimson on their crests and shadowed in their troughs. In the very far distance was the pencil trace of sandy canyon she knew as Ririba *laga*; far beyond it the desert sloped up to the wide dark lava peninsula called Dukana, continuing somewhere beyond it to other *lagas* – Wata, Bulal and Kore.

But in a good day's walk she might reach the Gabbra water hole, Balesa, beyond *laga* Ririba, if she could locate it and if she had no problems with hyaenas. There, digging deeply, she might find water. Another day's walk and she'd be in the deep canyons of Kore *laga*, where occasionally there was water. Leopards lived there, in the cliffs – surviving on the blood of their prey, the little desert antelopes, gerenuk and dikdik, who got their moisture from the desert scrub.

In Kore canyon, far above Kore *laga*, she'd made one of Klaus' greatest finds – a young woman's lower jaw, *homo habilis*, in a bed of exposed malbe tuff. The young woman had left this and nothing more – the jaw with which two million years ago she'd breathed, spoken, eaten, suckled at her own mother's breast. She'd died young, by a stream through lush savannah, buried by riparian sediments and volcanic ash, while the stream beside her cut down into a canyon that in time turned into desert.

With teeth so young and healthy, Rebecca had thought, it's unlikely you were sick – did you die by lion or by leopard, or in childbirth, the gift of a man you may not have loved, bringing forth another man perhaps, in the guise of a helpless child?

In the semi-darkness she watched the camels coming back, the boy-killer like any pastoral Rendille or Boran youth returning the family's herd to the *manyatta* at night. The men busied about the camels, the animals grunting and stamping. Steps whispered on the sand;

the boy knelt beside her. 'Here, *Mama*, you must be thirsty!' His pale burnoose leaned towards her; she clasped with bound hands the gourd he lifted to her lips. The taste was hot and putrid; she gagged but forced herself to drink, telling herself, this is strength, this is freedom.

There was not much, a mouthful of camel blood and milk in this gourd freshly rinsed with urine. Which man's? she wondered. The boy's? I need the salt. It's normal. They do it. It won't harm me.

It was down. She should ask for more but could not bear to. 'I have hunger – *njaa*.'

'There was only this,' the boy said. 'Soon we're in Ethiopia, then *chakula kingi* – much food.'

I will not be with you in Ethiopia, she promised herself, digging fingernails into her palms to keep from ripping open his face. 'No water?'

'You've drunk it all.'

'When will we be in Ethiopia?'

He hesitated. 'In two nights.'

'I won't live that long,' she thought of saying, to show she was weak and unlikely to escape. But if she seemed too frail they might tire of it all and simply shoot her. She bowed her head and his footsteps moved away; she raised her eyes to follow his sound into the darkness. If in two days you think you'll reach Ethiopia then you'll cross the frontier by the El Had water hole and over Selach Pass. And once you're across the border no one from Kenya can follow you. Nor do the Ethiopians care about any white woman supposedly kidnapped in Kenya.

The three Somalis sat peaceably by the sleeping camels, the red eye of a pipe passing between them. In Nairobi, Rebecca thought, the families of the dead still don't know. Living their normal happy lives, missing their husband, father, son or brother, not knowing he's dead. Now who'll pay their children's school, for their homes and food? Who'll drive down to Mombasa to tell the parents of W'kwaeme that the son for whom they've worked all their lives needs no further sacrifice from them? Klaus, stumbling round the desert beneath the bitter stars, holed up in a cave, surrounded by hyaenas – perhaps dead already, bones scattered – he'll be the one to do all this?

The night's chill grew fierce. She huddled shivering under the rock, burrowed in the sand that was like countless tiny particles of ice that would not melt, her wrists tied to one camel saddle, ankles to another, the men still talking in their liquid rasping language like the wild dogs wailing from the *laga*, their voices obscured by depth and distance. Wild dogs that slink into camp at night and rip off a sleeper's face before he can fight back – what will they do to Klaus, alone out there? The same as they'd do to me.

But self-pity only makes things worse, she told herself. You'll survive only if you think everything out and are lucky and stay strong and never waste time or sorrow on yourself. Only if you promise yourself nothing will defeat you, you'll never give up and *never* lose faith. Promise yourself you'll get out to pay for Milton's children's schools, the others' families. That you've made a decision just like you decided to leave Klaus, before this all arrived. Just like that: be strong, even if you aren't.

Sirius had risen overhead, a tiny, bitter moon, beside it Lepus the hare, caught between the hunter and his dog – maybe midnight, she decided; six hours to dawn.

Later the hiss of sandals broke a nightmare of Klaus dying because she would not make love. The Somali knelt beside her. It's coming now, she thought, leg muscles tensing. If I had a knife I'd kill you. The man rose noiselessly and stepped away.

After a few minutes she raised her head enough to see above the camel saddle anchoring her wrists. One man was sitting still, his cloak a sallow pyramid between the desert and the stars thick as snow against the blackness of space. The other two lay beneath their burnooses. She drew up her knees, dragging the saddle attached to her ankles closer, the sand swishing – but the man in the cloak did not move – until she could reach the rawhide round her ankles. The boy had spit on the knots to tighten them; now they snapped her chilled fingernails like steel. She rested, tried again, rested, watching the march of stars towards dawn, found an end of rawhide and worked it backwards through a loop and into a second loop till the knot loosened and fell away. Still her ankles were tied. She found the second knot; it was easier.

Blood rushed stinging into her feet; she bit a flap of leather on one saddle to keep from crying out. Her toes were on fire. The leather tasted of camel hair and sweat. The pain grew bearable; with one foot she pulled closer a chunk of lava she had located earlier at the base of the overhang.

Clamping the lava between her ankles, she rubbed the rawhide binding her wrists against it. The lava fell behind her ankles and was difficult to move up again. The angle was wrong and the stone's sharp edges sliced her skin instead of the cord. Back and forth she shoved her wrists over the stone, each time catching an edge of bone on the same razor curl of lava where long ago a volcanic bubble had burst, the rawhide sliding faster over the stone as her blood lubricated it, till one cord popped and the other slackened, pulse tingling her hands.

A camel snorted; she glanced back in terror but the sitting Somali had not moved. She crawled from the overhang along a steep, rubbled slope whose dark lava seemed to suck up all the starlight; looking back she was startled by the grim scar her footsteps made on the dewy sand, but no one followed; she had a moment of pure terror at the thought of them awaking and finding her gone, of their anger and what they would do when they caught her. Her strength melted; she ached to collapse and give it all away, to die. She sneered at herself, then laughed that she should sneer. Afraid of angering men again, girl? You coward, girl. You coward.

At her back was a slope of black lava descending from the Huri Hills, to the west before her the starlit Chalbi, with its dark wound of the Ririba *laga*, and beyond it the sentinel Dukana. Overhead the stars rotated west, Sirius now halfway to the horizon – was it three o'clock already? There were only three more hours of night left in which to cross the Chalbi down into Ririba *laga* and up into the Dukana, whose talus would mask her tracks and whose jumbled outcrops might provide shelter. The first breeze before dawn, tasting of dew, came bringing with it the roar of a solitary lion. Is that how the woman of the jawbone died, two million years ago? And why she'd left no other bones?

She turned from the desert and ascended the loose volcanic slope, avoiding the sharpest rocks. When she was sure her trail was impossible to follow, she turned, soon descending again to step out on to the desert a mile south of where she had first ascended. Gripping a sharp stone in each hand, she walked fast towards the black trace of the Ririba *laga* far out across the starry sand, looking back often, but no one pursued, glancing up at the stars as they slid inexorably westwards.

# Chapter 14

Through the dusty windscreen of the jolting Land Rover MacAdam watched the three empty petrol trucks bellow black smoke as they lumbered up the hill ahead. Boughs and creepers hung over the road and swayed when the trucks hit them. The Land Rover jerked and banged as Nehemiah steered it through and around the ruts and potholes; MacAdam held the bar beneath the seat to keep from bouncing. 'It's bloody well falling apart!' he yelled.

Nehemiah lifted his hands loosely from the steering wheel, letting it shimmy. 'This's a good one!' The Land Rover veered to the left.

MacAdam laughed. The panoramic purple Rift spread out below them as if the earth had cracked in half and they could see its distant other side. 'I was talking about the *road*, not your vehicle.'

'No difference.'

Longonot Crater, vast and jagged as a mountain of the moon, blocked the western sky. 'Still a damn shame,' MacAdam added, not meaning specifically the road that he and Nehemiah both remembered as much better before black independence, but Kenya itself that was falling apart, and he and Nehemiah seemed powerless to arrest it, no matter how much they talked or tried to change it.

'Some people are doing OK,' Nehemiah said.

'Like you?'

'I don't need much money.'

'M'Bole?'

'He's just one of many Ministers. You know that.'

The car whammed into a rut, stabbing pain across MacAdam's injured chest. 'He should fix some bloody roads.'

'He's tending to his cows.'

'His Swiss cows.'

'Maybe some are in the Bahamas. The Channel Islands.'

'Anywhere the feed's good.'

The land so far below was speckled with long-shadowed umbrella trees, its grass burnished by late sun. 'You should've shot the captives,' Nehemiah said.

MacAdam felt exasperation, remembered his feeling in the Matthews Range, that Nehemiah would understand. Now there seemed no way to explain. 'I felt so *alive*. I owed my life to one of them, who held his fire when he could have killed me.'

Nehemiah was indifferent. 'The sentence for poaching's death. So now they'll just be shot in Nairobi, and I'm in trouble with M'Bole.'

'Even a little time's better than none, when you're about to be shot.' But in this jangling, dirty vehicle, with the golden Rift spread out below, the battle in the

Matthews Range seemed unreal, even the scar-faced scared youth pointing his rifle at MacAdam's chest. 'Let me take the heat tomorrow, from M'Bole.'

'He'll chew on me, then knife you in the back. And your prisoners will still get shot.'

The road levelled, widened through conifer plantations, barefoot children herding cattle along the shoulders, bare huts beneath banana trees, flashes of cheap fabric like flags of poverty; a goat ran on a tether, a kid stumbling at her teats, trying to suck. Boys at the roadside held out rabbits by their ears, to sell.

A *matatu* passed the other way, its windows crammed with faces, five men hanging out the back and more huddled among potato sacks on the roof, the words 'Imagine Time' stencilled in white letters across the top of the windshield. Again MacAdam felt the absolute futility of it all, the haphazard unreality. 'I missed a man, five shots, up in the Matthews Range,' he said. 'The one who didn't shoot me. He was running away. M'kele killed him.'

'So he said.'

'What else d'he say?'

'That you missed that man on purpose. And that he's going to use his Ranger pay to buy himself a new wife.'

'How many's he got now?'

'He got three, four. But says he needs a young one, to warm him up again. Otherwise he be getting too old.'

'Like me—'

'You just *think* you're going soft.'

'I don't want to shoot at people any more.'

'As I said, what's the difference—'

'I don't care. I won't do it.' MacAdam glared at a leopard-striped tour van with pale tourists dozing at its windows.

'You wiped out a whole team of poachers! You didn't lose a man—'

'I lost Kuria.'

'He's not dead. He'll heal.'

'Not walk.'

'Many Maasai walk with a stick. A Meru can learn also.'

MacAdam shook his head. 'We took out seven poachers but three more got away, with the tusks. You know it won't stop till every elephant is dead. The problem's Africa – the world wants copper so Africa rips open its belly. The world wants diamonds so Africa sends its young men down mines to die for them. People want ivory and colobus skins and oil and slaves so Africa plunders herself for them!'

'The world wants game parks, too, Mac, full of animals. But I don't give a damn what the world wants – I care what *I* want.'

The road had narrowed, clogged with early evening trucks and buses winding down through the poor patchwork farms and shredded jungle of the N'gong Hills; Nairobi's lights poured out over the valleys below like diamonds spilled from a basket. 'I think I once believed,' MacAdam said, 'that I was better than most people, because I'd known what I'd wanted and got it. But it turned out I hadn't even known what I wanted . . .'

'Who does?'

Once more MacAdam had a sense of not belonging, alien, unable to explain. If he couldn't explain it to Nehemiah, how could he to himself? 'It's walking on nothing—' It felt like something wrung out of him, once he'd said it he'd go free. 'There's no reason, no real reason, for anything I do.'

'That buffalo make a big dent in your chest. Get it fixed, then see how you feel.'

Irritated, MacAdam started to say, 'It started long before this,' then stopped. He didn't care – it didn't matter when it had started or what it was. And he felt a traitor to Nehemiah's simpler vision, like a man who pretends to celebrate with his friends while in his mouth he tastes only ashes. He thought of the shattered butterfly in the Matthews Range.

'Like M'kele, Mac, you should get yourself another wife.'

'I got plenty of trouble with one.'

'That's because she's just one.'

MacAdam laughed and the laugh made his chest hurt. Thinking of laughter causing pain made him laugh again, hurting more. 'You're full of shit.'

'So don't you be!'

'Even full of shit I'm straighter than you.'

'Try it out, before you make conclusions.'

'You should speak.'

'It's when you have one you need another one. Not when you don't.'

Downtown Nairobi had already thinned out, at 8:30, broad Uhuru Highway the colour of weak mercurochrome beneath far-spaced halogen lights, its houses, shacks and factories peeping out with startled, tarnished faces. Nehemiah downshifted and slowed for the barracks. 'When's Dottie coming back?'

'She hasn't said.'

'You should take a few days off. Even in Nairobi.'

MacAdam shook his head, realized Nehemiah couldn't see him in the dark. 'I'll get stitched up, see how I feel.'

Nehemiah parked at Battalion HQ and walked with MacAdam between the buildings to the hospital. 'Your number two wife, Mac—'

'There isn't going to be one.'

'Get yourself a Maasai girl.'

The battalion doctor cut the bandages with which M'kele had bound MacAdam's injury in the Matthews Range, soaked them with ether until they pulled away without tearing too much of the caked black skin beneath. MacAdam watched as if his body belonged to someone else while the doctor severed the dead flesh with scissors and pulled back the edges of the wound. 'Broke your ribs.'

'How many?'

'Six or seven.' The doctor's curly hair was grizzled by the lamplight as he bent over MacAdam's splintered ribs to remove bits of bone and dead flesh with tweezers and wads of cotton soaked in ether. The needle seemed dull; the doctor forced it through the skin, tugging the black thread after it. The pain was severe and the doctor made little effort to lessen it, but to MacAdam it was as if the pain was happening to someone else for whom he felt no pity.

'You were lucky.' The doctor wrapped the wound in wide white gauze. 'Plenty people get stomped by buffalo – worse than a truck.' He seemed to disapprove, of MacAdam's carelessness, perhaps, in encountering a buffalo, or of a white man's intrusion into tribal conflicts old as human Africa. 'If he'd swung his horn a little closer you'd be dead.'

'The soldier Kuria Ikole,' MacAdam said, 'that they flew down from Wamba – you see him?'

'They take him right to Nairobi General.' The doctor yanked tight the last stitch.

'He's going to walk?'

'Not on two legs.'

MacAdam sat on his thin concave bed in the officers' quarters, a small room with a sink beside the window, a thin coarse towel hanging from a steel bar on either side of the sink, the linoleum smelling of carnuba, the window panes of ammonia, dust blurring the colour photograph of the President that hung like a crucifix over the headboard. He closed his eyes and had a sudden vision of this room, of a skeleton, its friendly jaw and head cocked in inquiry. Then he saw this skeleton from the rear as it hunched sitting on the bed, spine curved, and saw the sink and hanging towels beyond. How banal, he thought. That's not all I am. And the skeleton lifted its shoulders in a lonely shiver just as he did, straightened its spine so he could see its splintered ribs, reached out and knocked on wood.

# Chapter 15

She heard it coming up behind her but in the darkness could not see it. She stumbled, gashed a knee, kept running. Shale scattered, a footfall in front made her stop, breath thundering, hearing nothing. Before her the downslope of Dukana ridge looked out on a world of sand and stars with no place to hide.

The chunk of pockmarked lava in her hand was heavy, cold. She felt a shift in the air as the predator skirted her, was aware of the wind like water on her skin and the immanence of every molecule and moment, the imminence of death. The hideous hissing of footsteps and her harsh whispering breath were the same and only sound. Sure she would die, she ran downhill over rubble, sand, and splintered rock towards the desert and the far, darker core of Kore *laga* snaking across it like a crack to the centre of the earth. The noise leaped at her and she fell screaming, hands raised to claw. But it was only a horrible great bustard, wide leathery wings flapping up out of the canyon and round a cliff above her head and she smelled it now as she ran, the stink of rotting flesh the bustard had been eating, and in that stench of death she could smell her own. Then the paws came pouncing down behind her and she ran faster with death coming faster to catch her heels, but it was only falling sand and pebbles and she collapsed, utterly without breath or strength or hope, against a wall of rock, wanting death to come quickly without pain or recognition. Still death did not come. The land grew silent till against the silver glinting sand she could hear the passage of the stars. Faraway a leopard barked that high, dissatisfied deep roar it cuts off so sharply, as if its annoyance is too great to express, can only be appeased.

The rock wall was cold and sharp against her back. Below her the crabbed and rugged tumbled rock gave way to dunes that lapped this shore of the Dukana and rose and fell across the farflung desert. She could taste water on the wind, hear it splash the rocks and flutter on the sand, hush down these runnels and crevices of ancient melted stone. The wind cooled, bringing the metallic taste of night-damp sand and the wails of hyaenas gathering to the south. She craved to stay by this rock wall that felt so good against her back, but it would not dissuade the leopard or hyaenas, and once day came here she knew the sun would kill her quickly. She could no longer really remember if there existed such an absolute as water, no longer place the cause of this horrid, burning, exhausted dry flesh, this swollen throat sucking moisture from her lungs. Like someone who cannot swim wading deep into the sea, she left the wall of rock and, watching constantly around and behind her, walked out on the sand, the chunk of lava clenched like a knife, the horizon rising round her and shutting off the stars.

The sand rustled underfoot like galaxies of broken glass; a snake snapped at her from a boulder; jackals chattered like mad children. She got to her feet, fell, and stood again. She knew she had been walking along the Seine at night, the song of nightingales and owls in the leaves; a barge had come upriver, a smell of baking bread on the wind driving her crazy with hunger, but she could not understand where it came from. The barge passed, its cabin lights glowing on a line of wash that fluttered from amidships; through the barge's kitchen window she could see a husky woman bent over her stove, and realized the *woman* had been baking bread, but there was no way to reach this woman, no way to swim out into the Seine after this boat so quickly ascending, its wake lapping in condolence among the shoreline willows, the pre-dawn wind hissing over the sand.

It was as easy as putting one foot in front of the other. But yesterday whose tracks had she discovered stumbling haphazardly before her? Her own – she'd put one foot before the other till they brought her in a big circle back to herself.

The land darkened once again before her, descending into Kore *laga*'s great serpentine pit, the hyaenas calling faster now as they circled the foot of the Dukana and came loping towards her. She looked round frantically for something to climb, raised her hands as if to climb up to the stars, then ran down the *laga*'s steep cascading sands. The sound of something leaped down behind her, and knowing she'd die she ran harder, gasping with terror, to the bottom of the *laga* and glanced up but there were only the stars so high and narrowly framed above, the *laga*'s deep slit imprisoned by cliffs of sand, a dead end where a leopard would come padding on soft toes and grinning its huge jaws, where hyaenas could corner her, laughing and ripping flesh. She scrambled up the other slope, tumbled down again in sand and boulders and grappled her way up once more, earth crumbling and sliding beneath her, as if she were attempting to climb an avalanche, and feeling every instant on her back the ghastly grip of leopard's claws, the hyaena's fangs. But here was solid rock, there a slowly slipping piece of ledge she shoved past, fear driving her like a terrorized animal up the slick, impossible slope of sliding sand, the leopard's breath hot on the small of her back. But the leopard did not pounce and the slope lessened then levelled, opening to the stars, and she spun round gasping, and nothing was behind her but the *laga* gaping blackly and all around a sea of sand drowning the stars.

One minute the night was thick with stars, then the sun burst over the slag and battlements of Dukana ridge, blasting her with heat. Water appeared in hollows in the sand but sank from sight when she knelt to it; water trickled on the wind but she couldn't find it; water fell from heaven, touching her cheek, yet in the viridian sky there were no clouds, only growing fire. Pools of water glimmered on the sand; as she ran to them they retreated, and when they had tricked her far into the desert they disappeared.

She followed the *laga* south but could not remember why. There was some *reason* she must cling to, against this hunger to release herself to the softest, most sensual of sleeps. To the west the tall cliffs glistened in the risen sun, their scarps streaked with water; there was a stream – she heard it; a voice was calling her by a name she recognized but could not place.

The sun climbed quickly; step after step she forced herself across the blazing sand; minute after minute outspanned into infinite hours of unlivable heat and thirst, while the Dukana's brittle umber peninsula wavered round her, sometimes to the east, then straight behind her, then strangely to the west, marooned in the middle of the desert, once even before her, dazzlingly divorced from earth, a weightless dark phenomenon hovering over infinitudes white as titanium fire.

She realized she must get out of the sun, go back down into Kore *laga*, back to where the leopard waited, or die from the sun. She crawled and slid down to the Kore's narrow, vertical, shaded canyon. She remembered there had been a *geb* tree standing in a bend of the *laga*, hunched over a pool of clear water like an old man inspecting his reflection. A strangler fig had grown down over it, weighting its limbs and choking off its air, sucking moisture from the same tiny source. Before it would be a blade of outcrop on the right sinking into the bed of the canyon, and a sharp turn to the right upstream behind it, where ancient floods had split the basalt like an axe.

As it neared midday the sun's head poured down the canyon walls. Each time she fell she rose resolutely as soon as possible; only once did she get confused and turn back up the canyon. Why had she left the expedition? Why had Klaus deserted her?

Each step she was coming closer to it, the understanding. It vanished round every curve in the canyon ahead of her but she was catching up. She glimpsed a trace of movement around the cliff and ran to catch it, fell and ran again; the canyon floor widened where once a stream had barrelled round an edge of harder gneiss and now in its deeper deposits stood a gnarled *geb* tree guarding a scabrous pool. A dwarf raven flapped scrawking from its topmost bough.

She fell to her knees, parted the green scum and drank its tepid bilious nectar, lay in a trance and drank again, till her vision cleared and she washed her face and rested her feet in the hot alkali mud. She still could not understand how she had been separated from the expedition. Soon the predators would come. She climbed into the *geb* tree's low, stout crotch and began to eat its scaly, sweet yellow fruit.

How had she remembered this tree, when there was no way she could have ever seen it, if she had never been in this part of the canyon? How had she pictured it in her mind, exactly as it was now? She had a sense that someone had helped her. Who? Climbing higher, she ate till her stomach heaved, then gathered more fruit in her shirt. She was thirsty again, but feared to descend. She saw the bones scattered on the sand, tried to decipher the tracks around them, to find where the leopard waited.

When the leopard comes he'll climb this tree, she

thought. The cliff above was smooth and vertical. She'd have to continue south along this canyon till she found a way back up into the sun. South because if she could go for three more days, four days maybe, she might make it to Dabandabli, the police post at North Horr. No, not 'maybe'. She would reach North Horr.

She knelt again and drank till it seemed the pool would go dry. She gathered a few more *geb* fruits in her bulging shirt, holding them with one forearm beneath her breasts, took up an axe-rock in her other hand, and walked quickly, glancing often behind, southwards down the canyon.

Turning back like this she failed to see the leopard ahead as she stepped round a curve in the canyon. But she heard it snarl and jumped round to face it, raising her axe-rock. It huffed angrily at the bad human smell, glanced past her up the canyon, saw there was no one else and slid its emerald eyes back to her.

She tried to back up but the cliff wall bumped her spine. The *geb* fruits fluttered down her front and hit her feet. The ground was rocky and she tried not to fall as she stumbled backwards along the cliff and the leopard came at her. It was a big old leopard – how hungry is it, she thought, how much can it find to eat up here?

She saw she would not reach the *geb* tree. The leopard darted at her, eyes wide, mouth agape, yellow-black fur rippling down its shoulders, the easy swing of muscle moving into its pouncing gait, its white teeth smiling. She hurled her rock, distracting it for an instant, then she hunched down, teeth bared, neck muscles distended, claws wide, in that automatic position of pointless self-defence adopted by all primates about to be killed by a big cat. She was past thinking, past knowing, just flesh in its last desperate hunger to survive as the leopard halted and peered past her, hissed, spun round, and vanished down the canyon.

She knelt to pick up the *geb* fruits but her shaking hands could not hold them. It had not happened. Yet here were the leopard's tracks, the furl of sand where he'd spun round and down the canyon.

It was a small man, almost a boy, in a tan cloak, rifle in his hand. She felt no fear. 'You've just wasted time, *Mama*,' he said in his demotic Swahili, and raised the gun at her. 'Now we go back.'

She remembered. This was what she had fled. Klaus had not deserted her. Everyone was dead. She saw the universe as it is – pitiless, infinite; she had only imagined trust, faith, hope. 'You don't need to point that at me. I'll come.'

Warwar kept her ahead of him back up the Kore canyon and across the Chalbi's baking sands. The camels were tethered among boulders at the edge of the Dukana, where Ibrahim and Rashid rested in the shade of a goatskin stretched between four sticks.

# Chapter 16

Automotive exhaust rippled over clogged lines of midday traffic on Uhuru Highway, as if Nairobi's air were made of melting plastic. Every start and stop of Nehemiah's Land Rover brought new pain to MacAdam's bandaged ribs; to distract himself he bought a *Nation* from one of the barefoot vendors walking the lanes of cars. But these plaintive sheets of dead tree stained with English words and the photographs of politicians – people unfortunate enough to have forgotten the ancient warning that the camera steals the soul – seemed like a joke made tragic because no one understands it. The handshakings, earnest conferences, and faces wrapped in probity were simply a mimicry of the white world, angering him at both.

A Datsun *matatu* throbbed beside them, a half-ton pickup with a wooden crate into which some twenty people were compressed, others standing on the tilting bumper or squeezing out the cab. On the other side was a new blue air-conditioned Volvo with diplomatic plates, a single moustached driver in grey pinstripe, his air-conditioned windows shut against the air MacAdam was trying not to breathe. He envied the people walking beyond the roadside – women with variegated baskets on their heads, children running to catch up, businessmen in suits, and tribesmen dressed in rags and plastic bags on their way to beg for work at construction sites. The distant light turned green; the traffic edged ahead; the light turned red.

A stainless steel elevator at Government House took them to M'Bole's top-floor office suite.'There must be no *more* of this keeping prisoners!' M'Bole waved a broad palm that to Nehemiah seemed like a whiteman's stained with shoe polish. M'Bole laced his fingers and back-cracked his knuckles like stones snapping in a fire.

'No civilized soldier's going to kill his captives.' MacAdam had hunched forward in his chair and Nehemiah saw the antagonism building in him, in the challenge of 'civilized'.

'I don't want *"civilized"* soldiers, Mister . . . MacAdam.' This double slight seemed to please the Minister and he leaned back, the leather chair squeaking cooperatively, emphasizing his bulk. 'No one wants to kill, but this poaching's killing *us*. We have to make a stand.'

'You don't make a stand, Minister, by killing unarmed men—'

'Unarmed? That's not so, MacAdam—'

'—they're unarmed when you'd have us shoot them!' MacAdam lunged to drive home his point, then sat back, pain on his face. 'You do as you want. But I won't be with you.'

M'Bole levered himself up and walked along his office

wall hung with photographs of himself shaking the hands of many people, himself holding certificates of merit, himself smiling as he cut ribbons and placed paper crowns on young girls' heads. He stood with his back to the plate glass window, blocking the light, hands clasped behind him. 'You know your participation, Mister MacAdam – above the value of your experience *as a hunter of men* —' he stressed these words as if MacAdam might be foolish enough to think them a compliment, ' — is proof that we are a multiracial society using all our talents to protect the nation's common heritage . . .'

'You mean the international conservation groups and European governments are on your back about the elephants, and you want to project a unanimous, concerned effort.'

'We say the same thing.'

'But one of us doesn't mean it.'

'Meaning is what you *say*, MacAdam.' M'Bole looked down through the glass at the green lawns and tiny multicoloured figures far below.

'No, Minister, meaning is what you *do*. Siad Barre may be the "President" of Somalia but he doesn't pay his soldiers enough to feed their families – what would you do?'

'You and I both settled that question long ago.' M'Bole returned and sat. 'Mister MacAdam, don't you realize that sometimes governments are more important than people?'

'I can't think of a single case where that might be true —'

'And I can think of few cases where it isn't. These

men you captured, they'll be sentenced in a week and shot the day after.'

MacAdam got to his feet. 'Then you've got no further need of me.'

M'Bole waved a hand painfully before his face. 'Now let's not be precipitous—'

'We don't agree.'

'It's a necessary sacrifice.' M'Bole seemed to ponder. 'Like the millions of dollars' worth of confiscated tusks and rhino horn we burn, that we could be selling to pay for schools and wildlife conservation and all the other things we need so desperately . . .'

MacAdam's gaze wandered the room's fine carpets, wallpapers, statuary and fittings, swept across the vast ebony desk and back to M'Bole. 'If a man dies fighting he dies fighting. If I bring him in I don't want him shot.'

'There's other issues,' Nehemiah said. 'The G–3s, hot pursuit.'

'Into Somalia?' M'Bole's voice rose. 'Impossible.'

'Then how can we wipe them out? Isn't hot pursuit within the Department's power, according to the Constitution?'

'Not now. Not with civil war in Somalia.'

Nehemiah held his breath against the Minister's, harsh with raw onions and greasy with beer. '*Melay olambu enoyoto*,' he said suddenly, switching from Swahili to Maasai, which he knew the Kikuyu M'Bole would not directly understand, this tall, overweight farmer with his holdings in tourist hotels and mines and shacks for city workers, empowered to protect the elephants, whose sister used to send five thousand pounds of tusks a month, under protection of the Indonesian and Pakistani embassies, from Mombasa to Japan, Taiwan and Hong Kong. "*Melay olambu enoyoto*," he said. ' "He who talks loudly won't cross the valley." We won't get far without more action.'

'You speak Maasai to me; I speak Kikuyu back to you: *Mwaga gukua mwaruta mbaara* – "It's those who've not died in wars that start them." There are channels best approached diplomatically.'

Where everything is lies and stolen profit, Nehemiah finished to himself, furious that now MacAdam would desert the struggle, that he cared more for Somali prisoners than the future of Kenya, that the Minister would dismiss them and nothing would be gained. 'It's not enough guns.'

Leaning forward, the Minister nodded, as if glad this had been brought up. 'More will come as soon as we complete the loan agreement with Heckler and Koch.'

As soon as you have chosen your percentage of the herd, thought Nehemiah, How much will that be, your personal cut of the loan fees and payback? One per cent? Too generous of you. Five per cent? Somewhere in between. In the neighbourhood of ten to thirty thousand pounds. As we Maasai say, you milk the cow that feeds in your pasture – such a small amount on the international scale, but enough to pay the fees of a thousand children who otherwise cannot go to school. Are you really sure this thirty thousand pounds will do more for your people, Minister, in your Channel Islands bank? 'It would be better, wouldn't it,' Nehemiah continued, 'to buy fewer G–3s with cash and forget the loan, and have the guns right away? The thirty we just received, plus we could get what – another two hundred?'

The Minister nodded affirmatively. 'Believe me, I'd like to, but they prefer a loan. Building credit.'

Nehemiah decided perhaps this was not a deal the Minister had arranged. Was it forced down his throat by 'them', the Kalenjins around the President? He'd still get a piece of the loan though. 'The well-fed belly does not know the unfed one, yes? It does no good to waste money when we have it, just to ensure we can borrow it when we don't.'

Again the Minister flailed his hands. 'It's more complicated—'

MacAdam stood stiffly. 'You're busy, Minister – thank you for your time. Thank you also for Kuria's pension, for the attention you're giving this. Please reconsider the death sentences; two years of jail to one of these Somalis is an eternity; when it's over he'll go home and never dare to cross the border again . . .'

To Nehemiah MacAdam seemed to be playing in a hilarious tribal play the role of a man who attempts to overcome evil with goodness.

MacAdam took the Minister's suddenly outstretched hand. 'Perhaps you don't need to go into Somalia to find the poachers.' He smiled into the Minister's tiny, merry eyes. 'When one can find most of them here.'

'Exactly! That's why we don't need hot pursuit.' Bowing slightly forward, a hand in the small of each one's back, the Minister showed them out, like a gunman, Nehemiah reflected, sheltering behind his hostages, a pistol jabbed into each. From what, he wondered, do we protect him?

'You must reconsider, Mister MacAdam,' M'Bole said. 'You do your country a marvellous service by staying with the Rangers.'

'When the young Somali held his fire, didn't kill me, he taught me, he taught me . . . we're not meant to take others' lives – he didn't *want* to, he was better than that, and I've learned, learned from him—' Again MacAdam seemed, naively, to believe in the converting power of good, as if one man's experience could teach others.

'But you shot him!'

'M'kele – Nehemiah's uncle – did. He didn't know. I killed another man, in the battle. I don't like it, but I did. I'm still willing to be your hunter of men, as you call it, but to bring them back alive.'

M'Bole smiled. 'And teach them the error of their ways?' He halted at the door. 'I forgot to mention. You knew her, didn't you, Rebecca Hecht?'

Nehemiah saw MacAdam jump, try to hide it, turn. 'What about her?'

'Her husband, the archaeologist – he staggered into the police post at North Horr last night. Your dear Somalis shot their drivers and two students and took her hostage—'

'Where?'

'East of Turkana.'

'*Where* east of Turkana?'

'You knew her well?'

'What did he *say*, her husband?'

'All I've learned so far is that they took her in the

157

Chalbi. Somewhere by a place called Mailoka, Maikona, something like that. We're having the husband
flown down.' M'Bole raised a huge fist and tucked back
his suit sleeve to view his Rolex. 'Might be here now.'

'Who's on it?'

'On it? Marsabit police.' M'Bole turned back towards
his door.

'Marsabit police! She's an internationally known
archaeologist! You can't give it to local police with one
vehicle and three camels!'

'Who would you put on it?'

'Get planes on it!'

'We have. The plane'll fly back up there today, after
it drops off Hecht.'

'One plane's not enough—'

'We might send more men—'

'How many?'

'You won't be with us, remember?' M'Bole taunted.

MacAdam took a breath, steadying himself. 'What
do you want?'

'Mister MacAdam, what *I* want doesn't matter. What
matters is what's best for Kenya. I'd like to spare your
Somalis. I'd like, too, not to burn the ivory we confis-
cate. But we burn it because that shows we're serious.
Think of it, Mister MacAdam, in the African way.'

'Fine. But I want to call Wilson Field right now and
make sure that plane doesn't leave and to talk to Hecht
and then take the plane back up to Wamba to pick up
my men—'

'No more worry for these Somali prisoners?'

'I'll be back before you shoot them. Nehemiah, we've

158

got to get the men up to North Horr and on the Somalis'
tracks before they get into Ethiopia.'

'If they do,' M'Bole said, 'or into Somalia, that's the
end. No hot pursuit.'

'I pray that doesn't happen,' MacAdam said.

'If it does, we never heard of you. If they catch you,
they kill you. If you come back, we arrest you.'

Going down in the chrome elevator, Nehemiah
watched MacAdam in the mirror, the grey eyes narrowed under the thick, curly blond brows, the face set,
the stare that sees nothing. 'You let him walk all over
you,' Nehemiah said.

'That son of a bitch. He *knows*!'

'This is a distraction, Mac. The real battle's down in
the Tsavo, Meru, Amboseli, our last elephants—'

'You *don't* know, do you?'

'You tell me.'

'You want me to have a second wife, goddamn it?
She was it. Till she couldn't stand it any more and broke
it off.'

Outside Government House the air sizzled like
molten lead. Couples sat in tree shadows on the lawns;
the sidewalks throbbed with bright dresses and men's
dazzling white shirts. The Land Rover's door handle
was hot, the seat, steering wheel and air inside on fire
till they rolled down the windows and had driven as far
as Koinage Street, where the tall buildings and leafy
trees offered oases of shadow on the sun-brilliant street.
'That's why Dottie left?'

'She never knew. It happened two years ago.'

'You don't see her any more?'

'She won't see me. If she can help it.'

'Mac, you're all smashed up by buffalo and it's crazy for you to go. Stay here and line up some private aircraft to overfly.'

'I'm not staying here. I'll go alone, if I have to.'

Tourists in bush hats and Out of Africa suits clogged the crosswalks against the light. 'If you go, take M'kele. Even the clever-eyed thief cannot evade the one who tracks him – *kake miiolo enikichokini* – that's M'kele.'

'How many European've been kidnapped by Somalis in the last five years?'

The tourists thinned and Nehemiah shifted into first. 'Maybe ten.'

'How many have come back?'

The car nudged forward. 'I can think of one.'

'So we need that plane doing flyovers in outward concentrics till the second plane arrives and then spread out. With radio contact, two more planes patrolling the borders so they can't get across—'

'Mac—'

'How many Somalis are there? M'Bole didn't say.'

Nehemiah geared down and swung the Land Rover off Langata Boulevard and on to Wilson Field, halted at the gate, signed the guardsheet that the sentry handed through the window, resting it on the steering wheel. The engine muttered unevenly in the heat; a light plane droned over on approach. Nehemiah tapped the pen shut on the guard's clipboard and handed them back. 'They won't even let you keep the one plane, Mac. If you meet M'kele, Darius, and Gideon at Wamba that will get the four of you to North Horr tonight or tomorrow morning, then the plane'll have to swing back for four more of us. Maybe M'Bole wants you up there, out of the way—'

MacAdam paced the cool hangar where the voices of mechanics echoed off the quonset roof. The floor was sticky with oil and grit. She's already dead and that's all of it, he told himself. They raped her and killed her and the hyaenas won't leave any bones.

The plane from North Horr was late, must have stopped in Nanyuki. Sun the colour of poinsettia was sinking into sunset smog. There was no getting back to North Horr tonight unless the plane hurried, another night she'd be dragged across the desert. Unless she was dead. Of course she was dead. How many of them? M'Bole hadn't said.

MacAdam went into the office where Nehemiah sat radioing through to Wamba to tell the men to take the truck up to Marsabit. 'I'm going back to get the G–3 and more ammo and my backpack, and rations and extra canteens for everybody. Anything else?'

'Snake kit and maps.'

'Got them.'

'Not of southern Ethiopia.'

When he returned the Cessna sat on the apron. Nehemiah was talking in the office to an emaciated old black man in a tattered shirt who lay on a wooden bench while a doctor listened for his heart. Then MacAdam noticed he had grey whiskers and was not black but sunburned. It was Hecht looking up at him as if he were not there, as if he'd seen through and past him. You bastard, MacAdam thought. You let her die.

Hecht's voice was old and glassy. 'Attacked at dawn. Shot our two boys and two students – young man, Cambridge—'

'How many?'

'Of them? Oh five at least. Seven. More in the hills.'

'When? What did they say? Tell me everything about them.'

For a moment Hecht hesitated, a dislike, and MacAdam wondered if she'd ever told him, in retribution or else some marital reconsideration, some baring of truths that would lead him now to punish her somehow, punish him. But Hecht told it quickly, seemingly without rancour even for the Somalis, as if his desert odyssey had taught him the inefficacy of hate. 'Four days ago this morning. Hard not to get mixed up.'

'She's dead then,' MacAdam answered, more to hurt himself than Hecht, to hurt himself for hoping, for seeing her step across her kitchen floor to give him a last, worried kiss, for feeling again her first kiss unexpected and strong as an electric shock, her arms around him and her sweet, long hair against his face.

'They'll be sending a letter,' Hecht answered. 'I tracked them till they shot at me and said go back or they'd kill her.' Hecht pulled himself up on bony elbows. 'What more could I do?'

The plane sat on the apron with the pilot squatting in its shade, but a mechanic had dismounted the cowl of the port engine, had pulled the plug cables and was unbolting the head. 'Shit!' MacAdam screamed running towards him. 'I've got to use this plane!'

'Not tonight, Captain.' The Maasi pilot pointed to a

wide splotch of oil on the apron. 'She's got a busted rod.'

MacAdam bent over hands on knees and took a breath, forced himself to take another. 'You got one?'

'Another rod?' the Kikuyu mechanic said. 'Damn right, off this baby's sister—'

'Goddamn I'll fly that one!'

'It's dead, boss. Pieces.'

'How long?'

The mechanic eyed the oil on the ground. 'Two days.'

'Impossible. We have to leave tonight.'

'Even if the plane's done, Captain,' the pilot said. 'We can't leave till five. I can take off here in the dark but I can't land in Marsabit till dawn. They got no lights.'

MacAdam threw his jacket on the wing, turned to the mechanic. 'What's your name, son?'

'Keena Ogole.'

'Let's go to work.'

Ogole sadly shook his head. 'Waitin' on the other rod to come in from Kisumu. S'posed to be here, by six.'

The quonset was dank, airless. Through the open doors came the cries of soldiers playing volleyball, the crackle of small arms, the tread of boots against concrete. He looked out seeing nothing, ran outside, clenched his fists, came back, glanced at his watch, forgot the time. His body felt like a steel spring, wasted. The air was hideously empty. But he could compress himself into a pure perception that almost reached her.

# Chapter 17

A black rider on a black camel crossed the ridge, a black silhouette with a black rifle cocked across his shoulder. A second black rider dropped down from the ridgeline around a basalt cirque, nonchalantly cantering into rifle range. 'Three more on the right,' Rashid screamed, but now there were five, their black cloaks reddened by the low sun, leaning back in their saddles as their camels descended the talus of Daka Qaqala. 'Warwar, cover the left!' Ibrahim yelled, and Warwar ran forward, tugging the whitewoman's camel as Rashid swung round to defend the rear. 'Don't fire till I say.' Ibrahim added as more riders crested the ridge and raised their rifles in a signal to surrender.

'Keep going,' Ibrahim yelled. 'Don't stop till they fire!'

'Put down the whitewoman!' Rashid cried. 'We'll get on her camel!' He waved his rifle for the whitewoman to dismount but Warwar only ran faster, stumbling into Ibrahim. More Borani formed a line like trees blocking the rocky slope ahead.

'We're dead!' Ibrahim waved his rifle for the Borani

to stay back. 'Damn your whitewoman!'

Gripping the camel's jerking halter with his left hand as he tried to steady the rifle in his right, Warwar could not remember if the rifle was set to automatic. If it was, then the first shots would waste bullets and they needed every bullet for these black-caped Borani with their narrow desert-blackened faces. Except somehow he must save one bullet for himself at the end, must not be captured, must remember that, must not be captured, or the Borani would make him beg for death for days before they killed him. He wanted to unsnap the clip to extract one bullet to keep between his teeth for later, for there were far far too many Borani and this was going to be a horrible death and the fear inside him was so huge he could not breathe and the water came into his eyes, making it hard to see.

A Borani broke from the group and rode forward, waved his rifle in a big semicircle, the arm of his cape following the rifle round its ambit like a black wing. The Borani's voice was loud but Warwar could not understand. Wind chilled the sweat on his face. He was conscious of everything and nothing, of what it would have been like making love with Soraya, of a bird blown like a leaf, a pebble underfoot, the smell of rifles and now the dry palm oil the Borani rub their skins with, like sage and lemon, and the baked black clay odour of their capes, the white beads they wore like bits of skeleton showing through.

'Offer them the whitewoman,' Rashid hissed.

'Get down in the rocks,' Ibrahim answered calmly. 'Rashid, cover the woman. If they start to shoot, kill

her.' Ibrahim yanked his camel forward, the bull elephant's big tusks bouncing, raised his rifle in salute. 'We
come in peace,' he yelled, in Somali.

In Keena Ogole's hand the piston rod was like a broken
weapon. 'It's when he raised the torque, revving for
takeoff,' he said.

MacAdam swore at the gutted cylinder head with its
coils like intestines, congealed oil coating its brachiated
exhaust.

'Better down here than up there.' Ogole laid the
broken rod on a white cloth on the hangar floor, measured the substitute rod from the Cessna's sister ship
against it. 'Once it builds momentum, warms up, it's
OK. It's that *stress* – like if you had to climb too fast.'
The replacement rod seemed longer than the other but
Ogole nonchalantly began to pin it into its bearings and
reassemble the block. MacAdam paced to the hangar
edge, measuring the light left in the carmine and blue
sunset, with the black trees and rooftops cut clear
against it. In the wind he could taste her, from down
across the livid sands of the vast Suguta, over mountains
and savannahs and coiling rivers and jungles and icy
peaks, then down the last steamy hundred miles to Nairobi and across its acrylic smog to this breath of air with
her molecules inside it.

'Sorry, *Mama*, you got to go with them.' Warwar's eyes
sank pleadingly into hers, begging her to get down so
that he could mount the camel and run away, or hide
behind her back from the bullets that would slice like

white-hot smashing rods through his flesh, begging her not to mind being this sacrifice. The Borani circled closer, guns pointing like sinister petrified bones out of their black capes, their camels' jaws vengeful.

The hawk-faced leader's eyes were lit far back in his skull; his grin was the most frightful thing Warwar had ever seen. Like his eyes his voice came from deep within, a giant's out of a cavern, yet his body seemed nervous and eager for a reason to shoot. He turned from Rebecca back to Ibrahim, nodded at the tusks atop the two other camels, spoke curtly, and Ibrahim answered him angrily but with a hopeless acceptance in his voice that Warwar recognized as death. 'They want the tusks and saddle bags,' Ibrahim said.

Holding his rifle level, Rashid reached up on his camel, undid both saddle bags, and threw them on the sand beside the leader's camel. 'We come in peace,' he said also in Somali but none of the Borani edging nearer in a tightening circle responded.

'I've been kidnapped,' Rebecca called out. 'Will you take me to North Horr, or up to the Addis Ababa road?'

The fire brightened in the leader's eyes. 'They don't speak Swahili, *Mama*,' Warwar whispered. 'But don't talk. You're much safer with us than them.'

The leader spoke and another Borani dismounted, opened the saddle bags and handed the white bag of twelve thousand shillings up to the leader. Two others untied the elephant tusks and retied them to empty saddles of their own camels, took the reins of Rebecca's camel from Warwar's hand and led it to the leader. He finished glancing through the money, tied the sack and tucked it into his cloak, and pulled her camel to him. His eyes, bereft of pupils, emanated a coarse yellow light; then Rebecca realized it was one eye only that was like that, that it must be blind. Will they kill me now, she wondered, fighting over me, or slower later. Fear ran perspiration down her ribs and hollowed her lungs. The leader kicked his camel round, jerking hers after it; she gripped the pommel and glanced back imploringly at Warwar tiny and empty-handed on the sand. The motion made her hat fall forward and the strap slip and she jammed her chin into her chest to catch it but the hat spun away and plunged between the following camel's hoofs. 'Get it!' she screamed, but the Borani kept on riding and her camel jerked harder forward, snapping her neck. Now dust hid Warwar and the other Somalis, and her heart was full of terror and a rage to kill.

The Boranis' dust settled slowly on the wind. 'You who wanted it all!' Rashid shrilled at Warwar. 'Now see what you've got!'

'We were lucky,' Ibrahim said amicably. 'They'd sworn an oath of peace. We won't wait for them to change their mind.' He swung up on to his camel, holding the other camel's bridle for Rashid to do the same. 'You'll have to run alongside, little one.'

'They didn't take our rifles,' Rashid said. 'We still have the cameras and little cousin's "far-seeing thing".'

'I have to walk all the way back to Somalia?' Warwar called, running behind them.

'A fitting lesson, after you showed such bad judgement. It's by wanting too much that one gets nothing.'

Warwar panted with exhaustion and rage. The land danced round in his eyes. 'She was *mine! I* found her! And you let her go!'

'I didn't *let* her go, foolish child. I bartered her for our lives. Even for yours.'

'We could have fought them!'

'Three against thirty?'

Warwar's lips felt like leather bands over his teeth. 'At night we'll get them back. Tonight.'

'Into so many pieces they would carve you,' Rashid sneered. 'Making you eat each piece. How many would you eat before you died?'

'I promised them we'd go in peace,' Ibrahim said.

'They'll camp tonight. I'll find them.'

Ibrahim neared, reaching down. 'Come up with me, nestling. We're riding home, and in a while we'll travel south to the Kenya coast – there's still elephants – we'll get a few, and you'll have some precious shillings. Come! Life's what Allah gives us.'

Warwar shook his head and walked behind them to the top of the ridge, tears blurring his view of the line of Borani riding north up the valley into the Ethiopian heights, Rebecca's white shirt a spark against the darkness.

'The stroke won't be right, because the rod's too long. Changes the compression.'

'I don't give a shit long as it runs. I don't want to put down anywhere and I don't want to crash. Can it get me to Marsabit to pick up my squad and then up to North Horr?'

'You're asking me to predict the impossible, Captain.'
'What are the chances?'
'Like I said. Simon's not going to want to fly them.'
'He said he will. He doesn't give a damn either.'
'If he doesn't give a damn why you asking me?'

They rode into a wide valley with dark cliffs high above. Brisk evening washed over the stony slopes and down the middle of the valley. She smelled camel-dung smoke, then saw glimmers of flames and the outline of dark yurt-like tents. Children came running with whip sticks in their hands, chattering like birds. They clustered round her camel and gripped her ankles in their tiny hard paws. The leader dismounted, yanked her camel to him, took her arm and pulled her down. His grip was like a handcuff on her wrist as he led her between the clawing children and women's curious voices into a yurt, her head banging the hardened bough supporting the door. There was a dung fire in the middle of the floor; its smoke and an infected, warm, greasy smell filled the choking air. He shoved her down and she lay along one side, trying to breathe beneath the goatskin flap.

Two women entered, sharp faces and shining black eyes. One gave her a gourd of water, the other a flat piece of bark with a gruel of camel's milk and barley.

Where Warwar could find brambles for the two camels on the northwest side of the ridge they stopped for the night. Rashid had killed a lizard on a rock but Ibrahim did not dare to light a fire, so they ate it raw, in thirds,

Warwar with the head and neck as far as the front paws. It was rubbery as *geb* root but he got it down, feeling in the back of his throat a strange sandy taste which must be thirst or maybe only anger over losing the woman.

Every time he thought of going after her he trembled. Like a person keeping himself away from the edge of a cliff so he wouldn't throw himself over, he would not think about sneaking into the Borani camp and taking back his woman and the money. It would show them, teach Ibrahim and Rashid how to be men. True, he'd shown them before, at the Land Rovers, and they had not accepted it and blamed him instead. Even now if he rescued the woman they'd criticize him, say he'd increased their danger, but he was not going to think about rescuing the woman because then, fool, he'd try to do it, and the Borani would cut him up in pieces and make him eat them like Rashid said.

Nevertheless after he had staked out the camels and unrolled his own goatskin on a promontory of stone where Ibrahim had instructed him to guard, and as moonrise silvered the perfect blackness of the valley headwalls, he came to his conclusion, lingered a last moment in the goatskin's marvellous warmth, then rolled it aside, wiped dew from his rifle with his cloak, and set off north at a run, along the ridge above the valley walls.

The hawk-faced man came into the yurt and held out to her a string of charred intestine, goat or antelope; she ate it, not caring. He pointed to the fire and raised his shoulders in a shivering motion, asking was she warm.

He shook the water gourd and finding it empty called out for it to be filled and for a woman to bring a goat cape to cover her shoulders. Smiling, he sat across the fire and spoke as though convincing her of something, revealing good news, his teeth large and very even, lips wide and reddened by the coals.

'North Horr,' she said, and when he did not understand, 'Moyale,' naming the biggest Ethiopian town along the border, but he tossed his head up to one side, indicating that he did not know or did not want her to speak this way. Jabbing his right index finger into his cupped left hand, he nodded to show decision and swung his right hand in a circle that could have no meaning but this tent, this camp, our whole land. This was where she must stay.

'We'll give you many shillings! A million shillings!'

This word, too, seemed to hold no interest for him. He steepled tall slender fingers before him as he spoke, as if showing her a lanceolate wound that only she could heal. His face was young but gnarled as baobab, his arms like supple ebony in the subtle light; his breath, as he came nearer, had the fragrance of milk and flowers. She kept trying to recoil and now her back was hard against the goatskin wall.

He called out and the two women came in moments later with a leather flap of goat grease which they rubbed on her face and arms, making them sting. As if flicking dust from a table he waved them out. He stood and dropped his goatskin cloak, his enormous slender blackness heightened by firelight, held his fists together at his chest and ripped them apart, pointed at her blouse.

173

'No.' She realized he was dominating her by height and tried to stand, but the tent's sloping side constrained her; to stand she must move next to him. She clapped her hands and pointed at the door: leave.

Shock followed by mirth struck his face. He reached out and tore her blouse down the middle, baring her breast. As she dived past he grabbed her arm and knocked her down, fell on her and she snatched a thorn stick from the embers and drove its hot red tip into his neck. He yelled and jumped back and his hand came across the darkness and slapped like an axe against her face and the side of the tent came up and hit her as she fell. He lashed her wrists behind her against a side pole and stalked out.

Warwar came down the cliff above the village from the rear, from high up the mountain. As he suspected there was no one watching on this side. The village was a semicircle of twenty goatskin huts against the mountain wall, camels sleeping in a thorn enclosure guarded by two dogs pacing in hunger, but it was almost dawn and the wind came up from the valley. Imagining each footstep he made to be as silent as a leopard hunting, a hungry leopard robbed of his prey, he crept from the mountain wall out to the first hut, listened for a moment, went to the second, third and fourth, till inside the fifth he heard her breathing, different from the others, and not asleep. Beside it was a man's quiet respiration. He crouched to the open door and saw inside the glimmer of her shirt, a few coals smouldering heavily, a large sleeping shadow.

Moonlight cast a sallow path between the huts, sparkled on his cloak and seemed to make each motion louder. He ducked inside the hut, bent quietly over the sleeping man, angled his knife parallel to the man's ribs and drove it deep into the heart; the man lurched and swung out his fist like a tree bough, knocking him down, and Warwar rolled up to knife him again but the man moaned and fell back, heels hammering the earth. Warwar clamped a bloody hand over Rebecca's mouth. '*Mama!* Look,' he whispered, 'I've brought you your hat!'

She twisted away and when he saw she was tied he cut her free. 'If you stay they'll kill you. Where's the money?'

She scrambled over the Borani's corpse and stood banging her head. 'It wasn't here, not with him.'

'Hurry! If they catch us they'll torture us for ever!'

With a panicked last glance at the dead man she followed Warwar between the other huts and up the mountain wall and along the ridge beneath the dimming stars. Behind them in the Borani camp the dogs began to howl.

# Chapter 18

Nairobi's first lights were winking on as the plane climbed through seven thousand feet and swung north towards the dark wall of Mount Kenya above its dregs of cindery cloud. The port engine drummed steadily at 6500, flashing back occasional spurts of flame, but it had better compression and was a little cooler than the starboard side. MacAdam began to let himself hope it wouldn't blow, that they'd reach Marsabit and that the engine wouldn't snap the new rod when they took off from Marsabit with his squad and their guns and desert rations for two weeks.

The eastern savannah shifted from charcoal to deep purple; to the west a feverish orange moon sank into the Kiambu hills. The end of night, MacAdam thought, when the lion slinks into camp and clamps his jaws on your neck and carries you off with no one knowing. In fear of this we've killed all lions and now stupid cattle and egocentric goats graze the tall savannah to stones. In fear of this we create marriage and the ownership of women, so Rebecca could never come to me.

Light raced across the savannah, pockets of brush

standing out like the dark spots on a lion cub's belly when it rolls in the grass for its mother to lick it. Nothing so lovely as a lioness' love for her cubs, or the gazelle's for her fawn that the lioness will kill to feed her cubs. Nothing so lovely as holding you, Rebecca, naked all night in the Blue Posts at Thika, with the bedbugs biting and the twin cascades crashing beyond the flimsy walls, or holding you for a moment in a Grevillia Grove cloakroom while the maid waited outside with your raincoat, or in a corridor somewhere, the black and white tiled floor like a chessboard on which we never learned the moves.

Outside the window the savanah grew tamed by light; against the plexiglass MacAdam saw himself as a man defeated by his self-deceptions, his squarish face and bold chin a parody of resolution; see, he taunted himself, how the faults and fissures grow, the stress of joyless time? He was the man who'd kept it all inside, where it had rotted, poisoned him. He'd become the man of stone he'd always tried to be, right from the day his mother had sat weeping into her hands on the sofa, 'Your Daddy's gone, my poor darling. Oh God, Jesus, Daddy's gone . . .' And he'd been tough where she had not, hadn't he? His mother's tears, her print silk dress, the sofa fabric blue and gold, the patient parlour plants – they never went away, he could call them up at any moment. They came in the night, unbidden as the memory of Rebecca's small, strong white hands clenching his, of her soft, taut voice – 'Oh God, I love you, Ian! But I can't go with you. I *can't*, I *can't*!' He shifted from his reflection and that made his ribs throb as if broken anew; he could not breathe against the pain, wanted to rip off the wide bandages imprisoning his chest.

All grew dark; Mount Kenya had shut off the newly risen sun, its sweeping cloud forests wrapped in bands of mist, the podocarpus canopies far below like urchins on the ocean floor. Beyond the plane's wing, their velvet lustre darkened by the shadowed light, the bamboo forests of the mountain's middle heights oscillated like seagrass; above them the grass and lobelia slopes, chunked with bare rock like ruined ramparts, ascended into steepening barren battlements, till far higher, tall above the wing, soared the icy peaks named by the first white climbers in honour of three Maasai wise men, Batian, Nelion, Lenana.

'What's it mean, in Maasai,' he said to the pilot, 'when a woman tells you "*Meitalah elipoh oltunani ilke-jek aare* – A man can't cross two rivers"?'

Simon relaxed back into the headrest, his grin showing the standard Maasai gap between upper front teeth. 'What you been trying, Captain? Steal another man's wife?'

'What's it mean?'

'The woman's saying when a man takes a married woman, some day she'll leave him too.' Simon switched off the dash and running lights, donned his sunglasses from their case clipped inside his breast pocket. 'But this woman's already dead, isn't she, Captain?'

Like an enraged eye the red arc of the sun climbed over the eastern desert – the Somali desert. Already this sun was pouring its wrath into the blue Indian ocean

179

where swordfish and marlin cruised like silver-blue attenuated warheads in their green-gold depths; the sun chromed the wing like a sailfish soaring far above these jade forests of the Nyambeni Hills bleeding their red soil scars of human erosion. To the west lay the Mukogodo jungle and far, far beyond it the Laikipia plateau, and so far away he could only imagine it in the clear African dawn was his ranch, the place where he and Dottie had lived too long. Now it seemed she too depended on the clarity of his imagination.

Much further north the distant smudge of the Matthews Range hunched like the backbone of a slain prehistoric beast, where he had died and been given new life by the scar-faced Somali. But he had not protected his protector, and the Somali had died from M'kele's bullets and if MacAdam did not return quickly the Somali's brother would be shot in the Nairobi penitentiary. Even further north was the Losai Desert, then N'doto Forest, the uncountable wastes of Kaisut Desert, then Marsabit's mountains and clear crystal lakes, then the great deserts – the Dida Galgalu, the Koroli, the endless Chalbi, and unconscionably beyond them the blue-black Ethiopian escarpment.

The first time had been so rushed, her not wanting it, her dishevelled blouse and slacks left tousled on the stairs, her eyes wide as she held him back yet still wanting him, and he'd known if this was the only moment of his life, so be it. She had opened, filling up with him till they were one, made of her emptiness and his need, her blue eyes focused in his for ever, her perfect small breasts one with his chest and the illusion of time was gone, only feeling, sensing, holding, and the heat of sex washed in the joy of love.

'We mustn't do this ever again.' On her side, elbows at her ribs, hands clenched against his chest, she had refused to look into his eyes.

'It's all that matters to me now, this. For the rest of my life.'

'I feel so ashamed,' she'd said.

'It didn't feel good?'

'Good? God no. It felt beyond anything I could ever say.'

He'd nuzzled her hair that smelled like acacia honey mixed with the scent of her vagina from his hand. 'How can you stop what feels like that?'

Warwar climbed a pinnacle of rock but nowhere behind them on the gun-blue panorama of desert rock could he see the Borani. Below him the whitewoman sat disconsolately; through her torn blouse he could see her breast like a ripe fruit and it made his body ache and his mouth dry. 'No one follows,' he called, running down. 'Let's go!'

His hand round hers was wiry and enfeebling, as if exerting a magnetism that robbed her of her strength. It was cool and dry against her warm sweat and she wondered if that disgusted him. But his thoughts seemed enclosed in his black skull, with no link to hers. There was no point in asking herself if she had done right to come with him, for had she argued he'd have killed her, and had she stayed the Borani would have killed her far more painfully. But was it wise now to try to escape this boy-killer with his wide smile and iron grip, to snatch his rifle and point it at him? Or better to stay with the Somalis and hope for rescue or ransom, with the Borani now hunting them down? Would she elude the Borani alone? Wasn't she safer with the Somalis, who knew the desert and had camels for milk and could travel faster?

Ahead in a niche of rocks she saw Ibrahim and Rashid. Ibrahim rose suddenly, his face so wild with anger she feared he'd shoot her down. He whacked her aside with his rifle butt, yelling at the boy-killer who raised both palms in incredulous innocence as Ibrahim gesticulated at the ridge in new-bright sun and Rashid came running with the two camels, mounted one, his arm like a spring yanking her up behind him. Ibrahim leaped on the other camel, pulled up the boy, and kicked it into a run as the dark outline of the first Borani crested the ridge.

Below the tilting wing ragtag Marsabit huddled between its cedared slopes and wind-rippled turquoise *gofs*. Simon overflew the field one time to chase off a herd of gazelle. When they landed, M'kele, Darius, and Gideon – still with his one star-shaped broken eyeglass, MacAdam noted – were already waiting. M'kele had rousted the guard to unlock the fuel tanks and refill the Cessna; the yellow plastic cup filled with coffee which Darius offered seemed to MacAdam a drug – its bitter taste, and the sharp desert air, the tang of cedars and dry soil, of avgas and the hot new oil in the rebuilt engine and the warming aluminum paint of the Cessna, all seemed the current of the universe pumping through

him. Yet all was wasted, he told himself, if she was
dead.

Each time Warwar looked back from the rear of
Ibrahim's bounding camel it seemed the black-caped
riflemen were larger; now he could make out individual
riders; already one had reined in and dismounted to
fire, his bullets whanging and whining among the rocks.
With his right hand Rashid reached behind the whitewoman to whip his camel faster; they rode up a bould-
ered slope with traces of grass among the flashing stones,
on their left a soaring basalt cliff from which a cloud
of vultures scrambled, their cries like drowning men.
Ibrahim spun his camel round and leaped down, waving
at the others to spread out among the rocks. He shot
the lead Borani from the saddle and killed the second
rider's camel, then the man as he ran for shelter, then
the first camel as it trotted tossing its head. Now the
Borani had no rocks to hide in and they pulled back,
waving their rifles and screaming, some dropping
downslope to come round from below. Ibrahim
snatched his camel's reins and motioned the whitewoman up. 'Now we'll see if you're a man,' he yelled at
Warwar. 'Stay and keep them back till we cross the
ridge!'

Warwar looked past Ibrahim's pointed hand, along
the cliff. Below it the rolling slope was strewn with
boulders; at its far end the cliff crested in a ridge of
shattered rock leading westwards to the high black
Selach peaks. 'I'll die,' he shouted.

'Not if you're clever, nestling. *This* is how one

becomes a man. I've done it more than once.' Ibrahim leaped on his camel and snatched the whitewoman's arm round him. 'Meet us at the bottom of the canyon on the back side of Dibandiba. Don't let them follow!' He galloped off, calling, 'Flee before we reach the ridge and you're a condemned man. By all our laws and yours!'

# Chapter 19

As far as MacAdam could see down across Dida Galgalu Desert there was never a bush, a tree, a *manyatta*, camel, or man to break the bleakness, as if the plane stood still, for neither the black pitted rippling stone below nor the seared azure of the sky above seemed ever to alter. The sun had climbed higher, tilting its poisonous essence steeper down upon the earth, a raw white flawless ingot hotter than any human hell. MacAdam tried to turn in his seat without twisting his ribs. 'Thank you all for coming.'

Gideon shrugged. 'Blood's got no need of friendship.' It was the Kikuyu adage that links within the clan are stronger than those outside it, but his meaning was *we*, the clan of all Kenyans, even MacAdam, the whiteman.

'If it gets tight, I don't want any of you leaving cover, crossing open ground—'

'In the desert,' M'kele said, 'it's all open ground.'

The first bullet hit the rock beside Warwar's head, deafening him. He could not hear where the other shots were coming from and squirmed further back among the boulders, then ran along the covered edge of slope, against the cliff. He glanced over and ducked back, seeing nothing. Nor could he see Rebecca, Ibrahim and Rashid – by now they must have crossed the ridge. Trying to hold his rifle steady he fired at a flash of black downslope and ducked as a bullet then another smacked overhead, shaking the rock under his belly. His ears were ringing like bells on the bridles of a herd of camels, like their hooves on stone, and like a man sliding off a cliff edge Warwar felt life slipping from him. Not daring to stay, not daring to run, he waited in terror for the bullet that did not come, the first that would not miss.

When they reached the ridge Rebecca could hear the crack of shots and wanted to go back to Warwar. Then she realized what she was thinking and almost laughed in horror. Rashid's camel, for which Ibrahim had been waiting, sprayed her with its spittle as it galloped past and Ibrahim and Rebecca chased after it; before them expanded the whole nether regions of the earth, a blue, black plateau so vast as to hide the edges of the globe within it, a land of cracked crust and shearing canyons, endless. There seemed no way the Borani could find them in such a place, and nowhere they could hide.

MacAdam woke with M'kele bent between him and the pilot, map in hand, as they discussed in Maasai their course over a wide box canyon running northwards, the plane slowing, downdrifting, north-northwest, down to two hundred feet above the rocky rushing desert, till the canyon narrowed and deepened as though faulted to the centre of the earth. Suddenly, between a dry *laga* and its sheaf of sand an expanse of *commiphora* scrub, the smear of an extinct fire and two Land Rovers tiny as matchbox toys, one with a shattered windshield flashing in the sun. He felt the revulsion of one who has happened on a ghastly accident, who then with horror understands he is the next of kin.

Simon climbed three hundred feet to altitude two thousand, flew in slow circles wider and wider, then northwards towards the distant purple Ethiopian escarpment blocking the sky like the wall of a prison where once you step inside never can you leave. But nowhere below or out across to the far black horizons was there any trace of man.

Warwar scrambled upslope between the boulders and the cliff, hugging the ground against the bullets that did not come, at first daring to hope the Borani would not chase him, then fearing they were playing with him, only to shoot him easily from some vantage he had not perceived. But still there were no shots, no black-caped figures rising grimly before him. With his terror deepened by hope, he gained the ridge and looked out on the bleak stony world, gathered in his breath, slung his rifle over his shoulder and turned to run down the north side of the ridge. With a lurch, as if his stomach had been struck, he saw a line of Borani riding towards him, still out of range, but cutting off his retreat toward Dibandiba.

Simon brought the plane low over the scrubby wind-blown hovels of the North Horr police post and landed in a cloud of dust gilded by the sun. A lone blue Land Rover trailed its smaller scarf of dust out to meet them. MacAdam leaped from the wing, then bent double swearing with the pain in his chest, then became conscious of his hand clamped on the searing aileron and M'kele peering down puzzled from the wing. A burly Suk policeman dismounted from the Land Rover and opened its rear door for Darius and Gideon to load the packs and rifles. 'We'll pick up the camels,' MacAdam said, 'then drive to where the woman was taken.'

The policeman looked worried. 'Camel not come, sir.'

'What do you mean camels not come! We called through last night for six camels to be sent up, for us to follow the trail!'

'Trail disappears, sir. Camels all take by Gabbra, last week. Not enough food here so Gabbra take them Bura Galadi. Sure we bringing them back, tonight, fast as can come.'

'How the fuck were you following up the trail?'

'Trail disappears, sir.'

MacAdam leaned against the Land Rover, its dusty superheated metal a vague consolation for all that did not work, that would not *be*. Decide *now*, he told himself. This is where the fate of things is told. He bowed his head, took a long breath, forced himself not to think, then to imagine it all, what he should do. He spun round so fast his chest felt speared, reshattered. 'Tell me, friend,' he said to the policeman, 'how likely will the camels come tonight?'

The man's outspread hands were like an apology for Africa: if you need to believe, I will tell you what you want to hear. 'Two men leave last night, soon as call come through. Sure by now they have camels, coming back.'

'How many hours?' To MacAdam, everything seemed weighed in hours, life too. Remember, he reminded himself, she's already dead.

The man's pouched cheeks were a parody of calculation. 'Perhaps by sunset.'

MacAdam tucked back his bush hat; already the heat had soaked the band, was running rivulets of sweat down his cheeks and neck. Each breath of air seemed from a foundry. The lungs tried not to inhale it. 'Tell me, brothers, what are your thoughts?'

Gideon wiped his star-shattered glasses on his camo shirt. He too, MacAdam saw, was sweating. 'Either we all wait for the camels, or we all go in this man's vehicle to the place she was taken kidnap, and try to track them on foot. Or some go and some wait.'

MacAdam nodded. 'What would you do?'

Gideon bit his lip. 'I'm not CO, sir.' He looked up towards the sun. 'But I would like all to go.'

'You guys?'

'We all go,' said Darius.

M'kele watched the dusty runway by MacAdam's feet, as if the tracks began there. 'Trouble if all go, we likely never catch them. They have camels, five days' start. What chance is that?'

When MacAdam held his hands over his eyes the light turned pink within them, bright bars between the fingers. *Now* fate's told. If she's not already dead. 'You and I, M'kele, must go now to the place she was taken, pick up the trail. If they've covered it well there'll be time lost finding it. Assuming they've gone north, Darius and Gideon can bring the camels straight across, joining up with Nehemiah and the others when Simon flies them up, instead of turning south. That way you'll meet us, or follow our trail and catch up quickly.'

Regret shadowed Gideon's face. 'May not be the wisest way.'

'Even if they've gone north,' Darius said, 'will they not now already be in Ethiopia?'

When Ibrahim let her down from his camel Rebecca was so sore and weary the ground seemed to fall away beneath her feet. 'Dibandiba,' he said, and other words in Somali, but Dibandiba to her was only a peak on a remembered map, on a line between Kenya and Ethiopia; the other words she couldn't understand. But in his voice there was something more easily understood, an undertone of desertion, the way one speaks to someone whose fate no longer matters because it's been determined.

'Warwar?' she answered, as if her supposed concern for him would keep her one of them. Ibrahim jerked back his head in surprise. He spoke to Rashid, scoffing, and in the words she heard Warwar's name and understood they were speaking also of her. She suddenly had a sense of no longer being alone, of being part of *something*.

* * *

190

Surely the Borani would see him now, smell him in his hole among the boulders fiery with the sun, as they rode back and forth across the vast ruptured slope, the soft click of their camels' hooves and their savage birdlike cries nearing, withdrawing, and nearing again. Warwar wormed tighter down into the shallow trough between two halves of boulder split long ago by heat, his back and chest against two searing sheets of stone, his rifle too hot to touch at his side, and waited without hope for the circling Borani to find him. Now that it was too late he understood why Ibrahim had done this – now Ibrahim would be safe and have the whitewoman's ransom and Soraya to himself completely. Warwar would never take her by the spring or underneath the palms, while Ibrahim was elsewhere. Like all fools, Warwar saw, he'd devised his own demise.

# Chapter 20

From North Horr the Suk policeman drove MacAdam and M'kele in the Land Rover east and south across the Chalbi, raising a tall dust plume, till they picked up the ruts of two vehicles and Hecht's returning footprints west of the Huri Hills. They followed them north, the ruts sometimes diverging, sometimes doubled, till M'kele raised his hand sharply and the policeman stopped.

The hoofprints of three camels came suddenly from the east and paralleled the ruts. 'That's them,' the Suk policeman said.

MacAdam felt the bitter intuition of failure. He cleaned the dust from his glasses and, leaning forward between the seats of M'kele and the driver, watched through the windscreen as the twin grooves of the Land Rovers paired, diverged, and paired again, Hecht's lonely returning footprints vacillating along them, the walls of the box canyon rising steadily on either side.

Again he had the sense of her beside him, remembered how it felt to hold her. 'Klaus hasn't made love to me in two years.' She spoke into his shoulder as he held her close, fitting so perfectly the way he loved, her body's pressure responding equally to his.

'He's insane,' he replied.

'I even tried having my own bedroom – to shock him.' She laughed. 'I think he liked it better.'

'Why be married, then?'

'He likes companionship, support. We're very fond of one another.' Her hands drew up his shoulder blades, pressing them, making his body feel strong and light. 'And the boys – they're *our* sons. How can I divide that?'

'Does he love them?' MacAdam thought of them without remembering their names – one was a little older than the other, both with truculent, disinterested faces, thick bodies, and their father's puffy eyes and sarcastic smile.

'He's very good to them.'

'Dottie says he only loves himself.'

'He'd seem that way – until you knew him.'

MacAdam felt her defence of her husband stiffening, which angered him, but he told himself don't push it. Loving the scent and taste of her hair as it curled around her earlobe whose ruby and diamond pierced earring felt sharp against his cheek, he kissed the side of her neck. 'If I were married to you we'd make love three times a day.'

'You're married to someone else,' she said.

The car slowed, jerked, and stopped. MacAdam raised his eyes to the ruins of a fire, two deserted Land Rovers pocked by bullets, one with a shattered windshield. Equipment lay piled around them, the foodstuffs scavenged, their paper wrappings pinned to thornscrub by the wind. Footprints of hyaenas, sandals, and boots webbed the sand, among them slender sneaker tracks he took to be hers. On the far side of the vehicles from the fire, broken and gnawed bones were scattered, some still showing bits of dried black flesh.

M'kele circled the fire, the Land Rovers, then moved in widening ellipses round the edges of the camp. The Suk policeman hitched up his blue trousers till they were taut above his black combat boots. 'Four dead,' he said to MacAdam. 'We check to National Museum at Nairobi: two drivers, a student of Mombasa, and one of England.' The policeman kicked one of the bones as if dispelling doubt. It was a chunk of pelvis, MacAdam realized, as it scuttled across the sand, flies and wasps rising from it in alarm. 'They shoot dead the motors,' the policeman continued, striding towards the punctured Land Rovers as if MacAdam were incapable of seeing for himself. MacAdam picked an empty cartridge from the sand. 'Do an analysis on these?'

The policeman peered into MacAdam's hand. 'AK47.'

'Chinese, Russian, or Czech?'

The policeman shrugged. MacAdam handed him the cartridge. 'We'll follow the tracks in your vehicle till the terrain gives out or you run low on gas. When you get back to North Horr, send this to Nairobi, for ballistics.'

'I don't have much gas, Captain.'

'Don't worry, soon we'll have to go on foot.' He checked the sun – midafternoon – and reinvestigated the two Land Rovers. A small duffel bag half-open on the sand held her clothes – cotton shirts and jeans, thin underpants, white cotton socks balled in pairs, a comb and brush, tampons, a pair of Bata sneakers, a windbreaker. Dear Rebecca, you must freeze at night, he thought. He took her windbreaker, a change of clothes and toilet articles from the duffel bag. Feeling infinitely hungry for her, he emptied his backpack and put them at the bottom.

'What you doin'?' M'kele said, returning.

'Insurance.'

'It was the same three camels. They went the short way from Gamura to Balesa and came down the east side, there.' M'kele pointed to a sandy gully pouring down the cirque-like wall of the canyon. 'They tied up the camels in that *laga*; two guys went north on foot; the third, he came straight from east, the one with the light tracks. The one who shot the four people.'

MacAdam smiled at M'kele's assurance. 'How do you know?'

'Same rifle, *bwana*. 7·62mm Czechoslovakian, used by Ethiopian Army.'

'So where are they now?'

'Ethiopia, maybe, on their way across to Somalia.'

MacAdam finished reloading his backpack and lowered it carefully into the Police Land Rover, feeling it tug at his stitches. 'Maybe they're Ethiopians.'

'They have the wide sandals of Juba people. From the way they travel, how thin their camels – they're Somali.'

'Soon as we catch them they'll be dead.'

With the Police Land Rover it was at first easy to

follow the prints of the three pairs of sandals and Rebecca's sneakers, Hecht's heavy, wide boot marks skirting them. When they reached a narrow lip of lava that had poured down long ago from the Huri Hills, Hecht's tracks turned back and the terrain stiffened over the jumbled sharp rocks. They came to where the camels had been tied up in the sandy *laga*; Rebecca's sneaker marks disappeared; the track of the three camels and three pairs of sandals was like an arrow diminishing into infinity across the wavering sand. 'All three camels are heavily loaded,' M'kele said.

At first the Police Land Rover could move quickly across the desert, but now the trail snaked up into the Maikona cliffs and they had to drive many kilometres around them, the car nosing among boulders and canyons for a way up the rugged slope, till they crossed the sandy track known as the North Horr-Marsabit road. The sun had nearly set by the time they found the tracks again – now nothing but a chipped stone or crushed pebble here and there and once a camel's hoofprint. The Land Rover's gauge was on one-quarter; the Suk policeman's wide white eyes inspected the lowering horizon and the towering black abutments to the north. 'I'm low on petrol, Captain.'

Behind them, the North Horr-Marsabit road lay like a golden thread in the setting sun, a last link with the world of humanity. 'Wish I could go with you, Captain,' the policeman said.

MacAdam noted how the man's stomach bulged against the steering wheel, his fat thighs stretching his shiny blue trousers. You couldn't run a mile, he wanted to say, let alone two hundred. 'I need you to stay,' he said. 'When our camels come, send them, with Nehemiah and the other men, straight here.'

M'kele followed the faint trail at a run, swinging his rifle easily, his head slightly downbent to see the tracks, MacAdam ten yards behind. Despite the setting sun the heat was immense and the air burned MacAdam's throat. He wiped perspiration from his eyes and it returned at once; after a while his arm became too heavy to raise and he ran half-blinded by salty sweat, M'kele's image hovering before him, sometimes distancing itself, and he would hurry to catch up, M'kele always trotting with that slow, easy, rapid stride, his slender limbs effortless as a bird's.

At dusk they rested for a few minutes by a whistling thorn whose lower branches had been browsed by the kidnappers' camels. She's been *here*, MacAdam reminded himself, she's sat on a camel and seen this tree. He scanned the footprints: one kidnapper was young and light-footed, almost a girl, the one who shot everyone. One of the others had a slight limp; the third was heavier, with a long stride. Rebecca's tracks were nowhere. Maybe they'd already killed her, and it was her body they were carrying on camel back. Maybe they'd never taken her at all, her bones were back at the campsite and the camels just loaded with things they stole. He remembered her small footprints from the campsite; now they assumed a totemic value, like the last words of someone you've loved.

M'kele ran steadily, swinging his rifle loosely in one hand, MacAdam after, the G–3's web sling biting into his shoulder, each step tugging his chest muscles; he could not inhale deeply because of the broken ribs, and could feel the new stitches giving way one by one like an old sock unravelling, the blood mixing with sweat and soaking his chest.

Before dark the kidnappers' trail skirted a long lava slope laid down millennia ago by the now-blunted Huri Hills. M'kele stooped beside the tracks. Ah, he's tired too, MacAdam decided. But we'll keep going. The thought gave him new strength.

'Her tracks,' M'kele said.

MacAdam bent over panting but could see nothing but ripples of sand unevenly marching westwards, a series of random indentations angling across them. 'Where?' he gasped, hope mounting absurdly: maybe they'd let her go.

M'kele fingered the sand that cast down tiny runnels at his touch. He turned and ascended the slope, peering into the dusk. 'She came down here,' he called. Descending the slope he followed the indentations a few metres and called again, 'She's made a circle, escaped them; she's going west.'

M'kele checked the darkening sky, began to run, leaning forward over the tracks, faster and faster as Rebecca's direction firmed and MacAdam also could see the faint furrow stretching ahead against the violet twilight. It seemed possible now, she might be hiding at some water hole, or already sheltered in a Gabbra village, gathering her strength.

M'kele's shoulders sagged; he halted. Even he, MacAdam noted, was breathing hard. 'The others.'

MacAdam's joy escaped like water into sand: there they were, the camels, coming in from the northeast and linking up with her, as if they and she had been flung apart by chance and now were reunited. As if without the bad there could be no good, as if everything was paired.

'You remember the Somalis from the Ewaso N'giro?' M'kele spoke slowly, thinking this out.

MacAdam tried to remember what the Ewaso N'giro was; the words were familiar. Christ yes, the river. The Somalis – the poachers. Another lifetime.

'It bother me since we see these tracks today,' M'kele continued.

Then MacAdam knew before M'kele could say it. 'It's them.'

'The very same.' M'kele trembled with excitement. 'You see, we didn't lose the other poachers, after all.'

# Chapter 21

Since the last trace of red had vanished from the west there had been no sound nor smell of the Borani but the long dim rumble of their retreat. Warwar knew it was a ruse, that most of the Borani lay waiting among the rocks, but that he must try to escape now, before the moon rose. And he knew the Borani knew this too.

On this wide ridge under the stars he wanted to widen his cloak and fly away from it all, like a swallow to his nest and gladdened mate. He felt the sting of tears. Never had he flown above the sorrow of being without father and mother, and now he'd lost Ahmed. If one day he could make a new nest the past would go away. He would be the father he never had, and Soraya the mother. Their children would be beloved on both sides, their son Ahmed a wise warrior and leader of the clan.

But he forced himself to concentrate until the layout of this place was inside his mind as if seen from above, each little rock and crevice clear, the Borani in their black capes like prone chunks of stone, and within their capes as they glanced up to check the stars he saw their skulls coated in black skin. Then he found the widest hole between them and slipped quietly free, running downhill softly in the penumbra of the nearly risen moon.

MacAdam knelt exhausted to rest a moment beside a thornbush. He sat up suddenly, stared round – the moon had risen like a chiding eye. He could not understand, then remembered. His back prickling with fear, he wondered what had wakened him, reached to shake M'kele but M'kele was not there.

M'kele's pack lay on the ground but his rifle was gone. Bent low to minimize the target he presented, MacAdam sectored off the desert beginning now to sparkle under the moon, and watched each sector intently, but there was no movement save the quick veer of a single nightjar seeing him at the last moment, uttering its warning *churr* as it darted away.

There was no sign of a struggle by M'kele's pack. There were faint footprints circling the pack and moving westwards; MacAdam followed them till they joined those of Rebecca and the three camels.

You bastard M'kele, you sweet bastard, he thought. While I was too exhausted to travel faster, you were champing at the bit. MacAdam returned for the packs, lashed M'kele's to his own, and followed the tracks. From the length of the stride it was clear M'kele was running; his tracks made him seem both nearer and more absent.

When the moon had climbed part-way he saw a speck on the sand which soon became M'kele, coming at a fast lope.

'Christ, you should've wakened me!' MacAdam said.

'Sure, *bwana*, and you would've wanted to go with me. It's faster alone.' M'kele did not seem out of breath. 'They followed her across the Dukana and camped in a *laga* on the far side. One of them, the young one, went on foot and came back with her; then they put her on the camel again and turned north – they're going to Ethiopia on the trail by Dibandiba into the Selach hills.'

'Can we catch them before the border?'

'Maybe.'

'We've gained time.'

'Three days.'

'Want to rest?'

M'kele reached for his pack. 'Let's go.'

'At this rate, Gideon and Darius'll never catch us . . .'

The breeze shifted into their faces as they turned north, evoking desert scents and a lingering sense of Rebecca so fresh MacAdam was sure she was just ahead. As they climbed the soil became rockier, less sandy, littered with sharp volcanic debris that shifted underfoot and cut their ankles, but M'kele kept stepping on as if nothing bothered him, tireless and calmly resolute, now singing snatches of repetitive song in Maa under his breath, now chattering softly back in Swahili at MacAdam, now making no noise but the near-silent swish of his sandalled feet across the rock, the hiss of his canvas backpack, the rustle of his rifle slung across his shoulder.

Heartbeats thundered in MacAdam's ears. His pack lurched clumsily, the rifle a dead weight he traded from shoulder to shoulder, the pain like a rope of fire across his chest. 'M'kele!' he whispered.

Not slowing, M'kele looked back over his shoulder. 'Stop!'

M'kele halted, half-turned on his toes. His breath was coming in low steady pulses.

'We're near the border.'

M'kele gripped MacAdam's shoulders and bent him round, pointing. 'See that ridge we crossed two hours after moonrise?' It was unimaginably far behind: a charcoal line against a chrome and black palette. '*That* was the border.'

Without Warwar the balance was against her. These two would not let her go, nor much longer would they keep her. Yet without Warwar she dared less to escape. She saw his hands, his cloak as he hunched forward to eat, his swift small feet. His voice was permanently inside her. Why did they make him stay back there? Couldn't they see he'd never get away? He's saved us, she decided, given up his life for us. Now these two will kill me. The thought was so terrifying she could not inhale nor stop her wrists from shaking, nor turn round enough to face the horror at her back. She could feel the ugly smashing bullets and the knife burning across her throat, and was so afraid she refused to think of it. She would find a way to make them keep her, would be Ibrahim's wife the rest of his days and never once think that she'd done wrong. Or Warwar's too, if only he'd come back.

* * *

Like a bird Warwar fled south, away from Dibandiba spring, making his tracks possible for the Borani to follow in daylight. His rifle light as a wing, his feet soaring over the rocks as if each step could set them free, he reached a vast windswept table-land of rock, unmarked and brilliant under the moon, his fleeing form soon a tiny speck way out upon it. And soon after disappeared, with no trace left to track.

After many miles he swung north again, still not tiring; the slope thickened, rose into the Dukana hills; he slowed to a jog and picked his way among the rocks and canyons towards Dibandiba.

She was crazy with thirst but when she pointed to her mouth Rashid snarled and raised his rifle. Jackals were calling and he kept twisting his head to listen; Ibrahim came in silently from guarding and for a few moments, although she could not understand the words, she knew they talked about her, Rashid's voice rising in rapid irritation, Ibrahim's placid, deliberate. She caught the word for 'morning' several times; whatever they would do, they argued as to whether they should do it now or in the 'morning'.

'Rashid!' she whispered. 'Ibrahim!' If she called them by their names then she and they would be one family, intimates – how could they kill her then? They barely acknowledged her. 'If you want just leave me – I'll never say a word . . . be false.' She could not think of the Swahili for 'betray you'. But Ibrahim hissed sharply and kicked something that smeared her face with rough dampness; she raised her bound hands to it and smelled that it was dung.

Accept you're going to die, she told herself. The boys are old enough to do without you. Klaus doesn't care. The one man you dared to love you chased away – you're so good at killing your own joy. You learned how from your parents and no doubt you've taught it to your sons. Told yourself love's a fantasy, not how life's lived. You never lived expecting to be happy.

Tears burnt her eyelids, dribbled down her checks. It couldn't hurt any worse to *try* to be happy. Why had she settled for a loyal supporting role, first to her father's stolid wisdom, then to Klaus as his wide-eyed favourite student, so shy, so desperate for excellence that finally the highest mark he could give her was as assistant archaeologist and wife? That each of her finds became his, her scholarship his, as all the while he told her 'dear, you must publish more, put your name on things', when even her name had gone, had become his.

Wind chilled her sunburnt flesh. The bonds round her wrists and ankles had numbed her hands and feet again. Rashid came in from guarding and Ibrahim went out. Rashid watched her; she could hear him grinding moustache hairs between his teeth, heard his fingernails picking lice, his breath clogged and corroded by the desert dust. I *will* learn to be happy, she told herself. Even now.

# Chapter 22

The stars began to lighten, as if the finest veil rose between them and the earth. She realized she'd been dreaming of Warwar, in the dream hearing his voice, then woke to find him speaking with Rashid as if he'd always been there, as if nothing had gone wrong. How far back, she wondered for an instant, have things gone wrong? She sat up quickly and extended bound hands as if to embrace him, then dropped them. 'I was so afraid!'

'Don't worry, *Mama*, you were safe.'

'No.' Afraid for you, she wanted to say. 'Where are they?'

'The Borani? Chasing me far into the Chalbi. It will make them very thirsty.'

'*I'm* so thirsty. Please bring water.'

'There's none. Be strong.'

'Don't let them kill me.'

'I told you,' he said. 'They've gone!'

'No – *them*!'

When Warwar came to sit by the fire, Ibrahim moved aside to make space for him.

'Your whitewoman's been the root of all our problems.' Ibrahim squeezed Warwar's knee, consoling him for the loss that was inevitable. 'She's led us into the Chalbi, when we followed the Land Rover tracks. She's taken us north, to keep her and find ransom. She led us into the hands of the Borani, who stole our tusks and twelve thousand shillings. And if they hadn't sworn a vow of peace we'd have died yesterday – in ways so horrible you can't imagine. Then she bewitched you to return for her, causing them to break their vow and hunt us. All this she's done to us.'

Warwar shook his head. 'She's done *none* of this – she's been our captive.'

'Her influence, little cousin. Woman's influence is impure, and spreads around her like the disease that kills the camels, except that it kills men's honour and will.'

Warwar waited, telling himself not to argue. 'Perhaps because my mother's dead and I have no sisters I do not understand woman. But is it not out of her body that we come, like a calf from a camel? Who, then, creates the calf?'

'God does, nestling. Just as Allah has created thee. Woman is the vessel in which God's holy life is stored. When you eat wheat from the clay jar you don't praise the jar! When you light a wick in a cup of tallow to brighten the night, do you thank the cup?'

'If woman's the vessel in which Allah's holy life is kept, then what is man?'

Ibrahim cocked his bushy head, as if pleased by the question. He glanced at Rashid readying the camels, checked the horizon. 'Man's the sword of God, disembowelling his foes. Man is the plough of God, inserting God's seed. He is the house in which the clay jar of wheat and the tallow candle are kept.'

Warwar stood, staggered with exhaustion. 'Why have you not praised me, cousin, for standing alone against the Borani?'

'If you had not shot the people at the Land Rovers and taken the whitewoman, and worse, if you had not gone to the Borani camp to find her, we would not have had to fight them. How can I praise you for merely rectifying some of the harm you've done?'

'But I *saved* our whitewoman! The tusks and twelve thousand shillings are gone but in the Sudan we can sell her for much more!'

'*Ransom* her, foolish child?' Ibrahim patted Warwar's arm. 'We can't take her to the Sudan now. Not with your Borani hunting us.'

Pretending to adjust his cowl, Warwar pulled his hand away, sensing in the action both his own freedom and a freedom from any further protection Ibrahim might have given him. Cold fear fluttered through his heart; I'm better now, he told himself, I'm on my own. 'I'll take her,' he said. 'I don't fear Borani.'

'What you saw yesterday was a few riders pledged to peace!' Again Ibrahim reached out. 'Foolish child, I'm trying to reason with you!'

'And *I'm* trying to reason with you! Don't call me "foolish child"! I won't give up the bounty I captured – and recaptured – just because you're afraid!'

Ibrahim sighed, shook his head. His hands fell, hung

at his sides till he raised and crossed his arms. 'It's ten days' ride from here to Somalia, and more than twenty days till we'll be home safe in the Marrehan. We can't bring her that far.'

'Without her ransom we've gained *nothing*!'

'We can't risk Sudan. Even here, Ethiopia, is too dangerous . . .'

'This place will soon also be Somalia—'

'If we run into Gabbras on the Sidamo, I invite you to explain that to them.'

Warwar spat, making a camel jerk its head. He returned to where the whitewoman lay rubbing the numbness from her hands and legs. 'We go soon. If you have to make water or something . . .'

She stared up at him stupidly. 'How can I make water, idiot, when I'm dying of thirst?'

They have no endurance, he thought, no will. Their skin's so thin the sun goes right inside and boils their blood. Ibrahim's right: pale as cactus worms – how do they find each other appealing? He felt a sudden rage at her, for bedevilling him, drawing him on. Ibrahim's right: no one'll pay anything for you. Even if they do, you'll die first and cheat us of our ransom.

He turned from her and climbed the side of the ravine to where it turned to cliff, the far wall a single great blade of black rising into the dawn, its crest bloodied by sun. Kneeling on the rough rock spotted with bubbles, as if the earth's lung tissue had been suddenly exposed and petrified, he said his prayers quickly. But the words of the prayers sank into his mind and would not be ignored. *Who* was the innocent? Was it true that only man, not woman, is loved by God? If God loved woman, why did He give her such inferior station? Was it the lowly He loved the most? Why – was God afraid of men?

Again with a swallow's vision from above he saw himself crouched against the black stone, then saw the whitewoman, squat Ibrahim and Rashid, the disinterested camels, then they were tiny amid the cloven peaks and fractured land, the earth a patient beast of burden beaten and hungry, the blue-black sky where the stars encamp on their great pilgrimages of night; he saw even beyond their embers to the great sea without end that holds the universe like an embryo within its mother's womb. And what was God if not the mother of all this?

Beyond the ravine the black blade of stone grew bright. Halfway up its flank a single grey *commiphora* bush wavered in the heat which began to coil and tumble up from the maw of the ravine as from an iron cauldron sitting empty on the flames. His heart went out to this bush, gripping the rock, alone yet surviving where no other had, battling for a place to pass life on.

But I have not brought life to any children, he thought. My friend Biou is not yet twenty and he has given life to three sons. His cousin Sfey had two sons before he was eighteen. In a year I will be seventeen; they had wealthy fathers who paid the bride price. I have no father; it will be many years until I have so many animals. By then Soraya will be gone and I'll have to choose others: I'll soon be like the old men spitting in the fire while their young wives bend over for the warriors behind the thorn fence or on the way home from the water hole, their bodies slick under their black gowns.

He saw he would be absent from eternity. With an unexpected queasy feeling in his limbs, he took the last water gourd from Ibrahim's panier and put it on the ground beside the whitewoman. In her haste she knocked it over, its wooden plug rolling over the stones as the gourd glugged milky brown, but she snatched it and drank it empty, sucked at the pebbles where it had spilled, held the gourd upside down over her mouth for the three drops that came out. He felt ashamed, as if he'd seen her in an intimate act.

Ibrahim seemed huge, blocking the light. 'What do you, child, with the last water?'

Warwar could not keep the quaver from his voice. 'She drank it.'

'*She*!' Ibrahim's voice was a scream, a curse, his eyes wide in desperate understanding. 'You *gave* it to her?!'

He does not need this whitewoman's ransom, Warwar thought. He knows I do. 'Without the tusks and twelve thousand shillings, what else do we have?'

Ibrahim slowly drew in a breath, exhaled. 'Mount her behind Rashid. You behind me. I pray the Borani find us. So we can leave you both to them.'

When they stopped at noon she lay motionless in the shade of a camel, almost beneath its hooves, but when the camel moved she did not follow. Her hand when Warwar took it was hot and dry; he fanned her face with his sleeve, found four *hareri* sticks, pounded them into the ground, and stretched a goatskin over her.

'What's this?'

With disgust he noted how Ibrahim's thick yellow curved nails protruded from his tattered sandals. 'She needs water.'

'So do I, nestling, and Rashid. Even the camels need water.'

'*She* won't live!'

'She's eaten your soul. Look! He covers her like a lover.'

'If you want her money,' Rashid offered, 'we must take her to water.'

'She can't ride! We must bring water to her!' Warwar was shocked by his own plaintive, pleading voice. 'I'll stay – you're the ones who know how to find the Gabbra water hole beyond the baboon-backed mountain – I'll keep her alive till you get back!'

'We'll keep her,' Ibrahim said. 'Unless the Borani come. You go.'

'I don't know where it is!' Warwar noticed the woman's feet showing from under the goatskin, her funny white rubber-soled shoes like disassembled parts of a painted doll. As soon as I go they will kill you. Then there'll be no one to keep Ibrahim from Soraya. But why would Rashid sacrifice his share? Does he owe Ibrahim a deed? If I say I fear the Gabbras, want to stay, they won't believe me, will know I don't trust them.

If you hate a man, never let him know, he told himself. If you distrust him, don't let it show. 'Tell me where it is. If you swear not to kill her, I'll go.'

'It's on the other side.' Ibrahim pointed to the left of

the baboon-backed mountain rising above the lower Selach peaks. 'It's a cleft of white rock, you can see it, when you climb the baboon's neck.'

From Rashid's camel Warwar gathered three empty water gourds, then turned to Ibrahim's. 'Don't!' Ibrahim called. 'In case somehow you lose them . . .'

In case you fear I won't come back? thought Warwar bitterly. That I'll go to water with all the gourds then leave you here for the sun and the Borani? What would keep you from going to the water yourself? But without your gourds how far thereafter would you get? Do you fear I'll ambush you? Why would I not kill you now? In any case, your fear, your distrust, show how bad things have become between us. Do you see that? 'Watch carefully!' Warwar called. 'Pray I bring water!'

# Chapter 23

'It was Borani,' M'kele said. 'But they didn't shoot.'

'They gather up the cartridges. Afterwards.' MacAdam stared out on the desolate valley crisscrossed and pummelled by hoofprints. Don't be a fool, he ordered himself. This is just the pain that comes after an injured limb has finally been removed. If I could tell Dorothy she'd understand. If only I'd told her, all along. But it never would've happened, me and Rebecca, if I'd talked to Dorothy. If I'd told her, that would have meant a kinship existed between us, and then I wouldn't have needed Rebecca.

'They let them go!' M'kele shouted. 'Here! The Somalis' camels! The boy's still on foot!'

MacAdam ran to the camel prints angling north away from the Boranis' trail. M'kele's fingers on the tracks were like a doctor's parting injured flesh. 'But *Bwana*, the Somalis now have only two camels.'

MacAdam's backpack was like concrete; he raised a hand to slip off its strap, then noticed he'd already put it down. With a cupped palm he covered up a single track.

'Let's see what the Borani did to her,' he said. 'Then we'll kill them too.'

The sun had shifted into her eyes but her head was too heavy to move. If she could get away from Ibrahim and Rashid she could go to the *geb* tree and have water. As soon as Warwar returned he'd go with her. But if Warwar didn't come back?

At the *geb* tree there had been water in the little pool. How did she *know* exactly how it would be, before she ever saw it? How did she grow from a little girl in Papa's lap on the lawn of the house by the Seine to that assured, frightened young woman in Klaus' class at the Sorbonne, to a mother? How did something come out of nothing?

When Warwar came back he'd take her to the *geb* tree. Before Klaus, Petr had made her Hungarian meals on a hotplate in his narrow little *chambre de bonne* up six flights of stairs in the cinquième, looking out on the Arena of Lutecia. But all the things she'd done happily with Petr she'd paid for afterwards with Klaus.

The sun lay on her cheek like a pan of coals, burned into her teeth, made them so hot they seared her gums. Her arteries had emptied; she could hear the distant thump of her heart echoing along their desiccated corridors.

The dusk breeze brought the smell of dung smoke down the valley. MacAdam and M'kele turned from the Boranis' trail uphill among angular boulders where mambas and cobras had come out to enjoy the lingering heat, and whoever went first had to wave his arm as he walked among the boulders to warn the snakes and avoid being struck in the face. When they had climbed halfway to the ridge they shifted west again towards the smoke smell, till the Borani village and its backdrop of cliffs appeared round the shoulder of the slope.

Figures moved back and forth before a tiny fire; the shrill of children's voices echoed up the cliffs. But there were few camels in the thorn paddock; most of the huts had no fires. 'Out raiding,' M'kele said.

'Or letting the camels range.'

'Then where's all the men?'

'They wouldn't keep her, if they went raiding.'

'Some took her and the rest chase them.'

Again it was like a traffic accident of a loved one, where he was running towards the mangled wreck knowing she was dead inside, telling himself this clearly so there could be no mistaken hope. 'Maybe she's still in the huts . . .'

'I'll go down,' M'kele said, 'and have a look.'

MacAdam wanted him to, felt horribly ashamed. 'That's for me,' he said.

'Those ribs slow you. You speak no Borani—'

'We're not here to talk to them.' MacAdam searched the cliff walls for a way to circle the Borani camp and come down behind it. 'If you move forward, after darkness, to the front, and get down low in the rocks, I'll go around and down into the camp. I'll have to go hut to hut.'

'They'll catch you.'

'If I get in trouble I'll shoot or yell. Then you fire

from the front, divert them, so I can pull back.'

'There'll be no pulling back on that cliff—'

MacAdam felt fear for M'kele, realized he was transferring his own danger to his friend. 'If I don't come back, leave before dawn. Don't try to find me.'

The sun was down when Warwar returned from the water hole to camp. If Ibrahim and Rashid were going to kill him, now would be an easy time. He held the three gourds of water before his chest like a shield, his rifle slung loosely over his shoulder in such a way that he could grab it instantly.

Ibrahim, on guard above camp, came down smiling and took a gourd, pulled out the wooden cork and began drinking. 'Wait!' Warwar whispered, voice dry with heat.

Ibrahim lowered the gourd, sucked phlegm from his sinuses and spat. 'You've had plenty!'

'The hole was dry – and I had to dig – this's *all* there was. Look how you waste it!' Warwar tugged the gourd but Ibrahim would not let go. Warwar ran down to the whitewoman who lay motionless on her side, the goatskin half over her face. He tipped a drop of water on to his finger and touched her rough hot lips. He slipped a wet fingertip between her lips, to her tongue; she moaned and turned face down into the sand. 'Water,' he whispered in his hoarse, sun-dried voice. She looked up, seeming shocked, ashamed, or perhaps that was just the ugliness of her sunburnt face. 'Water,' he repeated, with his finger teasing a drop of it against her lips, feeling them soften. 'I brought you water.'

She lay on her back as he held her head sideways and let the water trickle into her mouth. When the gourd was half-empty he pulled it away, her head following it, hands grasping. 'Soon,' he said.

Rocks tumbled down behind them; he forced himself to relax; Rashid came and reached out his hand.

'This is for the prisoner,' Warwar said. 'Yours is with Ibrahim.'

'He said you have mine, that his was nearly empty.'

'He drank it all!' Warwar protested.

'*You* drank it, coming back.' Rashid snatched up the full bottle Warwar had laid on the sand, pulled the cork out with his teeth and sucked the water down, trickles glistening in his beard.

'Why do you do this?' Warwar whispered. 'She'll die – you'll have no money!'

'My money's not earned like *this* – sucking a white-woman's teats.'

'Then leave me with her, and the money will be mine.'

'Yours? This you could never do alone – write the words for them to send money! You can't keep her – already you sniff between her legs. Soon you'll be *her* captive.'

Warwar turned back to the woman, who was watching them with uncomprehending blue eyes. 'It was not I, but you, who could not keep her,' he said.

Rashid tossed down the empty gourd. 'This water's foul – you should've crushed in some *mawa* seeds, to clean it.'

Warwar lifted the remaining half-gourd to the woman's lips. 'You'll feel stronger soon,' he said in

Swahili. 'I'll bring you more.'

She felt the water seep into her coagulated cells. Her head throbbed; her stomach trembled; her throat ached. She opened her eyes to the desert sunset, saw Warwar, Rashid; all seemed new, or had she never seen what was always there? 'You should let me go,' she said.

Warwar corked the empty gourd. 'You'd die here, without me.'

'Bring me to a road, and leave me. That way you can go home. No one'll find you.'

'I'm sorry, but you're money to us.'

'Yet you're letting me die.'

'Tomorrow we'll go to the spring, where this water came from. You won't die. Unless you try to escape.'

She drew her knees up and rolled on to them, raised herself on all fours, lifted her head, sat back on her ankles. The desert was suffused with a topaz lustre sharpening each rock, tinting the lavender clouds above the savage, tattered peaks, each glistening bead of sand. The corona of a fallen sun spread across the jagged western horizon, and into her body and soul flowed a sense of forgiving peace, surpassing comprehension. Suddenly she saw and knew these three poor men in their ragged robes and hungry deeds, how they had been bypassed by time and were trying to catch up, but could never apprehend that which no longer existed, that which for them had never been, or had passed them by in a dimension beyond their touch or ken, that they, as much as she, were outcasts of time. She felt pity and love, placed her hand on the boy-killer's, furtive as a mouse under the sleeve of his cloak. 'Don't worry – we're all the same.'

She felt a moment's contact, a sense of what there'd been with the Hungarian boy in the *chambre de bonne* – of so many things ignored and not understood.

Warwar pulled back his hand.

'Tell the others,' she said, 'you mustn't fight over me. Tomorrow I'll be stronger and we can go to the water. Then we'll decide what to do.' Talking exhausted her, tore her throat; she curled into her niche of rocks and sand. 'Please give me my goatskin. I'm going to sleep.'

He spread the goatskin over her, her cheekbone awash with her strange yellow hair. Already she was asleep; he sat back on his heels and watched the stars one by one cut their way through onrushing darkness, till all was reversed, day was night, and the blackness glittered with all the desert's sands, each a tiny flame beyond the bounds of time.

There was a click of stones as Rashid led a camel uphill to tether it for the night. Warwar smelt this was the lactating female, could smell Rashid's sweet skin and the sour oil odour of his rifle, could smell the change in the rocks as the sun's heat left them, how the sand contracted and grew damp, noted the tang of the *commiphora* scrub from the far slope. As the wind no longer descended from the peaks but had shifted and was now from the west, he could sense the faint dampness of the little great lake, Chewbahir, four days' walk away, making him think of the woman and what she had said.

He stood, feeling a strange pain in his knees, picked up his rifle and climbed the slope after Rashid. A white shape blocked him. 'Good evening, cousin,' he said.

'You leave the prisoner?' Ibrahim answered.

'She can barely move.'

'You want to lose her again?'

'Last time, cousin, it was not I, but Rashid—'

'Your memory wanders. Because we couldn't trust you to watch her we made you go for water – despite your fears of the Gabbra . . .'

In a breath Warwar knew he was being drawn back into the old hostility, the old arguments, despite what the woman had suggested. But he could not disagree with Ibrahim, although Ibrahim lied, because this was how Ibrahim wanted things to be. He could meekly agree, but Ibrahim would see through that, too, see he had given up hope of concord and was planning treachery. He could argue, fight Ibrahim's lies, but that would only lead to deeper hatred. 'It has been a long journey, cousin,' he said. 'Please forgive me if I've angered or disappointed you—'

'I don't care enough to be disappointed.'

And Warwar saw that Ibrahim wanted this hatred, that he feared nothing more than trust and kindness between them, because it did not fit his needs. 'Please forgive me, nonetheless. I will do as you say.'

'Go back to your whitewoman.' Ibrahim's voice softened. 'Keep our bounty safe from hyaenas.'

Warwar went down to the woman and sat, rifle across his knees. Ibrahim will accept me as long as I'm a foolish child, he thought, when I do as he says and do not interfere. Like that I'm never a danger for him with Soraya. That way I will accept the fistful of coins he gives me when the woman is ransomed, and will never have cattle and goats to pay Soraya's bride price. Like that Ibrahim and Rashid will have much money. Although Rashid swears he cares not for money taken in ransom, did he not empty the pockets of the men I shot at the Land Rovers?

The woman shifted in her sleep, crying out briefly in her guttural tongue – a name, perhaps? Warwar tried to imagine a man covering her but could not. Even the hyaena, he told himself, loves its own kind. Even the whites – so mechanical, leaden, ruled by their strange, solitary dreams, with their rigid faces and tense eyes, they who always seem in pain or worry, who so rarely laugh or sing or dance or let the earth's heart beat freely inside them – can they too love? Not like us, surely, but at all?

Was he the woman's man, the tall, cowardly one we sent back after the attack? How could she love one like that? Perhaps he was rich, had paid a high bride price. Now he's gone back to his other wives, forgotten this one. How much money will he give? Perhaps he'd rather buy a new young wife, be pleased this one's gone. Like most whitemen he was so feeble and pale – did he even reach Kenya at all?

No matter, the whitewoman can write the words to bring the money. In the afterwards either I will or will not have Soraya's bride price. Would she truly rather have Ibrahim than me? What will happen with Soraya is hidden in time: already the stars know but will not say.

# Chapter 24

Approaching the Borani camp, MacAdam forced himself to slow down, to go silently, wanting to rush in and find what they'd done to her, telling himself there'd either be little left or she'd be already gone, under the sand. That they'd just kill him too.

But it was better not to think of that, better not to think at all, he told himself again. He must choose carefully each rock to step round or on, must keep to the shadows and watch for sentries and take care that his boots didn't rattle gravel or dislodge a stone, careful that his shirt didn't drag on an edge of rock or twang a thorn, that the wind stayed in his face and didn't warn their dogs, till their huts loomed lifesize below him in the cambric of the night and he could almost touch their roofs from the altar of the cliff, their smells of dung embers and oily bodies rising to him, the malevolent odour of their goats and the astringency of their camels' urine against the desert hardpan. But still nowhere could he sense her.

After many hours, when the voices ceased to percolate up from the huts and firesides, when the dogs had quieted and the camels had all knelt to earth and dropped down on their bellies, chewing their harsh cud of thorns and twigs, when the last child had cried out in her sleep and even the embers of the fires had closed their red eyes, he slunk down into the camp and stepped silently from door to door. But he found no sign of her. Wanting to walk out into the middle of the village, between the huts and down the valley, but knowing he'd be seen by a sentry and that this would cost M'kele's life, he instead retook his path up the cliff, round and down to M'kele, who climbed up to meet him.

'Maybe they take her somewhere else.'

'You know that's not true, M'kele. You mustn't say it.'

'Tomorrow we catch one, discuss it with him.'

'Later.' With the loss of hope MacAdam found a great exhaustion. He tried to remember when he had last slept and could not. Had it been four nights, or only three? Were his broken ribs hurting more or did the exhaustion only make them so?

And where, he wondered, does pain go, out in this universe of stars and space – what happens to the sorrow and the joy? If it's vanished was it ever there? 'Why don't we sleep, somewhere up the mountain?' MacAdam said. 'Tomorrow we'll track down the Somalis and kill them.'

'Then we'll have to be careful, going back. We're deep inside Ethiopia.'

One's never deep inside anywhere, thought MacAdam. Can't M'kele see this? We live on illusions, and call the real false. Only killing's not false; only killing changes things. Only killing heals. I was right not to kill the Somalis in the Matthews Range, but these will die for killing her.

They climbed the mountain to the ridge where the Somalis and their two camels had camped the night after they had escaped the Boranis. In the first rays of dawn the two camels' tracks showed they were hasty and burdened, their hooves leaving white gashes on the black stone, their strides wide and poorly placed among the rocks; then came the disordered tumult of the Boranis' hooves, of many camels running, then a cartridge glowing in the early sun. 'They've changed their minds, the Borani,' M'kele said. 'We're going to find the Somalis dead.'

'Then we'll go back. Once we've found her body.'

There was a place where seven AK47 cartridges lay like a broken necklace on the sand, where the young Somali killer's tracks wound like a lizard's among the stones, then finally vanished. No matter what they tried they could not find them, nor now those of the two Somalis still on camels. Holding his bush hat over his brow to block the sun, MacAdam stared down at the precise and meaningless contour intervals of M'kele's map. He felt the fire in his throat that precedes dying. Despite the agony in his chest he forced himself to stand, breathe deeply. M'kele must not die. 'We should go to the water, marked on the map – Dibandiba.'

M'kele forced dried lips apart with his teeth. 'It says there's water, sometimes.'

With the whitewoman alone on Rashid's camel the

Somalis crossed over the baboon-backed mountain next morning and reached the water hole at noon. Warwar lowered himself down its shaft to the cool mud at the bottom, happy to see it had slightly refilled from his excavation the day before. He restacked the branches of quadi thorn he had used yesterday, took off his *djellabah* and doubled its bottom end over the branches, and pushed them down steadily, increasing his weight, moving his hands to avoid the finger-long thorns plunging up through the wool.

Ibrahim lowered the water gourds to Warwar on a rawhide cord; coming down the long darkening hole they blocked the light. Warwar untied them and put them alongside the *djellabah* whose fabric was dampening as he shoved it deeper and deeper into its sieve of thorns and branches. He licked his lips and the sound was like sand over stone, magnified in this hollow, cool pit fragrant with crushed quadi leaves.

After a long time of pushing down, a grey mud began to appear through the fabric of his *djellabah*, and Warwar knelt to sip it. It tasted like rotten metal, grainy and sour; it slipped down his throat like warm honey and he could not stop sucking it, his face pushing into the wool. A horrible pain struck his spine and he leaped up screaming, knocking the gourds. 'Young scum!' Ibrahim thundered down the pit. 'Drink when your elders thirst? When the bounty woman will die?'

The fist-sized rock Ibrahim had hurled down on him lay in the centre of his *djellabah*, dampened on one edge. Wet ran down his thigh; he had a sudden fear it was urine, rubbed it with his finger and tasted blood.

Now Ibrahim will die: it was as precise a discovery as if he'd read it cut in stone. I must find a time and way to kill him, to make him crawl before he dies. But Ibrahim will know this and be waiting. Feeling naked without his gun, Warwar craned his neck to look up into the tiny glaring orifice half-blocked by Ibrahim's head. 'I give you my regrets, cousin. I was in such a hurry yesterday to return with the three bottles that I drank very little, thus had much thirst. I give you my regrets.'

'That did not keep you yesterday from drinking most of mine!' Ibrahim's voice was tubular, as if spoken from a jug. 'Fill the gourds quickly – you'd keep us all day in the sun.'

Ibrahim will change the truth, Warwar thought, and others will believe him. Already Rashid does. For this I'll kill Rashid too. With all the ransom for the white-woman I shall claim Soraya.

A film of briny pallid liquid was collecting on his *djellabah*. He pushed Ibrahim's rock into the centre of the cloak, deeper and deeper; after a while the water began to edge up around it. When there was enough he forced the first gourd down into the *djellabah*; the water noise rose inside it almost to the neck.

'The first is ready, cousin,' he called.

Ibrahim's head reappeared in the hole. 'Tie it.'

Warwar tied the cord and watched the gourd rise quickly, knocking pebbles down on him as it bounced off the pit walls, till it flashed into the sun and vanished in Ibrahim's hands. For a moment the hole was vacant; he bent and sucked quickly at the water, took a second gourd and began to force it down into the *djellabah*.

# Chapter 25

As through an ancient rippled window, Rebecca watched the rising half-moon dance in the fire's heat. How near it seemed, as if it had a part to play in all this, as if it *cared* about her.

Above the moon's glow Warwar watched an airplane's blinking red eye cross the night. Wherever man goes the whiteman looks down on him. From the great southern village of Nairobi, its people countless as the sands, north to the other vast village of New Flowers – Addis Ababa. But if it's true what the old men say, once the whiteman spread everywhere like the sleeping sickness or the disease that kills the cattle – now like the strange grass he brought he withers and retreats.

With the gerenuk rib he had been chewing he pushed a thorn twig closer to the coals, feeling their heat against his hand. How miraculous the thorn bush to keep the sun inside it, to warm us when we need it. How miraculous the gerenuk to eat the thorn and make his life so we can eat him and make ours. It is the spirit that warms – thorn and gerenuk and I and sun are one, and this rock made by the sun and the whitewoman – and where

Ibrahim and Rashid misunderstand is that in their hearts they place one thing above another and this gives them pain.

The thorn twig had burned and lay broken, the circles of its years bared like a skull's teeth. But the twig's thorns were still black and pointed – only the sharp endures. And only the hard can ever be sharp.

The gerenuk had not been sharp. It was young, had never learned how suddenly the breeze shifts at sunset in the mountains, how far a rifle's claw can reach. Ibrahim was sharp when he was young but grows less so. Although I'm respectful and call him cousin, he scents danger. But he's confused by matters of clan and family – for him the wind has always blown this way, as the generuk was confused by Ibrahim's scent below and so climbed up to me. Some people would rather keep a good idea of themselves, and think what they have always thought, than live.

Shifting his legs Warwar felt pain in his back where Ibrahim's rock had struck. Ibrahim must beg for life, ignobly, before I kill him. He must lose honour. For eternity.

But with water and food the whitewoman will be stronger, and Ibrahim will want to go tomorrow. In three days we'll cross the Addis Ababa road and reach the water hole at Abagobi, in four more days the Marrehan, the El God God, where Soraya is combing her little sister's hair, or helping her mother grind up new roots for the broth, or bringing in a handful of sticks for the fire, while the old men think of her and count their herds.

But the elders will never agree that the whitewoman be sold from El God God or any other village in the Marrehan. Knowing this, Ibrahim will be planning to stop somewhere in Ethiopia to send words to sell the whitewoman. This stopping place will be near a town where he'll not be noticed, where he knows someone to send the words, a Moslem he can trust. The only place like that is Moyale, five days away.

But Ibrahim's still too sharp to camp near Moyale; he'll hide the woman in the bush, somewhere beyond Moyale in the thornscrub and baobabs of the craters of Hardacha, where if he's hunted he can easily slip across the tip of Kenya into the Marrehan. Warwar let his eyes drift into the distances between the stars. Once Ibrahim reaches Moyale it will be too late, for he'll send his own words to Nairobi, and he'll win the money for Soraya.

The whitewoman sat wrapped in the goatskin on the far side of the fire, her chin on upraised knees. Seeing her like this in the near darkness it was easy to think her someone else, a person like Soraya. 'We're not far from Moyale,' he said. 'Soon you could be free.'

Her eyes shocked him with their strange mixture of kindness, pity, and hatred. 'But Ibrahim and Rashid would take you across Ethiopia,' he added, 'far into Somalia, to our home on the Ouabi Shibeli . . .'

'You're not from Ouabi Shibeli! You're border hyaenas.'

He made himself smile. 'These men will take you many days across the desert, maybe let you die. I'd be happy to leave you in Moyale.'

'You're not afraid these "men", as you call them, will

understand you?' she asked slowly. 'They haven't been to school like you – to learn Swahili?'

Unintentionally Warwar glanced uphill at Ibrahim and Rashid sitting by the camels, the pipe they passed back and forth winking as had the whiteman's airplane. He could feel Ibrahim's gaze. 'You know they don't speak Swahili.'

'Like snakes, they can sense you.' Her voice came out of the darkness of the goatskin draped over her head and shoulders. 'Don't you wonder why they left you back there, for the Borani?'

'Many times I've thought of that.'

'What have you decided?'

For a moment she seemed like the teacher in the concrete school, a woman far back inside him. 'With food and water you've grown very strong and independent – I must be careful not to let you have so much. It made you very kind and gentle to be dying.'

'You want everyone to die so that you'll feel no threat?' she asked.

'Four times I've saved your life – was that wanting you to die?'

She sneered. 'Four times?'

'From the leopard, from the Borani, from Ibrahim and Rashid when they wanted to kill you, then in bringing you water when you were dying of thirst.'

Her lip rose higher over her front teeth. 'You *took* me. I didn't ask for this. You killed my friends, sent my husband to die in the desert. You're scum, don't you *see* that?'

'If your husband were a man, even a "scum" man like

me, he'd have never let you go – he'd have followed, been there to save you when you ran away. Instead you got me.'

'You're not worth his little finger.'

'Do you love him?'

'Of course!'

Warwar smiled. 'Why lie to me?'

'It doesn't matter what you think! Can't you see that? Can't you see you're *nothing*?'

'And what is she who has no love?'

She looked away in resignation, anger. Warwar put new twigs on the fire. 'I'd find a better way to send you home from Moyale, instead of going all the way to Ouabi Shibeli.' He waited but she did not speak. '*You* make the words on paper, asking for the money, and I'll send them from Moyale. You can stay nearby, until the money comes.'

The twigs he'd placed on the fire began to blaze, tossing light and shadow across her angular, distracted face. He could see the ligaments beneath the skin of her fingers laced over her knees, and wondered what it would be like to penetrate her.

'They'll send no money for me. How many times must I tell you that?'

'No man would so disgrace his woman!'

'*You* killed him!'

'It was only a few days' walk. He had water. Are you really all that weak?'

Her face hardened. 'Why won't you just let me go?'

'If you make the words, in Moyale, once the money comes you'll be free.' He stood and glanced across the ridges of Gamud sharpened and lightened by the moon. 'There's lions on the slope below. Stay by the fire.' He climbed to Rashid and Ibrahim, a camel snorting at his approach. 'She's better. Tomorrow she can travel.'

'Love's a great restorer,' mocked Ibrahim.

'Why do you tease me so, my cousin?'

'Because he sees your ambition far exceeds your capabilities,' Rashid said.

'My ambition's to be a good man, and take my place in the clan.'

'You see, Rashid, you are right,' Ibrahim noted.

Warwar drew in a deep breath and sat disconsolately below them on the slope. 'When do you wish me to stand guard, cousin?'

'Later, when the moon's high. You will stay up here and watch the camels.'

'Till then I'll sleep.'

'Near your whitewoman . . .'

'No, there, overlooking the ravine. Wake me when it's time.' Warwar went down to the niche where he had shot the gerenuk and sat against the cliff with his rifle across his knees, the half-moon rising in his face.

Rebecca watched Rashid descend to take the boy-killer's place opposite her at the fire. As he gathered his burnoose about him and sat down, his look was one of curious distaste; he glanced between her upraised knees and hurriedly she dropped them, wrapped the goatskin tighter, lay down and closed her eyes.

It had been Rashid who had fallen asleep the night she'd escaped. If she'd found water sooner she could have stayed ahead of them, even reached Allia Bay on its breezy edge of Lake Turkana. She remembered the dining room of the main hall at Koobi Fora, the soft wind off the lake, the chair she liked in the corner of the room, listening there, a bottle of Tusker cool in her hands, to the cheery after-dinner conclaves of colleagues from all corners of the earth as they tried to unravel the fabric of time and identify the strands woven into it so long ago, to comprehend those long gone whose genes were briefly now their own. She looked up to fight the tears; the moonstruck darkness was just a cold reminder of the eternal wasteland of death that had so recently, like a hyaena edging ever closer to a dying fire, begun to prey on her.

Through the damp blur of near-shut eyes she watched Rashid settle himself more comfortably, his rifle on its strap across both shoulders, so there was no way she could steal it from him. I could hit him with a rock, she thought, knowing she had not the strength to do more than injure and infuriate him. If ever she wanted them to kill her that's what she'd do.

Rashid faced uphill for a moment, chin raised, his profile with its large hook nose, ridged brow, tall forehead, slender, wide mouth and dark, pointed beard seeming somehow noble, as if he'd been caught up in this by accident, and his thoughts were far away, poised on concerns of greater elegance. Men and women were two totally separate species, she'd realized, linked only by the ephemeral symbiotic needs of sex, companionship, and rearing children. Under men's superficial differences, the little kindnesses and considerations, weren't they all the same? If ever free of these hyaenas she'd have nothing more to do with men.

When the moon reached mid-sky Warwar awoke. Without moving he examined all he could see: the opposite cliffs drenched in vertical, nacreous light, their scarps and crevasses blackened by shadows, the ravine where he had shot the gerenuk, the walls of the precipice at his back. He felt a surge of fear but reassured himself.

He unsheathed his dagger, took off his *djellabah*, folded it and placed the rifle atop it, removed his sandals and laid them upside down beside the *djellabah*. While doing this he again went over in his mind the steps that the stars had shown him in his dream. Before Ibrahim died Warwar would make him crawl, cringe as a starving dog will beg for food or not to be struck.

The difficult part was to disable Ibrahim's rifle. Then in the morning, when Warwar shot Rashid, Ibrahim would snatch his rifle to kill Warwar but, shockingly, it would not fire. As in his dream Warwar saw Ibrahim's expression change from scornful rage to shock to realization as he faced Warwar's rifle, as he saw Rashid already dead and understood what would happen next. Would Ibrahim then beg, pray to Mecca, call him cousin, offer to give him all the money, sanction his marriage to Soraya? In the dream he had. 'Don't mistake the dream you live for life,' someone not long ago had said. Who was that?

Naked, he climbed towards Ibrahim, fast and silent, tasting the night air round the steel blade in his teeth. Now the whitewoman would be his alone; he might make her remove her clothes, be a woman for him –

238

who else of the clan had ever had a whitewoman? Even if it's a desecration as Ibrahim says, still one can desecrate oneself, the clan – one's also a man. The clan does not own one's soul.

Rebecca cautiously opened her eyes but Rashid did not move. He still sat with the rifle across his knees, the ringed finger of his right hand draped loosely over the trigger guard, the angle between the stock and magazine resting in the crook of his left arm. Although his eyes were closed he held his head high, the cowl of his white burnoose framing his long black curly hair, the embers lending his dark skin a reddish cast, as though lit from within.

When she slid her feet from under the goatskin Rashid inhaled quickly and she froze with fear, but his steady breathing resumed, his face held high and peaceful. Raising herself on her left elbow she began to fold back the goatskin, stopping with each intake of his breath, lying down quickly when, far away, a desert fox yapped and Rashid tensed in his sleep, raising herself again a minute later, till the goatskin was free and in a single motion she stood.

Two filled water gourds sat beside his knee; dreadfully she wanted to run downhill and round the huge craggy shoulder of this mountain and across the northern plateau for three days to the winding dirt track known as the Addis Ababa Highway – a truck would come, someone, take her to Faille, Moyale – she'd be home in a week. But to do this she needed all the water. To give herself determination she remembered her earlier thirst and, choking back a sudden sob at the thought of her sons waiting and worrying, she moved her foot round the fire and stretched out a hand for the closer water gourd.

Noiseless as a leopard Warwar crossed the ridge towards Ibrahim sleeping beside the tethered camels. Ibrahim lay on a bed of sand in a bowl of rock, his rifle by his side; to reach him Warwar had to descend the steep rocky slope without disturbing its loose stones and pebbles. Without clothes or sandals he was truly quieter but suddenly he feared snakes; the stars seemed to turn black; danger crouched in every hollow. He raised one foot, placed it by accident on a crumbly rock, removed it silently, regained his balance and moved the foot elsewhere. The jagged lava dug into the balls of his feet. Despite the night's warmth he could not stop shivering. The knife in his mouth made him salivate, his breath hissing over the blade.

Rebecca gasped the second water gourd and began to lift it away; its leather strap tautened, caught under Rashid's knee. '*Kitabu!*' he said, quite clearly, in a natural tone; after a petrified moment she realized he had spoken in his sleep. 'Book,' he had said, in Swahili. Did he speak Swahili, or was that some other word in his language? She'd been trying to put down the gourd because its strap had stuck under Rashid's knee, but when he had said '*Kitabu*,' he had also moved his elbow and now the barrel of the AK47 had shifted and she could not reach around it. If she let go of the water gourd it would roll against his foot.

From the hollow where Ibrahim slept Warwar could not see Rashid or the whitewoman, but in the morning,

Warwar told himself, Rashid would die and after Warwar had made Ibrahim beg for life then killed him, the whitewoman would be his alone, to do with what he wanted before he sold her.

All he had to do now was to cross the last few steps to Ibrahim's side, lift Ibrahim's rifle carefully from its niche by his elbow, carry it back up the slope, remove the little metal spearhead inside it which hammers against the cartridges, and return it . . . A rock beneath his foot crunched as he put his weight on it, but Ibrahim, sleeping the sleep of the just, did not move. Soon I'll have you, Warwar said, almost aloud.

Rebecca's arm ached from stretching out to hold the gourd, the other gourd clasped against her chest. She was growing dizzy and had to remind herself not to hold her breath, so near was her face to his. His breath was against her lips, her arm growing numb, and she hesitantly lowered the gourd, her elbow brushing the AK47's muzzle. Instantly his eyes opened, showing no surprise, a casual recognition as if they'd been long married and he'd woken with her in his arm. She dropped the gourd; in the instant of her fear, her face inches from his, his musty sleep-breath filling her nostrils, she heard the gourd hit against the ground and glug as the stopper popped; she leaped over the goatskin and down the rocky slope in starlight, twisted her ankle and tumbled, lost the other gourd, scrambled to her feet and kept running. Rashid unslung his rifle, whistled, 'Ibrahim!', tightened his *djellabah*, and ran after her.

Ibrahim woke when the gourd hit the ground, snatched his rifle and stood as Rashid whistled. He saw

Rebecca's glimmer moving downhill and aimed carefully, then from the corner of his eye glimpsed another shape, darker and faster, retreating uphill, saw it was Warwar naked, and fired. Warwar ducked as the barrel came up, and Ibrahim fired again, hearing a cry. Warwar dived over the ridge; Ibrahim climbed after him, forcing him upslope.

When he reached the crest Ibrahim descended to Warwar's sleeping place, hid Warwar's rifle among the rocks and kicked his *djellabah* and sandals into the abyss.

# Chapter 26

She ran down the stony slope and hobbled along the gully at its bottom, Rashid clattering down behind her. The twisted ankle drove a knife up her thigh into her stomach with each step; she couldn't run, climbed from the gully up a narrowing steep canyon and halted one-legged, trying not to gasp, her hands spread out against the steepening canyon walls, her fingers white as lilies on the rock. The first hues of dawn rubied the canyon crests, but all was dark below. The patter of his steps went past, returned; she heard his steady breathing coming up behind her.

Pinned in a corner of two walls she leaned out, trying to see up the cliff; there were ledges sticking out and gleaming rockslide chutes. She pulled herself up this corner as it steepened; something smashed down on her head, crushing it into her neck, and her hands slipped – she was falling outwards and grabbed at nothing, tried to pull back from the void sucking her down, caught her foothold as she fell, shoulder socket wrenching, stones clattering below her down the canyon wall.

Beneath her feet a flash of silver drove her scrambling

back up the wall and over the lip of stone she had just smashed her head into. Crouched on this lip, knees over the edge, back pressed against the cliff, she jammed her fingers under a chunk of rock but could not pry it free. She stood unsteadily, could not balance, twisted round for handholds up the canyon wall, tipping outwards, clamped her body to the wall. Rashid came closer. Knowing she'd fall, she scrabbled for grips up the slick vertical stone, slipped, slid and held, slid again, found a last hold and inched trembling up the cliff, angling herself to the left and up a skinny ledge. But when she slowed to listen he had swung after her. Her fingers found a loose rock and prised it from the cliff; it was heavy and off- balanced her.

The glow of Rashid's burnoose neared, moving side to side as he ascended beneath her. Her rock was too heavy for one hand but when she let go her other hand's hold on the cliff the stone's weight pulled her outwards. Rashid's breathing loudened, the scrape of his fingernails on rock. She squeezed further right and down the descending ledge, held her breath and batted her eyes to shake away sweat, gritted her teeth against the weight of the stone and the pain in her ankle. His dim outline passed directly below her and she pushed the stone outwards and away; it fell straight but struck the cliff above him, smacked the breech of his rifle and bounced past him down the chasm. He yelled; shaking with terror she crept down to the end of the ledge above a clear, sharp drop of cliff, and waited.

The sky above the eastern slopes crimsoned as the moon

slipped down the west. It's just a forced march, MacAdam told himself, sleep on your feet walking. Not going into battle nor retreating, just seeking water. And to make sure the Somalis are dead. Dead and very dead. For what they did to Rebecca, for killing elephants. For being the same ones on the Ewaso N'giro. If we had caught them there, split up and tracked them down, they never would've had Rebecca. We couldn't catch camels, Nehemiah said. But we are.

Water impossible to find. Darius and Gideon never reach us now. Halted at the border like respectable churchwomen outside a whorehouse. Ignorant of the sanctity within. He laughed, heard a jackal's bark and stared round shocked, but there was nothing.

Raise one foot in front of the other as the slope rises. Around each pockmarked ragged rock. Tense each descending ankle, step steadily with the weight, lean forward under the pack, balance the rifle, breathe deep and steady.

M'kele always before me. M'kele with his dangling earlobes tied up over his ears. His curly hair greying in the back. Who doesn't give a damn about Rebecca. It's not his fight, not his woman – he does it out of kindness. She wasn't my woman either. Time to say that. Elephants weren't my fight either but I pretended they were. I don't have any fights left. Must get back in time to Nairobi. So the prisoners don't get killed. But if they're the same as these, the ones who took Rebecca, why save their lives?

M'kele's seventeen children, 'twelve still alive'. His steady stride sucking up the miles. M'kele thirsting in the desert to help me with my vengeance. He who'd be the first to remind me the blood of enemies never assuages grief.

The dawn grew wider, engulfed the east, stretching euphorbia shadows across the gravelly sand. Birds were singing, doves cooed; far away a gazelle gave a warning double bark. Bees thrummed among the tiny purple flowers of the thorn bush.

Suddenly M'kele dived to the ground, waved his hand down. MacAdam ducked among the rocks and ran left, away from M'kele to the far side of this gully ahead that had somehow bothered M'kele.

Now he could smell it too. Camel dung. That's what bothers M'kele. Whose camels? He crept forward along the left side of the gully as M'kele advanced through thicker brush on the right, keeping parallel with each other so that if one of them needed to fire he knew he could shoot ahead or behind but never straight across.

M'kele stood, waved: they've gone. Who? MacAdam ran to the gully, picked up a piece of dung and rubbed it between his fingers: a day old. M'kele jumped down beside him. 'It's *them*!'

'They camped here. Yesterday.'

There were four holes in the ground where someone had driven sticks. Around them were the tracks of all three Somalis and prints of Rebecca's sneakers. MacAdam knelt beside them, not breathing so it wouldn't go away, wouldn't be a dream. 'They got her back. She's still alive.'

M'kele tossed a desultory glance at the sand peppered

with tracks. 'This time we won't lose them. Now *we* will kill them.'

'They got her back, from the Borani.' If he repeated it enough times it would have to be true.

M'kele glanced up, smiled. 'Tomorrow, Captain, *you'll* have her back.'

Warwar picked his way hurriedly along the far side of Selach ridge, his bare feet scraped and bleeding, his left arm nearly severed at the humerus where Ibrahim's bullet had shattered it, his legs quivering with pain. The curving shoulder of the mountain hid Ibrahim's approach, but Warwar's own tracks were easily visible as hasty dark blotches over the rocks. With no clothes he could not wrap his feet to hide his tracks. Without a gun he could not stop Ibrahim.

Hopelessly he examined the horizon grey beneath the platinum sky: no trees, no scrub, nothing to cut the wind or impede the eye, nowhere to hide but crags and gullies where his trail of blood would fast betray him. He sneered down at the curved dagger in his right hand, at its puny length and the nick in its blade.

Allah will not help me now because this is truly clan. I pretended it wasn't but it is. There *is* a link between Ibrahim and me: I can't deny him. Allah will not take sides within the clan except in cases of code; but here we have both done wrong. My pride will kill me. As Ibrahim said, I want more than I am.

He almost wept at the memory of last night when he had still been happily a member of the clan. Now he was alone and naked. Even if he escaped Ibrahim he could never go home; the clan would stone him to death.

Pride made me want to take the little metal spearhead from inside Ibrahim's gun. So I could make him beg, before I killed him. But Ibrahim would never beg: I wanted him to fear. Without pride I could simply have shot both him and Rashid tomorrow, from behind. Then the whitewoman would be mine, and the clan would look up to me, for no one would know about Ibrahim and Rashid except what I said, that they had been killed by soldiers. And I would have given money to their wives and children and been praised as a good man.

All this flashed through his mind in instants as he surveyed his bloody tracks across the rocks, the barren horizon, the dagger like a useless twig in his hand. I should have shot them plain and simple.

The sun's tip glinted on the horizon, swelled up in righteous anger, its first blasts striking his face and chest. It and Ibrahim – together they will kill me. Each will force me to hide where the other can easily find me. He felt Ibrahim's bullets striking his chest, even more awful than the one that had smashed his arm. Or will they take me back to the village? He saw Soraya watching from the crowd as the stones struck. Will she throw stones also? Perhaps my pride has fooled me even there, and even she has never cared.

# Chapter 27

Rashid climbed past Rebecca up the cliff, not stopping at the place where she had crawled to the left and down. His footsteps overhead negotiated the last steep section; he scrambled over the top and his sound vanished. He'll come down again, she reminded herself, as soon as he can't find my tracks.

The canyon brightened with sunrise; a fragrant warmth flowed down it from the peaks; between her feet pebbles glistened on the dusty ledge; the cracked canyon wall was chilly against her back. She leaned out and looked up the cliff but could not see Rashid; she crawled quickly back up the ledge and climbed down the canyon wall.

When she reached the gully at the bottom Rashid still had not reappeared, but where were the other two? Something thumped to the sand behind her and she flinched, expecting Warwar, but it was only a rock loosened by her descent.

She limped from rock to rock down the gully, trying to make no tracks in the sand and loose stones, avoiding even the rocks that might shift under her weight and leave a changed impression in the sand. Each time she looked back she expected to see the boy-killer or Ibrahim on his camel coming to recapture her. Or more likely now to kill her.

The sun struck her shoulders and neck, turned her hair to thousands of fiery wires. The gully died out in a down-plunging rocky slope; ahead the Selach's colossal southern flanks rippled down into the Sidamo Desert, towards the too-distant Kenyan border and the Chalbi. *This* is the way we came – so I can get back to the *geb* tree – if the leopard's gone I'll drink and then it's only a hundred more miles across the mountains to Turkana, if I can avoid the Borani. Oh if only I had my goatskin. The water. What will I do without water? Why did Ibrahim or Warwar shoot? Where are they? Warwar wouldn't shoot me. Were they shooting at something else? A lion? There can't be a lion because if there were by now it would have got me.

If I climb the mountain and go north toward Faille, Rashid will see me. Warwar and Ibrahim are up there too, expecting me to go that way.

Around her the plain, vast and indifferent, accepted her into its infinitude: wide, jagged, and empty past the bounds of time, its peaks of broken lava teeth and osseous mahogany buttes quivering with heat, the seared white sky, were the landscape of the childhood dream in which she first had glimpsed the horror, misery, and destiny of all life, and where she, like the ancient young woman of the jawbone, would vanish into the geologic whorl of time. This seemed only logical and fitting. Because it was fate. Dizzied by the sun, she stumbled down the slope whose every stone threw out a shock of heat, where no stone was big enough to hide her.

As he came down the cliff Rashid saw the place the whitewoman had turned left on the little ledge, which he had missed earlier in the poor light. He saw where she had climbed back up this ledge and redescended the cliff. Where she had hit her head on the overhang a single strand of her long straight hair had caught on the black stone, twisting in the downhill breeze like a spider's golden thread.

At the bottom of the cliff she had hesitated then turned south, downhill. Why, he wondered, does she walk this way from stone to stone? Her feet must hurt.

Soon the sun would strike her down; it was easy to follow the tracks but when he found her she'd be too weak to walk and he'd have to go back and get a camel. But why did Ibrahim shoot? To warn Warwar the woman'd escaped? Then where *were* they? How was it they were fools enough to go another way?

As he trotted upslope towards camp to find Ibrahim he reflected how unwise was this entire episode, how he and Ibrahim had become ensnared in the youngster's hunger for the whitemoney which was to come from writing words about the whitewoman. Warwar had been to the Mission school at El God God and had learned to crave what the whites craved. This was why the whites built those little hard dwellings made of the dirt that when you pour water on it turns to stone, thereby incurring God's wrath for locking up water inside this stone, and for building human places that remain, cannot be moved, are not annulled by time.

But it was not good to take whitemoney because slowly it whitened you too. You became like Warwar, desiring things you haven't made yourself, things made outside the clan: the loud black sound machines the young men trade goats for at Mandera, the bright necklaces and bracelets and the little sticks to start fires or shine light on the darkness. Warwar should be wandering the desert with his goats and sheep as Rashid had done, protecting his herd from lions, building it kid and lamb at a time, so by the time his solitary shepherd's years had brought him a knowledge of the stars, his herd would be large enough to pay a healthy bride price and feed his family. But the young men who went to the Mission school didn't cleave to the old ways, sometimes didn't even marry in the clan. They laughed at the ways their people had learned so repeatedly across the many hundred generations since Allah first raised them from the sea. Yet he himself carried a rifle made by whiteman hands; it poisons us and now we cannot live without it, he thought. And Warwar was his doing too, and Ibrahim's, for they had not been firm and gentle with him, nor proved to him the value of the clan's way. Simply because he never drank his mother's milk, nor walked in the shadow of his father, he'd had no one to show him.

But Rashid did not like to remember the clan because then he could not keep from thinking of Fatima, how sleepy in the early morning she rose to make him tea, how the smell of cool embers reheated with dry twigs and her odour of sleep and warmth were magnified by the fragrance of the dying night when she folded back the door flap, by the spicy tea warming his hands. He smiled seeing her wide brown eyes which always looked on his so openly and deeply. How true, what the Prophet said – everything shows through the eyes.

In years past there'd been so many elephants. Now because of Warwar and the whitewoman they had no tusks to sell at Daduma Addi, not even for a small gift to tell Fatima how he'd always thought of her, deep in his every day, no matter how far away. Nothing for the four boys and five girls she'd brought him out of her own slender body as a bough its leaves, the boys who watched his flocks and some day would hunt for tusks and defend the clan, the girls who would be mother to the clan as it is mother to us all.

Following Warwar's tracks, Ibrahim also was thinking of his wives, but with shame. He had not acted as a man and therefore dishonoured himself and thereby them. Shame because the young fool had led him by the nose, had insulted him without rebuke. Shame because he had made this long journey north with the whitewoman into Ethiopia, instead of turning south of Marsabit where still some elephants might remain, shame because he, Ibrahim, had slept and let the young fool approach and nearly murder him. Why had he come naked, with a knife? Had he been mating with the whitewoman, naked as a fish?

He stopped to inspect the jumbled landscape ahead, resettled the AK47 comfortably on its sling. The young fool's feet all cut and bloody but he hasn't slowed. Other splotches of blood on adjacent rocks, larger and less dirty – he was hit by my second bullet, in the left arm, or in the shoulder and the blood's flowing down the arm. Like a leopard or lion he'll be doubly dangerous wounded, expecting to die and therefore less afraid. Like a wounded leopard he can make a forward trail, then circle to pounce from behind, or like a wounded lion charge suddenly from the front.

Ibrahim wondered where Rashid and the white-woman were. The sun's heat weighed down through his *djellabah*; he picked up speed. Allah, let the boy not die before I reach him.

As at a thing profane his mind shifted away from the whitewoman, then kept creeping back. Like a boy, he warned himself, at the circumcision ceremony of an older brother. Like an inexperienced husband around the hut where his new wife is giving birth. The white-woman's caused all this – the young fool's envy for whitemoney, our flight into Ethiopia, the young fool's lust that he would mate with her, then sneak, knife in his teeth, to kill his clansmen.

Ibrahim scouted an outcrop from which a little *wadi* unravelled, but the young fool was not there. He tried to lick his lips but his tongue stuck to the insides of his front teeth. The splotch of blood on the first stones beyond the *wadi* was still sticky; he glanced back up the *wadi* but Warwar was not circling behind. The slope ahead shimmered and danced with heat, like the body of the whitewoman in Warwar's arms, her hot vagina clamping him. Satan. She has brought us all to this. As soon as I kill the young fool I'll kill her too. Only then can things be as they were.

# Chapter 28

'You walk like n'African.' M'kele took off his pack and lay down with it over his face.

'Spring'll be dry.' MacAdam dropped to his knees and fell down beside his rifle. Only stop a moment. She's just ahead. With them.

M'kele reached for the map in his pack but let his hand flap on the ground. 'The last ridge. This.'

Tuesday 12:34:41. 12 Dec. MacAdam tried to follow the seconds on his watch, but each time he fixed the number in his mind the next had already replaced it. 12:35:26. If it's after midnight – no, the sun's still out. Must be noon. If this is the Selach hills then we've walked two hundred kilometres since yesterday morning. Or the day before. No, we landed at North Horr in the afternoon. Spent that night tracking. She'd got away and M'kele found where they caught her. Next day we found where the Borani took her – last water. That night I scouted the Borani camp – second night. Then we walked all day thirsty to Dibandiba, and that night found the Somalis' trail again at the place where four sticks had been shoved into the ground. That was last night we found she's still alive. Or was there another day in between? It was Friday morning from Nairobi – where did the other day go? What other day?

He saw himself lying sick in another room while the family readied for a trip. Uncle Clyde in a striped wool suit carrying suitcases to the boot while mother hurried the girls through the parlour, each turning back for some forgotten trinket. The squat stone house in Ewen, its grim façade and frowzy shingles, trimmed holly trees to either side of the front door, the granite steps – the one at the bottom's cracked, catches your shoe – always feared some day you'd trip, but see, you never did . . . The copse of oaks, the hedgerows, the passage between the barn and fence muddied by trooping cattle – do you ever really leave the soil of your ancestors? Do you take it with you?

12:41:43. How many minutes since I started watching it – was it 12:39? No, it was 12:36. That's it, and the little numbers kept going. 12:42:16. Again he watched the little numbers but still could not recognize them in time. If it's not the middle of the night maybe it's broken. And that's the reason why I can't remember what day we left Nairobi.

12:47:09. 'M'kele!'

'Mnuh?'

'Get *up*!'

'Sleeping.'

If M'kele's sleeping it must be OK. M'kele jabbed him hard in the side and MacAdam lurched up angry. M'kele was a five-foot-tall black bird on knobby orange stilted legs, with a red neck from which a few pale feathers protruded like half-buried arrows, his yellow beak blackened with dried blood, that peered quizzically down on him, surprised he had moved. 'Scrawk!' croaked this M'kele bird.

MacAdam swung snarling at the bird. It jumped back, hopped into the air, wide awkward wings ticking the earth.

M'kele was back, pushed aside his backpack and sat up, waving flies from his mouth. ''S bad when the marabou he come to call.'

'Where *were* you?'

M'kele stared round the molten landscape. 'Where else?'

'You weren't *here!*'

The marabou circled overhead. It was not M'kele; there were too many, wide-winged in a column. He forced himself to stand, yanked M'kele's arm. 'They've come for us.'

M'kele licked his lips with a large black tongue. MacAdam felt a surge of hatred. M'kele's mouth was caked with white, like a camel's vulva.

M'kele lifted his G–3 from the ground, held it like a newborn across his lap, as if reading the maker's stamp. With awkward fingers he shoved the mode selector to semi, squinted up into the circling column of buzzard storks, his fatigue cap slipping back off his head as he raised the rifle and fired, the noise like steel walls crushing MacAdam's head. M'kele fired again, bang again. One of the huge birds exploded in a burst of fluff and meat, then another. As though caught by a wind that did not touch the earth, the others slanted off, while bits of feather, meat and bone drizzled down.

MacAdam found his glasses, glanced up at the Selach hills. 'Someone'll hear that.' M'kele's action seemed stupid, childish, could endanger Rebecca. MacAdam wanted to leave him.

'Showing the hawk the bow.' M'kele chuckled giddily.

'They'll come back.'

'And stay to feed on what's left of their brothers.'

'Just like us.' MacAdam knelt and shouldered his pack and rifle, made himself stand. Late afternoon sun reflected copper off the Selach hills; he staggered in circles till he found the track of the two camels and the sandal prints of the boy and the limping Somali, and without waiting for M'kele began to climb the shimmering slopes of lava up which they led, into the Selach hills.

The pain in Warwar's dangling arm was so great he tried to run on tiptoe in the vain hope of not jerking it. His stomach kept bolting as if he'd drunk tainted water, but there was nothing to vomit. His body, unprotected from the sun, had caught fire. The gashes on his feet had coagulated and broken open so many times they now flowed blood steadily, as a punctured gourd leaks out the last of its liquid.

Stumbling and running, running and stumbling, looking back and falling, raising himself from the sharp rocks and running onwards, he barely saw the mountains rise and slip down round him, changing from lava black and umber to ochre and crimson as the sun fell. He followed the north flank of the Selach hills east, the blunt shoulder of Gamud peak towering like an obelisk. In the immense north-descending rockslides ahead he was sure he could smell water. If he could reach it and there were no lions he'd find a way to live a little longer.

Far ahead a pair of doum palms caught the last jaundiced light sliding up the valley. With great precision Warwar memorized the entire landscape, seeing no trace of lions or anything that moved but a few gazelles out on the dusty plain, one watching while the others grazed the sparse combretum, a single eagle gliding far above, as if jealous of their company.

He approached to a hundred yards above the palms. Two augur buzzards sprang squawking from the top fork of one palm and sailed downslope; he moved closer, saw a dark stain of water on the sand. Moaning with joy he ran to the muddy, narrow pool, fell and drank.

He coated his sunburned body with mud, checked his back trail, and drank again. Locusts clung to the branches of *commiphora* and acacias round the hole; without bothering to break them open he ate them all, over a hundred, cracking their metallic thoraxes in his jaws, till his belly felt marvellously full and his body stronger, but his arm ached now almost more than he could stand.

The last light of the sun had climbed to the distant peaks as Ibrahim rounded the shoulder of the mountain and saw the two doum palms far ahead and below. Hiding among the rocks he studied the slope, trying to determine how far the young fool would move from the water hole that must be there, and where he could circle round to attack. From his ragged trail since noon it was clear Warwar was dying of his wound, of thirst and sun – he would probably not make wise decisions, nor had he the warrior's experience to set an invisible trap, but still Ibrahim must be careful. The young fool might be dying by the water's edge or else waiting, knife in hand, among the rocks ahead.

Ibrahim glanced west; at night the advantage of his rifle was much less. Should he go quickly towards the palms, hoping for a shot before darkness? Or should he wait, come in silently at night, unseen?

If he waited, Warwar might move on, and he'd have to track him tomorrow. If he moved in now, the young fool would see him and might evade him till dark, note where he was, and hunt him in the night.

The immense desert, empty as a bird's wing, inspired him with promise. As when going into battle he felt a rich completion, his entire soul's intuition of the beauty and brevity of life. I'll walk quickly towards the water hole and if he's there I'll shoot him. If he's not, he'll see me, that I've stopped at the palms, and he'll hunt me there tonight. But I won't be where he imagines; while he thinks he's hunting me I'll be hunting him.

Crazed by thirst and sun, Rebecca wandered south down the Selach hills. Somewhere ahead, in the tilting endless black peneplain shifting into darkness, must be the *geb* tree. The woman of the jawbone will lead me there again. If she cares she'll lead me. To save her children, because my children are hers. Thinking of her sons made Rebecca's eyes sting but she could not stop, her sobs a choking rattle.

With night returned her childhood vision of the black despair that rules eternity. Sitting on the green grass in her white frock, long pigtails warm with sun between her shoulder blades, her parents' voices near as the patio, she watched her tortoise-shell cat bring her a lump of molten green in his mouth, a dead hummingbird. The ruling principle of eternity was not good but evil, she'd understood, a purveyor of pain, pain made more tragic by the joy of life. Yes, the Master was truly evil and God just one of his disguises, a spy to ferret out the good and then betray it.

If there's only Hell it didn't matter; everyone belonged there. But if *everyone*'s imaginary then she was the only one in Hell. But there had been a way out before. The *geb* tree. But what if it was too far and the woman of the jawbone couldn't find her?

In the day's last chiaroscuro she moved slowly, weakly, avoiding the still fiery stones, the scorpions and desert cobras creeping and sliding from their crannies into the evening's cool. Walk quietly so you don't disturb them. No, better to make noise and warn them. But then the lions hear you. But they hear you anyway, or smell you on the wind.

Ahead a noise among the rocks made her crouch in fear. Footsteps, two people – how'd Warwar get so far ahead of me? Two shadows, rifles glinting, come to kill me. What if it's not *them*? If it's someone with water? 'Help!' she started to call, suppressed it, wind tickling her hair against her lips. She bowed her head to hide its glimmer. The steps paused, then moved on, paused again, as if seeking something. She waited, hardly breathing, till the footsteps moved further up the Selach hills and faded into silence.

M'kele's legs were tightening. No water for two nights and no sleep for three, just snatches caught walking when the ground's flat and the Somalis' tracks easy in the moonlight. Now the ground's steep and only rocks, no moon. No water. MacAdam faster and faster. Can't live without water. MacAdam a brave man but blue eyes no good for tracking. Like a lion walks and walks and never complains of the broken ribs. Easier to be that way when your woman's taken. But it's complicated about the woman because Nehemiah said she doesn't live in his *manyatta* although he protects her and is angry with those who took her. To understand these Europeans you must be one – see the world through their poor eyes, walk about in their weak, awkward, heavy bodies, love money and things as they do, with craving, unsatisfied, sad hearts.

The Europeans came to Maasailand boasting they'd killed God and hung him on a tree, as the leopard keeps his prey. We felt sorry for their frailty and the shame of killing the God who'd led them out of the desert as *N'gai* once did for us and the Samburu. We gave them food, some land to wander with their cattle, but the Europeans did not wander; their houses did not return to earth, and in trade for our gifts of food and land they gave us smallpox, liquor, and guns, killed a million Maasai, all of us except six thousand. Now the Europeans have changed many Maasai into black Europeans, wanting things and money, and staying in one place.

I, too, am too much European, with their schooling and the tribe's, but when this last year of Army ends as I have promised myself I'll go back to the Mau Escarpment, the Amala's shaded banks, its pools cool and brighter than silver, to wander with my herds the old way, see my children raise their families, enjoy my wives and take a new one, someone young and lithe with budding breasts and slender thighs – Joseph's daughter Celia, or some young beauty I've never even seen.

God's not a man you nail upon a tree. As it's said, God is he who separates the paths. And as it's said, the man who tries to walk two paths soon cleaves himself.

Unlike most Europeans MacAdam doesn't scorn us somewhere inside himself nor make himself silly with false friendliness. But like other Europeans he's crucified his God, kills what he loves.

Soon we reach the place beyond Dibandiba where water's marked on the map. Where these tracks go. But these tracks more than a day old: because of the Borani, the Somalis will have moved on. If there's water there, we'll live, and I'll take first watch so he can sleep.

Watching the tracks, M'kele did not see the muzzle flash but felt keenly its rod of fire rip through his intestines and throw him back down the hill, never heard the muzzle's blast in the complete agony crushing his stomach and pelvis, his mind telling him at first that he had been kicked by a camel, had strayed into one of the Somalis' camels, but pain exploded so horribly inside him he thought then he'd been struck by a rocket or by lightning, rolling, moaning, on his side, holding his shattered belly from which his life sprayed through his fingers. He heard the answering chatter of MacAdam's rifle, the ping of ejected cartridges on the rocks, and understood there'd be no sunny days herding cattle on the Mau escarpment, no grandchildren warm and giggly in his arms, no lithe young wife whose eyes, round and fearful, looked in on him as he died.

# Chapter 29

MacAdam was yelling for M'kele but he didn't answer and when he reached him he was dead. From uphill came the hurried snap of a bolt and the pop of a firing pin in an empty chamber; MacAdam dashed to the crest of the slope where a white-robed figure charged him swinging a rifle, and he shot him dead in the chest and dived between the boulders expecting the other Somalis to fire. Over his pounding blood and breath he could hear only camels stomping nervously in a gully where they seemed tethered. He could smell water, a faded fire, camel dung, the hot stink of blood and grease from the dead man's cloak, the burnt oil and cordite of his own rifle. Where were the other two? He mustn't let them kill him or then he couldn't kill them for M'kele.

The camels quieted, ripping and munching branches with the sideways grind of their jaws. Blood from the dead Somali trickled down the rocks. The dead man was skinny with a pointed beard, probably the one who limped, his mouth agape at the surprise of death, of how rapidly it claims you. His burnoose was dark across the chest as if he were empty there and the black ground showed through. His rifle lay beside him, the magazine full with an empty cartridge in the chamber, a dent across the breech, where the ejection mechanism had jammed after the first shot.

MacAdam dismounted the Somali's magazine and threw it far down the hill; it clattered against the rocks and a jackal barked a warning across the ravine. He circled the top of the hill and found only the two camels tethered in the gully, who huffed at his smell.

He went back to M'kele but he was truly dead. He sat with M'kele's grizzled head in his arms, but M'kele had no interest in condolence. MacAdam returned to the dead Somali and in widening circles scouted the camp; there was no one there at all, and after a while he found a water bottle and drained it and stumbled to a distant niche in the rocks to sleep till dawn.

Warwar's pain grew ever more horrible. One-handed, he had wrapped his feet in palm fronds so they made no blood trail when he left the spring between the two doum palms; he tried to fortify himself with the vision of Soraya as she leaned out over the well at El God God, her slender, strong arm revealed to the shoulder, her back straight as if the bucket were weightless, as if all tragedy were nothing beside the joy of living, but even she could not diminish this agony. It made him want to lie down, collapse, give up, walk empty-handed to Ibrahim and beg forgiveness, explain he'd heard a noise in camp, had gone with his knife to check it, naked and barefoot because he'd wanted to wash with a little water from the spring, and although Ibrahim would upbraid him for the water he would not kill him just for that. But a man shows his lies in his eyes, in the cut of his lips, and now that Ibrahim had drawn his blood he couldn't give mercy.

And had not Soraya stood by while the others stoned him? Had she not, tentatively, then harder, thrown sharp stones? If it had not happened why did he remember it? He couldn't be sure, as in his body he could not tell which was the pain from the bullet and which from the sun.

Ibrahim was very thirsty, smelling the spring at the doum palms, but in the darkness unable to come in because of Warwar. If the young fool's still there I must kill him quickly and drink. I must not take pity on him as I have been thinking. If he came with a knife it was to kill me. Unless he had been with the white-woman. I must kill him just for that, for mixing flesh.

But he's young, and wild because he had no father, and now his only brother's dead. How much better, years ago, for the clan to be his father. Then none of this would have happened. In my pride and love for my own sons and those who are my dead brother's, could I not have given some to him? And now I think he flees because he's guilty, when perhaps he's only injured and afraid. If he calls openly to me I won't kill him but will first speak: he who has strayed furthest from the clan must be most welcomed back.

Deepest night, when the leopard hunts, the time of greatest danger. Don't be weakened by thinking. Ibrahim turned south, up the black shoulder of the mountain, intending to approach the doum palms from above.

Warwar walked until he could walk no more and nestled himself in the rocks. In the night, with no blood trail, Ibrahim could not follow. Gratefully he sank back among the cool, soft rocks, the dagger in his hand, and tumbled into sleep.

When Ibrahim neared the doum palms he listened for a long time, hearing only the hum of insects round the spring, the whisper of wings overhead as two tambourine doves landed in the palms, cooing softly together, the minute rustle of sand disturbed by the wind between two rocks, the shifting of his homespun *djellabah* as he breathed. How sad to be here, in an alien land, hunting your own kind.

Before sunrise MacAdam checked the Somali camp but could find no sign of Rebecca or the other two Somalis. The dead man, like M'kele, had hardened in the form of his death, as if our last moments somehow define our posture for eternity. The two camels were very irritable from hunger and drank avidly when he brought them a little water. Near them he found a large lion skin busy with scorpions, and in the camels' panniers two Nikons, magnifying glasses and a worn leather case containing an assortment of archaeological brushes and probes. Rebecca's wide flat sneaker tracks marked the sand by the extinct fire. He wanted to force the Somali to say where she was and had to keep reminding himself the man was dead. Either the other two had taken her or – he would not think of an alternative. He stood where

the dead man lay and looked out over the desert beginning to yellow now with first day, the body of M'kele a
tiny clump far down the slope, the wind from the south
damp and fragrant.

A movement out on the plain caught his eye and his
heart leaped, but it was just a string of hyaenas come to
share the feast; he went down and covered M'kele's
body with heavy stones while the hyaenas sat expectantly, ears perked, out of range.

Now it was light enough and he returned to the camp,
descended the water hole, filled all four canteens, and
put them in his backpack. Keeping M'kele's rifle, he
again circled camp until he found Warwar's trail of
blood and Ibrahim's tracks following it north. He pursued them a short way then returned to camp and continued circling, almost missing the wind-muddled traces
of Rebecca's sneakers leading downslope and west, the
prints of the limping Somali atop them.

He saddled the female camel, tied M'kele's rifle and
his own backpack to her saddle, set the male free, and
tugged the unwilling female by the halter rope along
Rebecca's tracks. The male ran snorting in circles round
him and the female, obscuring Rebecca's trail, charging
and baring his teeth at this strange person suddenly in
command of his heifer. Without guilt MacAdam shot
him in the head, the camel sitting shocked then flopping
over as the rifle's echoes brayed up and down the hills.

The she-camel sniffed the dead male, pulling back
her upper lip, and, keeping her head down, followed
MacAdam. Beneath a precipice MacAdam saw the
limping Somali's tracks coming back, knelt and sifted

the sand, trying to invent an explanation other than that he'd killed her and now was returning.

When he reached the precipice she had climbed he tied up the camel and followed her, knowing at the top he'd find her body scavenged by hyaenas among the rocks where the Somali had shot her – scraps of flesh, bloody clothing scattered by the wind.

Under the overhang a thread of golden hair twisted in the wind; he took it in his lips and held it there as he climbed, till the slope eased and he put the hair in his breast pocket. Without hope he went higher but there was no sign or track of Rebecca; he climbed back down, tried a side-sloping ledge, and found at its steepening edge the two solid imprints of her sneakers side by side in the dust.

At the bottom of the cliff he could find no sign that she'd descended. Again he climbed the cliff and searched in widening circles far above it, but there was no trace or smell of death, nor could he find her tracks. Even if a lion had carried her off there would be blood, even if the jackals had licked it off the rocks something would be left, if only their scattered, deep-clawed prints.

A malachite sunbird alit twittering on a desert rose, its feathers iridescent in the rising sun against the rose bush's round red flowers. Warwar threw a stone but missed, the bird darting off in an emerald flash; on the bush a gout of sap appeared where the stone had cut the thin bark. After a moment's thought Warwar crawled to the bush, found a sharp rock, and began to make parallel gashes up and down its trunk.

When the pus-like sap had filled all the gashes he gingerly collected it on the rock and, watching for Ibrahim, returned to the spring between the doum palms. Ibrahim's tracks were everywhere, and the imprint of his knees in the sand beside the tiny pool, together with the tracks of a lion and two gazelles that had drunk this morning. Warwar knelt also and drank as deeply as he could, then stirred the poisonous sap into the water. Suddenly he was thirsty again. He glanced round as if to locate another spring and saw a small white shape, descending the mountain, that could only be Ibrahim.

He waited until Ibrahim was close enough to see him but was still beyond range, then hobbled on his frond-wrapped feet away from the doum palms at an angle so that Ibrahim would pass by the water in pursuing him. But Ibrahim swung east to avoid a *wadi* and passed by the palms without drinking. His voice, tiny and sharpened by the dry air, bounced over the rocks. Warwar halted.

Ibrahim stood at the foot of the *wadi*, put down his rifle, and waved both arms over his head; his widening cloak, at this distance, made him look like a *namaqua* dove settling to earth. Leaving his rifle, he began to walk towards Warwar, gesturing and calling.

Warwar looked down at his naked body for a place to hide the knife. Hurriedly he knelt, partially unwrapped the palm fronds round his feet, laid the dagger against the strip of skin and muscle which was all that held his shattered left arm, and awkwardly lashed the fronds round it, holding their ends with his teeth, then tying them off till they completely covered the knife. The pain made him nearly unconscious and again he felt very thirsty.

Ibrahim was nearer. 'Yes?' Warwar called, his voice sounding peaked as an old woman's.

'Come closer. I have no gun.'

Warwar tried to imagine where Ibrahim could have hidden a second gun: the first stood propped against a rock at the foot of the distant *wadi*; truly Ibrahim had carried only one. There was no way he, Warwar, could reach it before Ibrahim, yet if Ibrahim returned for it Warwar could easily escape beyond range. A chill wind cut his face; he glanced at the sky: tall, puffy cumuli tinged with grey had collected over the eastern peaks.

'Are you hurt?' Ibrahim cried.

'Not badly.'

'Come – let me see.'

Warwar eased nearer. 'Why did you shoot me?'

The wind grew stronger, driving pebbles before it, making him tremble. 'What did you wish to do with your knife?' Ibrahim answered, close enough now Warwar could see his jagged, pockmarked face.

'I felt impure, and had gone to wash with a little water from the well. There was a noise – I went past you to see it – the whitewoman it must have been. Then you shot me and I ran.'

'I think you were coming to kill me.'

'I'm not the Devil's child. Why would I kill in my clan?'

'There are many reasons, perhaps—'

'Any one of us could kill the others with his rifle – if

I'd wanted to do such a horrible thing that's the only way to do it.'

Ibrahim watched him, *djellabah* tugged by the cold wind. 'Where is your knife?'

'Lost when you shot me.'

'How is thy arm, then?'

Warwar could not still his shivering. 'It's broken, but I've splinted it. I must get out of the sun.'

'We'll go back to camp. Rashid must be afraid for us.'

'You won't shoot me?'

'I was sad that you tried to attack me. Now I under-stand you did not and my faith in you is healed. Come, we will go together as father and son. In camp I'll try to heal your arm.' He raised his cloaked arm in welcome, like a bird's wing, Warwar thought, making him feel cold and bitter.

Ibrahim returned, keeping ahead of Warwar, to the doum palms. Their shade was chilly; the wind gnawed Warwar's aching arm. 'Stay here – I'll go for my gun,' Ibrahim said.

'You do not drink, cousin?'

'Nay – I'm full from this morning – but thee?'

'I too.' Half-hidden by a palm trunk, Warwar began to unwrap the fronds round his broken arm, hiding the knife among the fronds on the ground beside him. 'I must rewrap the arm.'

Ibrahim edged closer. 'First you must wash it.'

'Yes. Help me, cousin.'

Ibrahim knelt before him and carefully untied the last frond biting into the swollen black flesh. It's like he's praying, Warwar thought, leaning his good hand back for support on the ground among the discarded fronds. Ibrahim tipped forward, rebalanced himself and Warwar drove the blade deep into Ibrahim's extended throat, yanked down and squirmed aside as Ibrahim fell, choking, stumbled wide-eyed to his feet, clenching his disgorged throat in both hands, blood spurting. He leaped at Warwar, fell on one knee, stood and, arms agape, plunged face down on the rocks. Warwar backed away, the blade dribbling down his leg. The earth darkened; the sun was gone. A coal-coloured wind agitated the palm leaves; fat black clouds half-covered the sky. Warwar looked down sympathetically at Ibrahim's corpse. 'You should not have shot me for no reason.'

He went to the *wadi* for Ibrahim's rifle, came back and removed Ibrahim's *djellabah* and sandals and rubbed off the blood with sand. He took Ibrahim's damp wrist and dragged his naked corpse into the brush. 'I was naked and you were clothed. See how Allah has punished you: for you are naked now and I am clothed!'

From the pouch of Ibrahim's *djellabah* he removed a bow with a string of camel gut, a plaque of baobab and a rod of *geb*. Even doing this gave him terror, but there was no other way. To make himself brave he looked into Soraya's eyes. 'Do it or you'll die,' she said. 'There is no other way.'

With the plaque pinned under a rock on one side and under his foot on the other, he pushed the rod vertically down on it with his chin, shoved palmfrond shreds around it and began to spin it back and forth into the plaque with the camel-gut bow. The rod kept slipping from under his chin, making him lose balance and jerk his smashed arm; finally a thread of smoke began to coil up from the fronds, making him spin harder, till a tiny coal appeared. But he blew too hard and the fronds scattered. Weeping he collected them, spun the bow furiously; the fire started and this time he blew more carefully, till he could add more fronds, then chunks of bark.

When the fire was burning steadily he placed Ibrahim's *simi* in the flames until it grew red. Keeping Soraya's eyes locked on his, and clamping a stick between his teeth to keep from screaming, he laid the *simi* against the wound, shrieking as the black flesh sizzled. Do this or die. Do it or Soraya will marry someone else when she'd rather be with me. Make me do it, Soraya. He drove the blade through the open fracture and sliced round it, sinews popping and new blood welling out to hiss on the steel as he jerked the *simi* to pry the broken bone apart. Screaming he bit through the stick as the arm swung by a flap of underskin that parted and he fell back, convulsed, not knowing time or place or self.

# Chapter 30

Wind whistled in the grey thorn trees, chilling her bones. The sky sank down over the peaks; a flock of swifts blew by chittering, flailed by the wind that cut through her torn shirt. 'This one's the best!' her father said, handed her down a yellow rose, 'What perfume!' A rose thorn caught in his cardigan and he tugged it carefully free.

Night must be coming, for it to be so dark. She must find a place to hide. No trees here, no cliffs. No water. Tomorrow she must go back to the water hole, or die. She inhaled a rose – 'No, *papa*, this one's better.' This one here by the château wall on the bank of the Seine – 'like lemons and honey!' A great beast roared out of the sky – the anger of a God making her crouch instinctively – '*Mais c'est quoi, papa?*' He pointed the yellow rose at a black spot hurtling across the sky, '*Ce n'est qu'un Mirage!*'

Again the great beast roared out of the sky and she fell down in fear; it flashed the desert white then dark again, images of scrub and rock seared by the lightning so she still saw them when they were gone; thunder hammered through the hills and reverberated rumbling and dying out in dark silence, but in its after-image there'd been something – a distant figure, camel – Death on a camel following her trail. The wind quickened, spraying sand and skipping rocks and pebbles over the lava. A thorn bush genuflected before it, tried to stand, bent again. It *was* a tiny camel and rider, negotiating now a split steep monolith where she'd rested, when? This morning? Then what had happened to this day, that she'd come so short a way? How had Death found her trail?

On the bare black desert there was nowhere to hide. Wind screamed in her ears and yanked her hair; she ached to fall down, die, be blown away like the scraps of acacia the wind banged into her face, the branches cavorting helter-skelter through blowing sand.

Like stones the first heavy raindrops shattered on the rocks; she faced up opening her mouth; one hit her nose and she licked its spray; one smacked painfully into her eye and she cried out, bent forward with hands over her eyes, rain whacking the back of her neck. When she looked again she could not see Death and, covering her eyes, raised her mouth to the rain, lying against a concave rock to drink it in. A tongue of fire split the sky; thunder crushed the earth and the rain crashed down, pummelling her shoulders, knocking her down but she got up and ran, for now the rain would hide her tracks and Death might not find her.

Warwar twisted his body this way and that but could not escape the stinging stones. Everywhere they struck blood welled; even Sfey and Biou, even crippled Jisha, hurled sharp rocks, even Soraya, the veil tumbling from her eyes. Wakened by his screams he sat up stunned; lightning sank forked roots into the earth; the people of El God God were gone, their stones but the hail roaring down in hard white chunks, his blood only the rain.

Rain and hail made the lava slippery and she kept falling on its knife-edges, blindly stumbled through the opaque pelting curtain as if beneath the sea. She looked back, hands like a visor over her face; the rain cascaded off them in a rippling glassy sheet through which even the nearest rocks were barely visible. Louder than the rumbling rain a hoof struck stone. Death rode out of the mist almost atop her, his camel bolting. Death leaped from his camel yelling her name, she ran but he caught her, speaking words she knew but couldn't understand; his hand swam through walls of rain and bit her shoulder and she sank down saying do with me what you will. Death kissed her with cold lips, his beard like sharp sand, his arms like steel bands around her. She felt her heart fluttering against his chest, his rough face snagging her hair. He *needs* something, she thought. Death needs us all. Unafraid she looked into his eyes and saw it was MacAdam.

'You're alive, you're alive!' he kept saying, holding her too tight, but she knew it wasn't true, Death's reassurance, this man who had been hers and now that she was dying dreamt him. And as he wasn't real she finally could tell him what she never would have said, how every day she'd missed him, wiping a dish to put on a shelf or patting down a child's errant hair or raising up a petrified bone to see it in the light, or suddenly awake at night, and he always her first thought – the void I made by sending you away, and what I did is the opposite of pregnancy – put an emptiness inside and let it grow, and now it's come to term. And now I'm dead I'm with you.

MacAdam made her sit beside him on a lava headstone, and from his camel's saddle brought a folded cape and spread it round her shoulders, but she saw it was *their* goatskin and tried to throw it off. 'They're gone now,' he said, above the roaring rain. 'We're going back to Nairobi.' Little by little she let herself believe, it's truly you, Ian, out of the desert, as he told her of the plane's broken cylinder rod and the camels not ready at North Horr, the days of tracking over the desert, M'kele beneath his pile of stones at the water hole on Selach mountain.

To him every thing was sacred – her lips, the look in her eyes, her wet brow and tousled hair, her cold fingers linked to his. It's not fair, M'kele. I would not take her in return for your death. I wish it had been me, but you're dead, dear M'kele, and I can't help that though I caused it.

The rain grew listless, drained away. The sun beat down and the water rose back up from the rocks in gauzy sparkling will-o'-the-wisps, as if it had been lent and now must be returned.

When the rain ceased Warwar crawled from his shelter of rocks into the sudden sun. Every stone glistened with new life; he felt washed clean. Every soul, the Prophet said, shall taste death. Dying we awaken, see life was a dream, happy in paradise to see life's gone, that anguished hunger. He noticed the spring between the doum palms – with fresh water on its surface how innocent it seemed. Was he also innocent on the skin yet still poisoned beneath? Or was he like the grass that after five years without rain would now burst up between the stones to make the camels heavy with young, and increase the wild herds so that even the lion brought new young into the world?

He stood unsteadily, the new world wavering. His shattered arm ached unbearably and he reached to hold it with his left and saw it was not there, remembered that he'd cut it off, saw that he had not died, and sank weeping to the ground.

The air was very sharp and MacAdam could see all the way down the Selach Hills into the Sidamo desert, a thorn tree thirty miles away diamond-etched against a tawny slope, and beyond down into the shadowed Kaka Qagala and off the horizon, beyond the Kenya boundary to the endless Chalbi. The far bronze cliffs and agate canyons glowed; each bead of sand sparkled like new loam. The breeze tasted of a thousand joys. One by one and then together the birds chanted, warbled, whistled, and cooed, like a rare desert plant bursting into life after the rain.

Steam rose from the camel's pungent fur. He untied his backpack from the saddle and took out her clothes he'd put there so long ago, before M'kele had died, back at the Land Rovers, and now M'kele's dead and I have to tell Nehemiah. Feeling like a voyeur he gave them to her, then turned his back, tightening the camel's saddle, not to see her put them on. This is foolish, he thought, turning towards her but she was dressed, the clothes too white, too large yet insufficient; she gave a grimace-smile, shocking him with remembrance: the face making a resemblance of pleasure while the teeth show distaste and the eyes pain. Seeing death's rictus again on M'kele's face he wanted to sit down, bury his face in his hands. So many hours across the desert thinking constantly of you, Rebecca, praying for you, expecting you dead, but I would not give up M'kele to have you here. Months and years when never passed a day I didn't think of you, hardly an hour, and now you sit on a lava chunk, hands pressed between your knees, a scrap of wind in your hair. And yet I couldn't prefer you to M'kele, don't have the right, can't have you now because I lost him.

'Your friend who died,' she said. 'I wish you hadn't come.'

'He was Nehemiah's uncle.' He realized Rebecca was not Dottie, would not know Nehemiah.

'If I'd only known it was you, coming this way, yesterday. . . It isn't worth it, what you've done.'

'It's done now. He would have said it was his job.' He looked down, saw the sands, a billion little tongues of truth. 'No, he never would've given up his life, like this.'

'Then we took it from him. Stole it.' She looked away, that way of hers of staring out over nothing, planning a desertion. 'When will we meet your men?'

'They must've turned back at the border. Ministry orders. Anyway, we have to go back to the water hole, up there.'

'But if *they've* come back?'

'The kid's injured and the other's chasing him. Odds are they're far away and the kid's dead.'

'His name was Warwar.'

'The one who shot everyone?'

She looked down and he felt sad, for her.

'How badly was he hurt?' she said.

'Arm or shoulder. Those must have been the shots you heard when you escaped.' His voice belonged to someone who cared about casualties and targets, who thought he *wanted* to go back, the me she hates – the dull provider, the military mind working things out. 'From the water hole we'll head round Gamud peak to the Addis road at Faille, and get a truck to Kenya.'

Warwar leaned against a doum palm and lapped the last trickles running down its trunk. His body was cooler, free from fever, since he'd cut off the arm; he felt light and off-centred. Having only one arm will make me a brave man in the eyes of the clan – did I not survive the whites' bullets and live, while Ibrahim, nearly an elder, died?

Ibrahim, now rendered into splinters by hyaenas – all but his blackened skull jawless on the sand, eye sockets gaping in dismay. Even my arm they've carried off, snarling and snapping among themselves.

But I can't return to the clan until I kill Rashid, for he'll want to find Ibrahim's body, will ruin everything.

And Rashid has the whitewoman. I must stop him before he kills her.

# Chapter 31

Before dark they found an overhanging shelf of rock against which to light a fire that could not be seen, and nearby acacia scrub with buds of new growth for the camel to browse. There was a little water left in one canteen to mix with the maize meal from M'kele's pack and cook *ugali* that they ate in handfuls without waiting for it to cool. 'Tomorrow I'll shoot us something.'

'I've been dreaming of a francolin – roasted on a stick.'

'Sure.' He hadn't seen a francolin since North Horr. Even doves would do.

She leaned against him, her hands under his arms and round his back, speaking into the warm corner of his neck. 'If I'd had more courage I never would've left you. Then all this never would've happened.'

It gave him pain to think of all the years he could have wakened each day beside her. 'It was harder, stopping us like you did.'

'I was going to live without you; that was that. But it's like a stream, you cover it over and it just flows underneath, and everything you build on top caves in . . . And you dry up, you're nothing.'

He tried to see over her head, watch the sunset-orange desert. Already, she thought, I'm losing him. 'That's why in a way it didn't matter, with the Somalis.'

'You had the kids, Klaus.' It did not irritate him, he noticed, to say this.

'The kids were *my* excuse, remember?'

'I always thought it was ironic – that I'd tried to show you the joy of life, the purpose, when all along you'd had a deep purpose of your own, one you never shared with anybody.'

'Rubbish.'

'I who had nothing, bringing you my gift of nothing because you weren't content with what you had . . .'

'You're over-dramatizing.'

'No, I've thought a lot about it, in the desert. Since M'kele died. Funny how you never know how close you are till someone dies. Same way I felt when I was tracking you.'

A hyaena called, out on the desert, making the tethered camel hiss with fear, and in the firelight he saw her shoulders rise in repugnance. Why couldn't she see killing and love are one, that each demands the other? The camel lipping the new grass, the combretum root flaring on the coals, the dry wind's scents of dust and lava and its memory of rain, the voices of hyaenas, night birds, and the stars – death and life are two halves of the same truth – couldn't she see that?

'M'kele says we should get out of here. Watch for the Somalis and Borani, find water and get up to the Faille road and back to Kenya.'

'And when we get back to Kenya I'll keep doing research at the Museum and live with Klaus and you'll ranch on the Lerochi and we'll be shy with each other, every five years, when we meet.'

The sand felt loose beneath him, as if he might fall through. 'Your kids aren't a reason. Not that they ever were.'

'Klaus won't let them go.'

'He doesn't care.'

'He does when he might lose them. When he can use them.'

'No one's like that.'

'Klaus is. Nothing stands in his way.'

'Except danger.'

She shook her head, making him feel a child. 'That's not fair.'

'But true.'

Her palms felt small and cold on his face. 'You and I went through this so many times, and never reached an answer.'

'We never went through it far enough. All the way.'

'It never ends. I cried and cried and ached for you so hard I thought I'd break. I won't again.' She undid the buttons of his shirt, careful not to tug the fabric. 'As soon as we have water I'll clean this – it's so infected.'

'It'll wait.' He caressed her hair back down into her collar, took his rifle to scout the perimeter of camp in a silent radius of a hundred yards, then back to check on her and out again, further now, crouching and watching, bent low and slipping soundless between the rocks, sheltered in the shadow of a basalt boulder where a sagey herb grew in a little dark crevice. Dig deep here and there's water, he thought, memorizing the place. A slimmer moon was trying to climb Gamud's southern slope, pricking out its detailed silhouette as of a ruined castle. Andromeda rode the peak, interrogating him. 'I'll watch her,' he promised. 'She'll get back.' Something darker than the night passed below the peak. He thought of shooting to scare it off but held his fire.

'What did you see?' she said when he returned.

'Nothing.'

'Nothing kept you a long time.'

'I'd have rather been with you.' Hasn't that been true for years? He felt cross with himself for saying it. But you bring it out in me, Rebecca, love and the refusal to lie about it. As the firelight brushed her hair, her cheekbone shadowed, he saw written on her face a harsh docility that would turn from any man she loved. In her hunger to be free she'd always be alone.

He watched her pulling at a strand of tangled hair, caught in herself. Right at the start, Rebecca, I learned you make *me* free because I desire you so, to be with you, so much I can't ignore it, *have* to be the way I am. And the more I become who I am, with my harsh incessant striving, the more you, fearful of your freedom, recoil. He felt a surge of anger and frustration.

'It's like I'm lost,' she said. 'And they're calling me.'

'Who?'

'The hyaenas.' She spoke as if he should have known, drawing the goatskin around him so it covered both their shoulders. 'They know some day they'll have us.

But they don't know when. So they keep calling, hoping it comes soon.'

'They've talked about us, decided to wait till tomorrow to see if one of us dies.'

'They always know, the Maasai say.'

'They're great optimists.'

'All scavengers are.'

The wind shifted; like water, he thought, flowing round us.

'On my way to the *geb* tree the hyaenas kept following. They never attacked but I couldn't stop imagining what it'd be like, eaten alive.'

'They start with your legs.' He snatched her thigh, fingers like teeth.

'Don't!' His hand inside her thigh made her mouth go dry. *He doesn't know what I'm thinking. I don't care if this happens. Oh yes I do.* Her fingers touched his leg. 'What about Dottie?'

'She'd rather have England than me. I love my kids, too, but that doesn't make me want to be with them.'

'But you'd take mine?'

'I'd take your kids to be with you. That's a fair trade.'

'A she-camel and two calves.'

'But I'd have to see how you ride. See if you kick, and check your teeth.'

'I'm thirty-four. You don't need to check my teeth to know that.' *How wonderful to kiss him, the soft rasp of his beard making electricity inside her. Like* it *would feel coming in. It's been so long;* she could not stop her hand from rising up his thigh. 'You aren't afraid someone'll see?'

The feel of him beneath the khaki was too big for her hand, made her wrist, her body ache. Swollen in her hand, it belonged to her. That had been lost. She kept holding and squeezing it and his lips roughed hers, his tongue in her throat hot like *it* would be, and now it was free of his clothes and she could hold it in her hand all the way around warm and hard but everything was in the way. She was pulling down quickly the clean underwear he'd brought and the earth was sharp under her but she kept holding it lifting her body to him so *it* could fit inside, it was *there* now, splitting her, slow, go slowly God go slowly and yet come quickly, lacking for so long, and already it was happening, the coming, making her so hot and wet inside that he slid in faster, pushing her apart, filling and completing, and again she came, sharp as a sword the pleasure driving up inside her and he kept forcing her open so far inside there was no end to it, all the way filled up making her think of bullfighters only they live their lives all the way up Hemingway said, hard like a rock inside her, it *was* hers now and this time she'd never give it up, never give *him* up, how could she, his scratchy hair butting hers and the thick round warmth of his balls ramming her and she came again, this time washing everywhere in waves and never is dispersed and yes, she prayed, make it always be like this.

This is all, he realized, all that counts, inside her, driving to completion, her whimpering an admission of so vast a truth it linked him to her for ever, her teeth against his neck, her breast in his hand and her belly wet to his, the pumping agonising joy that becomes the only and all truth, knowing he could hold it let it go, feeling it soar out into her, lift her, lift them till they were together and alone, where no one had ever been. Like God he looked down on the universe and saw that it was good, but less than this, and he felt sorry for poor God.

When they returned to where they'd been he was still hard inside her; she was so wet he could not feel her, only feel within her. How insane, to do anything but this, he thought, moving down to lick how wet and smelly hot she was, her come mixed with his, making his lips sticky and slippery that he rubbed against her lips and into the corner of her neck, making all of it smell good. He held her buttocks in his palms and then licked and licked gently and slow, rising, shoving, carving her with his tongue as her body arched and writhed and subsided and he came into her again, exploding at once, the way the stars die, and how can this be so much and suddenly be over? I'm free, he thought, alone, seeing the scar-faced Somali and M'kele, the lives he had to live for them.

The hyaenas had stopped calling. He slid his body from her, pulled up his trousers over his throbbing, aching penis that stuck damply to them, took up his rifle and scanned the night. 'I love you. More than the entire universe has ever loved.'

She lay with knees bent up, the cool air like another orgasm. She could open to the night, the world, take it all inside, be mistress and mother of it all. 'There is nothing but this.'

He knelt, caressed her, bringing her fingers to his lips.

'And there's lions and hyaenas and other enemies, and we're going to be very careful of them so we can live, and do this again and again and again and never stop. And almost never stop.'

He took the rifle up to sit beside the overhang, seeing and unseen, the tent of the stars unrolled down to the peaks around him, her scent stronger than the desert's on his body and his face. If the hyaenas had stopped calling there was danger. If the danger were the other two Somalis there was no way they could approach across the star-bright rock without his seeing them. If it were Darius and Gideon he'd hear their camels and his camel would whinny at theirs, but they hadn't come north of the border nor could they find them if they had.

There was a flicker of dark distant movement against a starlit rock; he caught it with the corner of his eye but by the time he turned his eyes it was gone. He watched the starlit rock for a long time but nothing moved near it.

After a while he stood and stretched, back muscles sore and tightening. His broken ribs were too painful, made it hard to breathe. He thought of the Cape buffalo in the Matthews Range crashing faster than a huge truck at him through the bamboo, its horn smashing his chest. Why, he wondered, didn't the poacher shoot me? Because I *wanted*. Now that I have what I wanted, what do I want?

Warwar too was attempting not to think of his pain as he lugged Ibrahim's heavy rifle along a flinty unvegetated reef of stone shouldering down from the mountain, its roughness blistering his feet through Ibrahim's worn sandals, that flipped loosely because they were too large and because one-handed he could not lace them properly. I'll have Rashid tie these before I kill him. If he doesn't know. But if he doesn't know, why kill him? But to rescue the whitewoman how can I help but kill him?

Thinking like this he tried to divert his pain, trying also to focus his thoughts on Soraya, but he could form no clear impression of her black eyes above the black veil, nor the outlines of her face he had seen openly in the years before the veil, nor her slender strong arm raising the bucket from the well. That will all come back after we're married, he decided. But then, why do I have to marry *her*? Did she not stand idly by while others stoned me? Did she not also throw sharp stones? There's Halia, Usuf's first daughter: who's to say I can't have her?

No matter how he tried, Soraya's features became Halia's, longer, more slender, the cartilage of her nose concave as bone. But Halia's skin was far too pale; she had the whitewoman's nose, Soraya too, and the whitewoman's frank abusive gesture of throwing back the look in your eyes although she doesn't love you. But after I rescue her from Rashid she'll have no choice but love me. I'll be her maker and she must love me for ever.

Rifle on his knee beneath the wheeling stars, MacAdam tried to stay awake; the camel huffed and snorted in her dreams; jackals were exchanging news along the distant ridges; thirst climbed steadily up his throat. He tasted his fingers heavy with her scent, loving the taste but not wanting to lose the smell of her by licking it. Thank you God for her. I will protect her, God, he promised, no matter what. I can live with both of them, her and Dottie. I have enough love in me for both. When you feel like this nothing can stand in your way.

At first light he would wake her to stand guard an hour while he slept. Just an hour would be paradise. Tomorrow night we could reach the water hole on Selach mountain – where she was before with them, but now she'll be with me. Then three more days to Faille.

No use to think about what will happen after Faille, not now with the stars losing their edge, the jackals quiet and dawn's first breeze rising with the odour of honey up the crevices and gullies. To *be* is all, not in sorrow or in joy but much more deeply, simply to breathe in and out the wonder of the coming day, so complete all sense of self is lost.

# Chapter 32

The sun like a vast low-lying thermonuclear explosion
seethed up over the east, melting the air, the stones, the
shrivelling, seared brush, the simmering sand. Of the
earth there was nothing but blackened ruins, broken
teeth of buttes and peaks and collapsed, charred canyons, shadows to mark the former existence of *things*,
like the human silhouettes printed on the ground after
Hiroshima.

Dust rose from the camel's hooves as if there'd never
been rain. Walking beside the camel, MacAdam tried
to keep his mind separate from the pain in his chest by
thinking that Rebecca must get home, he must not let
her down, that any movement in this land might be
Somalis. No matter how carefully he watched the rock
and scrub, the dry sky with its distant tinged cirrus and
lazy innocent spiral of two short-tailed bateleurs above
the crags, even if he saw every scurried trace of elephant
shrew's tiny splayed feet and string tail over the sand,
or the klipspringer's rear hoofprints shoved deep by a
fast, frightened leap, a burst of cut-throats chittering
with fear from the bush ahead – no matter how much

he saw he wouldn't see enough, for every moment can be death: the change of shadow on a stone, a trace of dust, a smell, a hint way back in the brain, the camel turning her head or raising her ears or slowing for one step. . . He carried the rifle only in his left hand now because of the broken ribs, watching ahead and behind and on all sides, near and far, reminding himself of the klipspringer who is never for a moment safe – a lion behind the thornbush, a leopard on a branch, cheetahs or hyaenas to run you down in shifts, a human's poisoned arrow or loud stick, a mamba, viper, cobra, or adder to kill you for coming near. Kill you any instant, night or day, while you eat or sleep or drink or mate or care for your children, as soon as you're tired or sick or unwise or for a moment unlucky or not totally attentive.

The camel undulated on, jerking Rebecca forward to the left, then backward to the right, on to the left, back to the right, like the trance dance of the Samburu, how they accentuate the prison of the flesh till they can break through it to a plane of pure perception, the loss of thought, the loss of want. Till they revive, she remembered, when this numinous state cannot be recovered.

She wondered what the camel thought of death, what it wanted: to get this human off its back, to have water, grass and brush to eat, the company of other camels, shade beside a stream beneath the tamarinds and date palms.

High above, a silver glimmer against the blue – the morning Air France from Nairobi. Paris in five hours. People up there having coffee and croissants and reading *Le Monde*. How far we've come from those first stories round the fire, about antelope herds, tubers, berries, of where the lion feeds and where he hunts us, the first words far back in our heads, this sharpening of brain and tool – for what?

Warwar became aware of El God God and the cracks of morning sun through the straw and brambles of his hut, the bleating of kids for their dams as night's coolness arises from the ground. But across the enormous shrivelled earth as far as he could see, to Mega's radiant peaks and the shimmering hardpan of the north, there was no hut nor calling kids, only the fire in his chopped arm, the awful thirst and dizzying heat inside him, the diffident company of hyaenas sitting on their haunches a hundred yards away, waiting for him to die.

Thirst was like a hook in his throat. It yanked him up, dragged him across the hot gravel, blocking his mouth, pulled him along the steep side of Gamud peak back the same way someone had once chased him with a gun, before he'd purged his evil, but he could not remember who or when that was.

Thirst made him keep looking back to check his way by the far angle of Mega's peaks, and as he did he saw how close the hyaenas had come, the nearest one's drool sparkling in the long corner of her jaw. He tried to shiver the rifle off his good shoulder but it wasn't there: he'd left it somewhere, gone on without it – and now the hyaenas knew. He stared disconsolately down the slope to where he'd left his rifle, but could not see it, could not remember where it was or was it back in El God God?

The hyaenas were too nervous as they circled – too near now – he turned back down the slope, holding his good arm up against its shoulder like a rifle, clasping his fingers like a barrel pointing to the sky.

Each rock looked the same; there were no tracks; he'd gone too low and climbed higher – no, this was too high; he descended then realized he'd always been too low; at each step the hyaenas came another closer; they've already had my arm, now they want the rest. His body seemed promised to them; he tried to think what they'd given him in exchange.

The rifle was between his feet; he'd almost missed it. He lifted it quickly to his shoulder and checked the breech to make sure the hyaenas had not unloaded it; glancing reproachfully over their shoulders they withdrew, regrouped, and followed from the rear.

Into MacAdam's mind sprang a medieval image of a servant leading his lady's horse by the halter, the lady in fine clothes, the servant in buckskin, and he laughed out loud, startling the camel. In the dream of going round the foot of the bed and stepping on the lion, would I have asked Rebecca what to do about the lion? he wondered. Never – instantly I would've known, acted without thinking. But once I'd lived a while with her I'd make her just like Dottie – someone to bounce things off of, someone to think for me. That's how I left Dottie, so long ago. That's why she drinks. Is she drinking now, does she need to, far north in London under the grim cold sky? Africa made her drink. Africa and I.

He'd left Dottie long before he knew Rebecca, ceased

to care all the way down. Rebecca was a symptom of the disease Dottie had perceived long before he had; like him she'd taken what medicine she could.

There'd been an oaken dowel in the medieval beam above his bed that as a boy he'd always tried to pull out but never could, a sailfish he'd killed fishing off Kilifi, its terrored eyes, the rainbows draining from its bloodied sides. We're always reaching for the mystery, he thought, but it will not submit, or fades to nothing in our hands.

# Chapter 33

At the foot of the long slope leading up to the water hole MacAdam halted and let the camel browse. He wanted to sit but the rocks were hotter than the sun now low in the west and coppering the peaks. Across the entire earth he could see no trace of man; yet in the countless crags and crannies a thousand men could hide. Water was how the desert would bring everyone together. The antelope's daily prayer, weighing the mortal need of water with the mortal danger of obtaining it.

She did not speak, seemed stunned and dislocated by the sun. He gave her M'kele's rifle. It felt like a bad omen and made him think of Nehemiah again. 'There's forty rounds in the magazine and one in the chamber. The mode selector's on semi, which means it fires every time you pull the trigger. I'll come back after dark. I'll call before I come in, so don't shoot me. If the Somalis come and you can't hide, shoot at them. That might keep them down till I get back. Any time you want me, fire four single shots a second apart. Stay over there, where that whistling thorn grows out of that lava slab.

Don't put the gun down where it can fall over and go off, hit you.'

'I won't shoot myself. Or you.'

He put the last half canteen down beside her, absurdly thinking how he used to hide the liquor bottles from Dottie. 'If you hear shots and I don't come back – or if I don't come back before dawn, ride straight north, to the left of Gamud peak then, keeping the peak behind you, with the sun on your right in the morning and the left in the evening, and at night with the Great Bear straight before you. Watch out for lions—'

'Not the Great Bear, the Pole Star.'

'That's how you find it.' He turned to the camel, rubbing the soft spot at the top of its nose and talking softly to it in Rendille and English, as if giving it instructions also. She felt deserted, that just as he turned his back now so he would some day betray her for the grave, by dying before her.

'Before we know it,' she said. 'We'll be in Nairobi.'

As he climbed the slope in the gathering dusk her words took on another meaning: if we die, the words could say, our bodies will be brought back to Nairobi before we know it. This made him try to be doubly cautious, but the fever of his wound mixed up his thoughts so that he had constantly to recall where he was and the danger everywhere, the thirst so great he had to hold himself back from running to the water hole, drinking just drinking no matter what, for he was sure the Somalis had departed – he'd killed the last one, the one who shot M'kele. This reminded him that M'kele had died because they'd been incautious and exhausted, and for a while he made himself lie watching, but saw no danger.

There was an evil, flatulent smell; ahead a pile of rocks rose in the gloom, and he circled wide to the right, thinking of M'kele buried there. She and I will smell like that too, he reminded himself, when we die. Unless the hyaenas and marabous pick us clean. Above the ravine he reached the main slope where he had shot Rashid. There was a different smell here, not the swollen putrescence of a body covered by stones and heated by sun, but sun-dried bones and scraps discarded by vultures, hyaenas, and jackals. Better to live on in them, some day scattered across the desert in their bones, living again in those that eat them, and on and on. As he thought this he was advancing silently to the crest above the water hole, seeing nothing, hearing nothing, smelling only the desiccated camel dung from before, and the entrancing overpowering odour of water that threatened to pull his body to it like a magnet, no matter how much he feared.

But he made himself watch till he was sure the hilltop was vacant beneath the new, bright stars, then crept to the water hole and lowered himself to the bottom, knelt and drank. He circled the area once more, still seeing nothing, and began his descent towards Rebecca.

As she sat by the whistling thorn, the strange, oil-smelling rifle beside her, the camel snoring softly, it occurred to her she'd always been alone like this. Maybe we're all always alone, she wondered, only reminded of our solitude by the occasional appearance of others, their mirages, but each time we begin to believe they're real we find ourselves even more utterly alone.

The way I've hungered, she decided, for a lost father in a man, but instead got sex and children and the slavery of the kitchen, when all I wanted was his dispassionate warmth, the linkage of our souls. But *needs* all separate our souls; like a fish rising to a lure maybe I was doomed by the flashing thing I thought would feed my hunger.

With a hiss of gravel a snake crossed the lava. Let him come, she thought. A shooting star darted over, lost itself in the blackness like the sound of the snake dying out among the lava pebbles. She felt the part of her soul taking over that would console her in the face of death.

But she'd been happy with *him*, cared about *him*, reassured him he'd return. Maybe she should drink some water. The idea of water was repugnant. The idea of having one personality, linked, was foolish; different selves began to swirl in her, rising and speaking, sinking and twirling on.

*There* – a sound. The camel heard it too. A lion, maybe hyaenas. The beast-child Warwar returning like a devoted lover. She took the cold, evil-smelling, heavy gun in her hand, a thumbnail absently scraping at a gout of blood hardened to the barrel. She placed the butt against her shoulder, the weight of the stock and barrel almost toppling her.

The sound was closer. If it's a lion and I fire he'll run away, or he'll be angry and charge. If it's Warwar he'll be warned and will sneak up on me and this time he'll put his knife into me and I'll be his for ever. She strained her eyes, seeing nothing but the great dark slope blanketed with stars. When he comes I'll kill him.

Wasn't there a story, once, of someone who killed her own son by mistake? Don't we do that giving birth? Do I want him back? How could Rebekah love Jacob more? Her hands, on the rifle, began to sweat.

Descending the slope MacAdam fought against the hope growing inside him. As he'd expected there'd been no Somalis at the water hole, and no sign they'd been there since the night he'd killed the one who'd shot M'kele. Night before last. This meant he and she could rest here tonight, drink their fill, water the camel, leave at first light. The cleft in the rocks above the water hole was easy to guard. The map showed a spring on the north side of Gamud peak; they'd fill the canteens again there, have enough water to reach Faille.

'*Faille*'s French for "flaw",' she'd said. 'Or geologic fault.'

'It's the only place we can reach. It's a Galla word.'

'Meaning what?'

'I don't know Galla.' I pray there's no flaw, he thought, I don't believe but I'm happy to pray anyway. I don't believe in anything because I've never found anything that's true, and now I see *that's* the only thing that's true. I'm happy now to realize nothing's true and that I've been faithful to that.

The rocks were crumbly going downhill, bounding ahead like hares out of his way. No worry for sounds now – the Somalis gone – no lions. If we're very smart and very careful perhaps we'll make it.

# Chapter 34

Warwar approached the water hole from uphill, the northeast, back the same way he now remembered fleeing Ibrahim. God sees what will happen with men though they do not, he reminded himself. Only God knew, when Ibrahim shot and then hunted his clansman Warwar, that two would leave the water hole but only one come back, that the naked martyr would return in the garments of his hunter. The victim conquers, for God is just: the proud and evil find an early grave in the bellies of hyaenas.

He watched above the water hole, eyes and muscles weak with thirst, but there was no sign of Rashid and the whitewoman, only a disassociated sense of death difficult to monitor on the downslope wind, that and the dried camel dung and old fire and here, near Warwar's feet, the place where Ibrahim must have spattered his drops of urine before lying down in his crevice in the rocks.

Yet the place was made evil by the sense of something he could not understand, a lacking, perhaps, the lacking of absence. Yes, the place was not as empty as it should be, the night avoids it – why? The scent of death – whose? Nothing that threatens now, he decided, holding up Ibrahim's cloak as he descended the last steep pitch and climbed down the hole to the water, fell to his knees, and gratefully sucked in its bitter, brackish warmth.

She aimed the rifle at the noise coming downhill. Waiting made her very thirsty and as soon as she killed this thing approaching she'd drink some water. She would not drink it all because if he came back and there was no water at the water hole or if *they* were there, he'd need it.

A rock crackled down and smacked against a boulder. He's trying to make noise, she told herself, so I won't shoot. 'Ian!' she started to call but held her breath. The camel nickered, its tether twanging as it strained its neck towards the sound. It can smell him. If it whinnies in fear then he's a lion or hyaena and I'll shoot. If it calls to him then he's a Somali and I also have to kill him. I'll miss and he'll kill me but I have to do it anyway.

'I'm coming in,' he called.

Her finger descended towards the trigger. Don't the Samburu teach that the lion will dress as a man and take his voice, talk himself inside the *manyatta*'s coil of thorns? The Devil says he's God and we believe him. Her finger found the trigger.

'Rebecca!' he called. 'It's me!'

'Yes, come!' If it's not *you*, you'll die.

Visible now, a shape against the darkness; her heart pounding made the rifle jerk up and down. I'm crazy, she told herself, there's too many of me. Some which love and some which hate and some which fear nothing at all. Kill him and I'll never be alone. 'Is that you, Ian?'

'Of course it's me! Who'd you think – Haile Selassie?'

She leaped to her feet, rushed forward, the rifle clattering, 'It's you!'

'Who else?' he laughed, his whiskers tickling as he kissed her, his arms binding her together. 'There's no one at the water hole – we're going. Where's the canteen? Quick! Drink up!'

Seeming to see perfectly in the dark he gathered up the other rifle and untied the camel and she took his hand and followed him up the slope down which she had fled from Rashid so many years ago, before the rain turned Death into MacAdam, before she had climbed the cliff and hid on the tiny ledge and Rashid had climbed past her, after the time Warwar had shot Milton and W'kwaeme and the others at the Land Rover, and the Somalis had taken her across the Chalbi, and she'd escaped and the little woman of the fossil jaw had led her to the *geb* tree where Warwar rescued her from the leopard, and the Borani took her to their village, to the hut of the hooded man whose neck she'd branded, whom Warwar killed as he slept, Warwar who then brought her water, walking faithfully beside her camel up to this water hole where he climbed down to get her more water and Ibrahim struck him with a rock and now Ian says Ibrahim has shot and hunted Warwar, and her body felt warm and sad but she thought don't care.

There was no feeling but a numb joy, as after love – when, she wondered, did I have love? Sex fills me up and afterwards I'm twice as empty – the emptiness I had

309

before and now the new emptiness of his absence inside me. '*Merisio ereposhi o eseriani*' – don't the Maasai say that? 'Being full and safety are two very different things.' Why should I go home with *him* and grow old with *him* when everything will be the same?

But how can I measure with no measure but myself? When every other measure I would use is measured by me? Above her a mass of rhyolite loomed like a sleeping camel against the rocky, naked slope. Here I tried to find shade but could not. It was noon and there was no shade anywhere.


Warwar awoke in his sleeping place on the side of Gamud, throat afire with thirst. For a time he convinced himself to lie still, not climb back down to the water hole in darkness, prey to lion, leopard, hyaenas, or Rashid, but then it came to him simply that death was better than such thirst, so he took the rifle and started down towards the water hole. Trusting to the dissuasive threat of his noise and the final deterrent of the gun he walked quickly, scrutinizing the scrub for movement, the wind pushing at his back.

Life's to kill and be killed, he remembered Ibrahim would say; he of little caution lives few years. But there comes a time you no longer care, you've so long been careful this time surely you'll be lucky – it did not matter this time if he finally gave in, ran towards it, let his body overrule his soul.


After MacAdam and Rebecca had drunk their fill he'd lit a fire and hitched up the camel in the little gully leading to the water hole. She sat on drawn-up legs, half-sideways, one hand on the ground, the other curved in her lap; he liked her way of looking down as she spoke, of hiding things and not speaking of them unless he probed. But each claim of common experience he made only caused her to draw back, as if her self was far too nascent still to share, or even she did not yet dare to know herself. It's not that, he decided. The illusion of love must be accepted by both people, or it soon comes to grief.

Thinking this made him hunger for her again, the ache so long instilled, but crazy now, with all this danger. And you're a fool to try to penetrate the mystery, he told himself, *pin* it down, convince yourself a moment is for ever. You've always hated the unseeing people crouched over games of chance and profit in some dim corner of life's bazaar, counting up their markers while life goes on all round them in multicoloured splendour. But how different have you been, savaging all illusions but your own?

When you were with Rebecca before, you knew you'd never have her, that she'd never leave the satisfying solitude of a failed marriage to give herself to anyone. She as much as Klaus was architect of what they had. And you had Dottie: someone you loved and who loved you but you wore each other down, deadened each other. You forsook Dottie by putting Africa ahead of *her*, and she withdrew the only way she could.

Then why live with either? he thought, looking at her, at Dottie in her. They wear us down, domesticate us like our sheep. It's our prick and loneliness that draw our claws, they and the errant inexplicable need to love. The poacher in the Matthews Range *spared* me and I didn't shoot him later, on the ridge, but M'kele did and now M'kele's dead and I killed his killer, and if killing's so inseparable from love I have no need of either.

This he thought between the seconds, while seeing her and hearing her voice and thinking about her words and thoughts, and listening for hyaenas or a change in the wind or in the pattern of the camel's breathing, a nervous clack of hoof, while he was tasting the wind for the smell of danger, reaching out a hand from time to time to check the G–3 beside him, its black barrel shroud shimmering with starlight and the fire's votive glimmer.

If there's nothing to believe in where do joy and beauty come from? This sense of harmony, everything fitting, of not being apart?

If everything that lives feels, why kill? He started in surprise, looked round to see who'd lifted the cloak from his shoulders. But there was no cloak and no one there to lift it, and he shivered, drawing in his shoulders. With a ripping of brush and grating of teeth the camel resumed eating; far to the north a jackal had wailed. MacAdam's heart reached out towards the jackal squatting on the hard earth, his muzzle raised to call across the dangerous night for a voice like his. Wish he could be like me, safe and warm with another of his kind.

# Chapter 35

It came before Warwar saw or heard – the smell of camel: Rashid and the whitewoman! He halted, mouth agape with thirst.

When there was no sign of Rashid he crept closer, till he could see a camel's hump against the starlit rocks. The female: now he could smell her but could not smell or see the male. He decided perhaps he was grazing lower, or further west, beyond the wind.

Staying east he circled the camel till he could now smell the smouldering dung and twigs of Rashid's fire. But Rashid would not light a fire unless he's killed something to eat, yet there's no smell of meat or any food. Maybe he's going to cook it or maybe he has the fire because he fears a lion. Or has he lit the fire to watch the whitewoman? To strip her clothes and use her, even this instant? Or is she dead, when I vowed to protect her?

He tried to swallow down his thirst but could not, remembering the well at El God God shrouded in its grove of tamarinds, *geb, guider, quadi*, and desert dates. Water transparent and smooth as a dawn breeze, soft

313

as woman's skin, jewelled like mica cold out of the cold centre of the earth. Cold slaking this thirst. The villagers all stoned me, Soraya too, her eyes taunting me through her slitted veil.

Thinking of her sons, Rebecca half heard the camel nicker as MacAdam went to check it, the nervous stamp of its hooves, its wanting to be free. Her children were a dream she was unable to recall, but she saw how her distractedness had for years driven her from the older one, he with his father's judicious surface, how she had treated him with a distant tension while believing she loved him intensely, how her tension and rejection had blocked closeness with the younger boy, except at moments when he forgave her. If only, she thought, I could be with them as I *feel*.

'What's got you nervous?' MacAdam said to the camel in Rendille, laughing at himself, for as this was a Somali camel how should she know Rendille? 'It's just the tongue I've learned for your kind,' he continued, but the camel would not listen, straining at her halter and shifting her hooves on the scratchy corroded lava. She shoved her bristly jaw at him, sniffed his breath to see if he were fearing also, then shrugged away, impatient with this whiteman too dull and insensate to scent what anyone could scent.

'Ah – it's lion? Coming in from the north? Worry not, my pretty, he won't come in on us here, not with the gun and fire, not unless it's a big male and he's old and very hungry.' He scratched behind her ears but she snatched her head away, pawed the rock, jerked her halter. He took up the gun. 'I'll go see, my pretty,' What will I do with you, he wondered, when we reach Faille?

The great bowl of the stars was redolent with fragrances of brush, cooling stone, and wind from the peak. His hands on the rifle smelt of the camel's fur – if it's a lion he'll come in on me, MacAdam decided, thinking I'm a camel. I'm getting scared, seeing danger behind every rock now I've something to live for. If it's lion I'll shoot above him and he'll run, he's not a fool, to have survived up here. No reason to kill him.

What's that – flicker of motion against that distant slaty lava slope, a ripple of starlight brighter than the earth? Why would he try to approach across the shale? The world silent, nothing but the change in the character of one boulder among many, a hundred yards away. The lion moving east to circle us downwind, study our scents. If he's old he should know better than to cross the scree. There was nothing but the cool feel of rocks as MacAdam settled down among them, nothing but the sense of where, from the corner of one eye, he'd seen the movement of the lion.

In the silence of the desert night the lion could be many things; MacAdam knocked on his rifle stock then realized, that's silly, it's not wood, but high-grade plastic from some German factory, How strange that now my life depends on a weapon made in the land that killed my father – how the killing goes round and round and never stops, new alliances, new enemies, always thinking now we know who's right, who's wrong. . . This gun fabricated perhaps by a survivor of the Falaise pocket, where four hundred thousand frightened German boys sought a way out of the Allied massacre, taking with them at Fourneaux Woods fourteen soldiers of the South Wales Borderers, including a burly cheerful moustached lieutenant named Aubrey MacAdam, he, my mother said, who always used to knock on wood. My father only lived to twenty-seven, twenty years younger than I am now, yet I always think of him as older, wiser. What would he do, here? Would he have chosen to be here at all?

It was difficult for Warwar to squirm one-armed among the rocks, with Ibrahim's rifle like a prison ball chained to his one hand, with his thirst making him dizzy and weak, making the stars and rocks dance and confusing his sense of smell.

He would tell Rashid that he and Ibrahim had surprised a Galla trying to steal the camels. We chased him all night and the next day then that evening the Borani ambushed us by the spring of the two doum palms. I finally killed them all and then cut off this shattered arm, but Ibrahim was killed. That will give me a few days to get better, when Rashid can heal me, before I have to shoot him. Or I can lead him to the doum palms and let him drink the water.

Before him Warwar saw a clear chute of scree, with no cover. The black stone at night scintillated like flint, reminding him of death, his death, which could come soon now if Rashid shot him, if there was a lion. When I am paid my wages on the day of Resurrection, Warwar thought, how much will they be? Will I be removed from the fire? What if there is no fire, no wages, just nothing? How can nothing *be*, when by its very nature it *is not*?

Impossible to cross the scree chute without being seen, if Rashid's sitting guard. With his anxious nature he would be. Why did he never come to help us when the Borani ambushed us at the doum palms? He stayed here, mating with my whitewoman. That's reason alone to kill him.

MacAdam watched the boulder that had moved, and all around, and everything between it and the scree, but nothing changed. If the lion's coming he's stopped to analyse the scree. If he turned around he could circle camp and come upwind from the ravine. Or west across the wind, once he's circled to check us from below.

If the lion was waiting to cross above the scree that would be the best time to shoot over his back and scare him. Even though that would scare *her*. But I've been gone too long already. She's already scared.

If the lion's circling to come upwind he'll reach her first. But if he crosses the scree this is the only place to stop him. Till that last quick charge when he won't be scared off.

The wind hit MacAdam's right cheek – it had shifted east of Gamud peak. Now if I swing further west I might pick up his scent. If he's still there. And if he's not there that means he's circled and will be coming upwind to camp. She and I'll back up against the rocks and he'll come from wherever he wants to and I'll have to shoot him.

\* \* \*

If Ian would come back now, she pleaded. I need him. I'll admit that now, I need him. If he'll just come back now I'll tell him how much I've loved him, heartbroken, all these years, that every day I've missed him, his tense smile, his grey eyes so sadly shocked by life. That he bears it all up. That I love him so. Dear God, please understand. That I've been afraid, cold. And because I've been cold nobody's loved me. Except Ian – no, even Klaus, too, he's loved me. And the kids . . . they've all loved me – what am I to do? What am I to do, God, if he won't come back?

The rifle slept like a snake, lit by the coals. As if it could wake and strike at any moment, whenever and at whom it wished. Oh make him come back fast, she begged. Emboldened by the firelight, a dusky scorpion crossed the rock where MacAdam had sat, its arachnid tail held high in warning.

Her body was frozen, knowing something approached. Ian, please come down soon. She could not move her hand towards the rifle, seeing it ready to strike, feeling already its fangs in her hand. No, I'm fine, she told herself firmly. It's just the night.

# Chapter 36

From his new position MacAdam could still not see the lion. He licked a finger and wet the insides of his nostrils but smelled only the stones and the sharp coolness from the peak, the *commiphora* breathing the recent rain back out of their brittle trefoil leaves, the red, rocky soil awaiting tomorrow's sun.

A heavy listlessness made him want to stay. Or will the lion go down after Rebecca? He pulled his eyes away from the slope and crawled a few paces, turned back and raised his head to look again. I should stay here, something tells me. She's down there, she has the rifle. Reluctantly he shifted downhill between the clustered boulders to the hilltop where he'd shot the Somali, where the rocks were smaller and if the lion came he'd see him. Which means the lion won't come this way. If he's too smart to cross the scree he won't come up this slope either. He's old and wise but doesn't know this place. A refugee from up north, Ethiopia's last lion.

This means he's very smart and very experienced, and probably very hungry to be doing this. A flake of

319

the Somali's bone tinkled underfoot. If the lion circles to the east the camel will smell him. So he'll come from the west. The southwest. MacAdam imagined the lion moving towards camp, head high against a black mane, eyes inquiringly empathetic, the statuesque stealth of his kind, the power that can make itself invisible.

Warwar came upslope through the deep rocks. The camel stirred as he passed downwind, sensing rather than smelling him, the familiar notion of him. He wondered again where the male was. The male would never stay out alone, leave the female. Criminal if Rashid lost him – a strong young male like that.

Beyond the camel the sandy gully led round an angle of stone on which Warwar could see the reflected glow of Rashid's fire. Why's he so afraid?

In case Rashid was not sitting by the fire but guarding among the rocks, Warwar stayed in the shadows, slid the rifle forward, set it down, slid one-armed silently alongside it, raised and lifted it forward, put it down and inched up beside it, the rocks scraping his ribs, the water near, almost in his mouth.

His heart was hammering so loud he feared Rashid would hear it. For a moment the fire's reflection on the gully wall profiled an animal cut into the rock, a long-horned, broad-shouldered ancient beast as on the cave walls of Marrehan, put there by God to tell men of the old ways. As he shifted closer the animal became a crouching leopard, shoulders tensed to strike, long haunches rippling back. This was a bad omen but he pushed nearer, almost in the open.

There in the fire's glow sat the whitewoman, wrapped in the goat cloak. Sliding his head and shoulders into the gully Warwar came closer but could not see Rashid. He's up there watching. If I come into camp now he could kill me; then I'll never get water. Despite this thirst it is better to wait for him to come, then shoot him easily. With the whitewoman loosely in his sights Warwar settled among the deep rocks, his stub arm aching terribly.

MacAdam decided maybe the lion had circled below the scree and had smelled the rifle and left. Maybe he wasn't hungry. What if it wasn't a lion? He glanced at Leo rising in the northeast, head and shoulders above Gamud's crenelated peaks. Be careful, Leo said. Careful of what? Of what you haven't thought of. Of what you don't expect.

He crept towards the water hole, avoiding the sandy patches for the rustle that they made against his soles, silent on the loose, rough rock, till he could see the fire and Rebecca beside it, the coals reddening the goatskin draped round her and reflecting dully on the curved wall of the gully beyond.

Of what you see but don't expect and therefore aren't seeing. She seems to be sleeping. The lion isn't coming from the north or east because of the scree and the wind, nor from the south because of the open lava, so he can only come in through the deep stones between the gully and the lava. From the southwest quadrant. Where I see no movement. I'll go down, see her, check things from there.

As the fire died the rifle-snake crept closer. If she put more dung on the coals the gun would retreat, but she could not reach towards the pile of dung or the snake-rifle would strike her hand. It had been watching like this for a long time and soon it would kill her. If *he* would just come back – but, no, he's got a snake rifle slung over his shoulder, and it reached out lovingly and sank its fangs into his neck. I'm just thinking this because it *seems* true, but really there isn't any snake, only this rifle, and soon I'll reach out and pat it, to be sure.

But if Ian doesn't come and the fire doesn't die, if it's true what I've always feared, that there's no end to evil? Then I'll wait for ever for this snake to strike, and the fire will grow darker and darker but never go out, and I'll get thirstier and thirstier and colder and colder but never die, and that's what happens after life, that's what it means to be in Hell.

MacAdam took a last look before dropping down into the gully and the water hole. The lion won't come up behind because of the wind, unless he scorns our sense of smell but knows we have a gun. Then he'd stalk me from behind. But what if all the time I thought he was hunting her he's been hunting me?

He felt immediate dread, his back tightening in terror as he spun round, and there was the lion huge and black in the last electric instant of its leap, tawny coat and rippling muscle, forepaws like mountains to sever and destroy him, great jaws to chew him down, and finger tightening on the trigger he regretted this loss of Rebecca and all the desert dawns and cool highlands of his life, sensed the lion would kill her too and pulled the trigger as the barrel was coming up, a shot that ricocheted against rock and made the lion grunt and swerve, MacAdam firing three more shots that leaped and sang among the stones, his ears ringing with the blasts that then echoed back from Gamud peak. The lion had vanished. Wounded. Now he's coming in for sure.

Warwar ducked, trying to hear between the rifle's echoes for a footstep, any sound, but when the echoes died away there was nothing, no moans, no sound of camels, nothing. The gun was not Rashid's, but a different kind he'd never heard before. Four shots ricocheting at three different angles. Had someone shot Rashid? There'd been no thump of bullet hitting flesh, no clatter of dropped rifle or slap of body falling down. No running, no voices. None of the accoutrements of death.

When he looked up the whitewoman was gone.

# Chapter 37

Expecting the lion's leap he ran downhill, afraid it had already killed Rebecca. When he leaped into the gully she wasn't there. 'Rebecca!' he screamed, 'Rebecca! Rebecca!' He ran up out of the gully, couldn't see her tracks; M'kele's gun fired and he ran towards it, the lion streaking at him as he raised his gun but then he realized it was she grabbing him. 'The lion!' he shouted, trying to see above her head and looking all round as she hugged him.

'I thought they'd shot you, so I grabbed the snake and came to kill them. It was *them*!'

'*Who*?' Shadow, in the rocks beyond the gully – the lion?

'The ones who shot!'

'That was *me* – at the lion!'

'What lion?' Her teeth were chattering and he tried to warm her with his arm, pushing her toward the fire. 'It was *them*,' she pleaded.

'Who?' The shadow moved, beyond the gully. He shoved her aside and fired, the bullet smashing off a rock. The shadow gone – imagination – why had the lion come that way? How'd he get beyond the gully?

She jammed her foot against a rock. '*They*'re down there!'

'*Who*?' Still nothing behind. He'll come upwind.

'The Somalis!'

'You *saw* them?'

She locked her leg against the slope. 'The one you just shot at was a Somali.'

He threw his and M'kele's guns over one shoulder, snatched her up and ran down to the gully, dropped her and spun round: there was no lion.

'Pick up all the dung you can find,' he said – 'I'll guard you.'

Ignoring his thirst Warwar tried to decide what had happened. The whites had just killed Rashid and one of them had now just shot at him among the boulders and a sliver of bullet or rock had gone into his side, not deeply, but bleeding and painful. There were at least two whites plus the whitewoman – he had heard the second rifle that spoke with a deep sharp voice like the first – guns he'd never heard before. When he killed them he'd have their guns, but they'd not be easy to kill. He could hear the voices of one whiteman and the whitewoman now in the gully – he sounded excited and she afraid – but where was the other whiteman, who'd shot the second gun?

The fire ruddied the dark cliffside of the gully, bringing to MacAdam's mind the word 'Masada' but he did not think about it or about the crushed ache of his chest or the dizzy nauseous hunger for sleep. If the lion comes down the gully I'll have at least a second after he comes round the rock before he gets me. Time for three shots fast or two well-placed, or none well-placed if I'm startled. If he comes from up the gully it's not so easy – he'll leap on me from this side so I have to swing the gun and there's maybe time for one shot. Which means he'll come that way because he knows it's harder for me. Or he'll figure I'll think that and he'll come up the gully instead. No matter which way I think he'll come, he'll come the other way. Or he'll wait on the overhang till I move out to feed the fire. If he comes across the top he can't leap on us directly because of the overhang but will have to land first on the ground then turn to leap on us. Despite the angle that gives time for two shots. No matter which way he comes he'll wait till I close my eyes for one second or turn to look at her or stop watching in all directions at once. 'Why'd you shoot, up there?' he asked her.

Beside him, pointing M'kele's gun up the gully, she seemed to feel as if fundamentally he'd failed her. 'I dropped it. It fired by itself.'

If the lion's so hungry why didn't he kill the camel? Unless he's too old or hurt or he's an Ethiopian rogue used to eating corpses from the wars up there or in Sudan. How'd he attack from the east and moments later be going down the gully on the west? Unless he has a female hunting with him?

'Ian, *please*!' She wanted to tell him about this snake that could change itself into a rifle, but he wouldn't believe it. '*Please* let's go!'

327

'So he jumps us in the darkness? Kills me first and then comes after you? Or so the camel goes crazy with fear, and we lose her?'

'The camel's not afraid because she knows it's *them*! The one you shot at above the gully – if he was a lion he'd have scared the camel!'

'The wind's changed, to the north. He circled from the south.'

'I don't care,' she yelled, shutting him out. 'We won't live to see tomorrow!'

He nodded at the stars. 'It's already tomorrow. Soon as it's light we cross the ridge. Two more days we'll be in Faille.'

She turned her back, made him disappear. He has no right to keep me from going out there. I'm a separate human being just like him. If you're a passenger in a car and the driver's driving crazy you've got the right to make him stop and let you out.

Nothing to stay or go back for. Hyaenas in the night, packs of wild dogs fattened on desert refugees. This man a stranger. All strangers. Get back to France I'll leave him. Not going back to France. Yes, take the boys and go to France. Over her shoulder she sneered at this stranger behind her. 'You won't *live* to see Faille.'

Either you have power over your life or you're its slave. If you're its slave then your life has nothing and you become slave to a slave. On and on the generations, each new life deeper enslaved. That's what Allah means by Hell.

That's where I'll go if I let them kill Rashid without

revenge, take my whitewoman. Warwar thought this in the voice of the elder he would become, an old man wounded in many wars and rich with plunder, his one hand still deadly with knife or gun, surrounded by his young laughing wives and grandchildren glossy as bullocks in the sun.

As the night paled he forced himself to approach the gully, near as he dared, smelt its smouldering dung and the whiteman's sweaty hair and the sour odour of the whitewoman, but there was no sign or smell of the other whiteman who had fired the second gun, so Warwar withdrew till he was beyond view, lying on his back in agony as night gave way to day. He awoke from a strange dream of peace to the distant clack of camel hooves on stone, raised his eyes above his clutch of rocks to see a whiteman leading the whitewoman on a camel north up Gamud towards the ridge. He stood and aimed the rifle, but it was too far and the barrel would not stop shaking from being held across his stub arm, and he remembered the other whiteman and ducked quickly. The two whites with the camel cut left towards a saddle in the ridge, the sky dawning orange above them.

Still he could not see or hear the other whiteman. Keeping low, he advanced to the edge of the gully. There were only the tracks of one whiteman in strange-toothed boots and the whitewoman in her flat rubber shoes and the prints of the camel. Perhaps the other whiteman has taken the male camel and gone a different way. Then it's safe to drink.

He ran to the water hole, glanced round; there was

no danger; he ducked down it and drank.

When he could drink no more he climbed out of the gully to watch the camel and two whites cross the saddle and swing right along Gamud's northern shoulder. He returned and searched the gully but found no other tracks, nor any on the slopes nearby, then, slightly lower, in loose lava sand the imprint of an enormous lion paw, larger than a man's head. Anew Warwar felt fear, and knowledge of his missing arm and the blood smell it made, and the fresher blood smell of his waist where the stone or bullet fragment had pierced it. The whiteman did this, he reminded himself. He who killed my clansman Rashid. He searched the rocky slope: there was no glimmer of Rashid's cloak or the dark lump of his body – the lion had taken him off.

He sat on a rock and traced in his mind the way the whites would go to reach the road: there was water only in one place, and once they drank that water they would go no further.

He remembered the dream. Soraya had married someone else but one night came to lie with him and he grew full of love for her again, and said, 'why did you stone me, with the others?'

'No one stoned you. That was just your dream. You're loved by everyone.'

He felt warm and satisfied, went down the water hole and drank himself full again. He urinated against the rock which had changed, the night before, from long-horned ancient antelope to leopard, then forced himself to drink again.

Even though earthly life is but delusion Allah wishes

us to act as if it's real. Shouldering the rifle, Warwar began to ascend the mountain.

# Chapter 38

MacAdam walked sleeping, waking every few minutes to glance round, when the camel altered her pace at his side, or the ground shifted. In daylight the lion wouldn't follow, nor was it likely he'd track them to attack tonight. Since last night Rebecca had remained aloof, as though he'd failed her in the deepest way, and he was no longer a person who mattered to her. But I never did, he reflected, dozing as he walked.

He liked this exhaustion because it left him free: there was something in him too tired to fight back. He could admit there was a commonality he and she would never share, her alienation that he'd never breach, and the part of him that would reject this was too tired to defend her.

I'd just be another Klaus on which to paint her disappointments, someone to blame because the world's not as it seemed when she was fourteen. The world's made sorrowful by too much thinking, too much wanting, like the Somalis killing elephants so the Japanese can carve their tusks into trinkets people buy because they want to do what's done, because they're blind men at the feast, believing what's believed solely because others believe it, those who also never tried to see what's true. A thousand generations, more, of lies. As if life's a contest to be the most alike, the least alive.

Dorothy never banished me from her heart like this one does, any moment she pleases retreating into her disenchantments. Dorothy never disgraced me by sullenly doing my will against her own; Dorothy doesn't blame.

And even if it's too late for me and Dorothy, too many wrong turns too long ago ever to mend, why do I need or want to be with anyone? Sell the ranch, split it with Dorothy, buy a boat in Mombasa and sail the Indian Ocean, wherever the wind goes. Hike from Kashmir through Nepal to Sikkim and Bhutan, as I've always wanted – walk like crazy Grogan from Capetown to Cairo.

Like the desert wind the world grew infinite with possibilities. Why live as if you *have* to do this, or that? When you die all the *having* disappears – why be prisoner of it now?

'For two years I haven't been able to forget her,' he'd said to Nehemiah that afternoon outside the barracks, before the broken piston rod, the desert, dead M'kele. 'She intoxicates me.'

'Hey, Mac, look into your Latin,' Nehemiah'd answered. 'In-toxicates. Poison.'

It's easy to love someone who's not there, you can make her what you want. Isn't love slavery too? Why *need* anything at all?

In the bitter little granite church on the bitter Cotswold heath, in driving wind and rain, he'd clutched his little coat round him and clamped shivering bare knees, bit his tongue when they sang, 'Love like the golden daffodil is coming through the snow, Love like the golden daffodil is Lord of all I know.' Why, he'd wondered, be grateful for so little? When there's so much more?

Every death you make claims you, as every joy. I didn't kill the lion and the lion went away. It was right not to shoot the prisoners. Have no enemies and no enemies will have you. 'A man's nothing without enemies,' dear M'kele'd say. That's Maasai talk – I can't live for you, M'kele.

By late afternoon they rounded the shoulder of Gamud peak and their shadows stretched far ahead on the ground before them, the shelved rocks and distant vistas of the desert draining back the sun. Ahead MacAdam could see the tiny fork-branched outlines of two doum palms against the yellowed rock: this would be the spring marked on the map, last water until Faille.

This was the desert's edge; already there were more animals. A jackrabbit scurried through the scrub, tiny puffballs of dust hanging in the air behind it; he could see a single distant giraffe browsing the crown of an acacia, and occasionally the sinuous track of a snake or the hurried splay-footed prints of a honey badger. A long-tailed whydah fluttered over, dropped his wings to perch on a gnawed umbrella thorn to watch them pass. Nests of weavers hung like miniature Luo baskets from the umbrella thorn's branches; sunbirds and barbets flashed their golden wings like reflections of the desert, and a pair of yellow-billed hornbills fluttered from a euphorbia.

Soon the female hornbill will lay her eggs in a tree hollow and seal up the hole with mud and wattle, leaving only a tiny hole through which the male will feed her and the young until they're old enough to fly. Over how many million years has this evolved? Now as Africa dies the last hornbills die also, and their different way of caring for each other dies as well.

What goes through the male hornbill's heart as he scours the desert all day for food to bring home to his family locked in their tree? What if he's killed – what happens to them?

Don't those children grow best whose parents stay united? '*Pookay olayoni oloyonisa osina*,' the Maasai say, the best man is the boy who was eaten by trouble, but trouble comes to us all, without a parent's desertion. What if my father hadn't died in the battle for Fourneax Woods? There's no way it would have been better for Rebecca's sons to leave their father and come with me; no matter how selfish and unimaginative Klaus is, he's *their* father; it's he, not I, who brought food to their closed-up nest.

Nor can I pretend that Africa's not lost – the hornbill, elephant, lion, hyaena, sunbird, cheetah, and all the other thousands of species doomed by the plague of man. Africa, the Amazon, every wild place, nearly all vanished now, the last vestiges gone in my lifetime. And this has broken my heart for so long now, because I've loved the wild, loved animals, the forests, each tree and bush and river and hidden spring, those I know and those I'll never see, each heath and wild shore and the herds of wildebeest and zebra far as the eye can see, and then beyond, then beyond that, outspanned beyond time – the magnificent multiplicity of earth reduced now to these few outposts, these last cornered survivors of rain forest and savannah to be eliminated in my days, before my sons are old.

And for what? For mindless teeming humankind choking in its smog-bound anxious cities, this mass which follows itself around in circles, doing what it tells itself to do and what it can't help doing. For the fools who bring medicine to Africa without birth control, like giving a patient a drug which makes him feel good while poisoning his future. For the automobile, the newest tyrant to which poor man is vassal, that kills his cities, strips the land, poisons the very air and future so now even the climate is withered, the world becomes a desert and the desert turns to Hell.

Humans in their groping inessential cruelty seemed not evil but subjects of an infinite condolence. He smiled up at her, appreciating the beauty of the slanting sun against her hair. I could share her with a thousand men, share her with all life. Nothing would matter. 'I don't care. I'm free.'

'Of me?'

'Of you, too. But I was thinking of how I've loved Africa, the whole earth, and ached because I knew it's lost, and now I don't ache any more, because I accept it's truly lost and there's nothing I can do.'

'What if I'm madly in love with you and follow you everywhere?'

'You're never madly in love with anyone. You won't let yourself, Rebecca. I've been happier with you, more *myself* than I've ever been before. But being myself, seeing myself, I see that it can't be.'

She rode in silence, as if there were a transparent wall between them and nothing he had said had reached her, or if she were not really there, a two-dimensional celluloid image projected beside him.

'When I almost died and the woman of the jawbone brought me to the *geb* tree, I thought that I could live alone. The Warwar saved me from the leopard, then from the Borani, then from the other Somali, from thirst. Then you've come all this way to bring me back, and your friend M'kele died – all this was one person giving to another. I've realized it was possible,' she added after a while, 'that if we had a long time, together, I could learn to give myself to you.'

His heart wrenched. Have I been rejecting so I wouldn't be rejected? Could we be together, all our lives? He reached up to take her hand; his motion alarmed her camel and it snapped back at his face, his glasses flying off, crunched beneath the camel's hoof. 'Bloody hell!' he yelled, forgetting the sense of peace he'd been feeling. The glasses were crushed; he tossed them away and glanced around, eyes stunned and unreliable. 'It won't matter now. Soon we'll reach the spring. We'll get water there and keep moving. If we go all night we'll be in Faille by noon.'

From the shoulder of Gamud Warwar watched the tiny camel and two whites inch across the golden savannah, their long shadows cast before them, the deeper shadows of the western hills slinking up behind them.

He was exhausted by his fast direct climb over the peak, which had allowed him to travel only a third of the distance the whites had come, in the same time; yet he felt energized and elated by the coolness of the heights and the vast panorama over which he ruled like an eagle, as God must see the world.

He rested briefly, checking the rifle to ensure that the magazine was properly connected and a cartridge seated in the chamber and the sights clean and the ejection mechanism working. He was pleased at how well already his single arm did the work of two; as he manoeuvred the rifle across his knees he had barely noticed now the absence of a second hand. Yes, I have severed that which was unclean; now nothing mars me. She who was my white sister has cast her lot with he who tried to kill me; she also I shall sunder. God has brought me over the mountain to destroy His enemies; He will not fail me now.

There were recent bone chips near the doum palms, reminding MacAdam that our greatest needs entail our greatest dangers. There were tracks of several antelope since the storm; they had barely drunk. The spring, small and eroded under its ledge of stone, seemed hardly to have profited from the rain. 'How much in the canteens?' he called.

'Two full ones and a bit.'

'We'll drink them then refill them.' Roping the camel to a palm trunk, he knelt and dipped his bush hat into the water and held it to the camel. She sniffed the water, curled her white-pink, bristled lips to bare her yellow teeth, huffed and craned away.

'She drank a lot this morning,' Rebecca said. 'She won't be thirsty now for several days.'

MacAdam wet a finger and raised it to his lips. 'It's brackish, that's all. The other was sweeter.'

She handed him a canteen. 'Let's drink all we have and refill the canteens. We'll drink this brackish stuff tomorrow, if we need it, before we get to Faille.'

'So French of you – the best wine first.'

'This is no marriage feast.'

Her words stung but he told himself soon he would be free, glancing up at the peak all dark-silvery and crimson with sunset, seeing there a flash of wing or something white among the rocks – a beisa oryx, maybe; without his glasses he couldn't be sure. Maybe he should shoot it and they'd have something to eat. But no, he would not shoot it, wouldn't kill a creature in the wild again; once more he felt at peace and finished drinking the canteen she'd given him, no longer mindful of her retort but looking out across the northern peneplain to the imagined locus of a town called Faille, where all this would end. Dear M'kele, if we'd only caught them on the Ewaso N'giro.

'Years from now,' he said, 'do you suppose we'll look back on this with longing?'

She knelt to fill her empty canteen, 'Not I.' She tied the canteen to her camel saddle.

The sunlight was fading from the land and rising up the eastern peaks; its shadow brought a cool breeze from the north; far above an eagle circled, crying. It must be he I saw, he thought, among the rocks.

'God, I'll always miss this,' he said. 'No matter how far I go. I'll miss M'kele and always grieve his death, and Kuria, whom you don't know – I'll miss you . . .' Seeing her now in the peak's reflected light he knew how much he loved her but that she was lost to him, lost for ever, and was glad, saw the sunset and was glad. 'No matter where I go, I'd like to always—'

He had thought the words already, 'live like this', but never said them, never thought again, for Warwar's bullet travelling at three thousand feet per second took all his thoughts away in a moment of infinite pain, smashed them into pulp which it sprayed upon the rocks, her face, the doum palms, the camel, and the noise and her scream and camel braying all were one; he was dead upon the ground as she held him, weeping for what would never be.

When she saw the boy-killer walking down the slope she had the sudden recognition of enormous sin: I've brought this down upon us. I am the death of love. For eternity I will escape and be recaptured and everyone I love will die for me. She scrambled over MacAdam and ran into the desert.

Warwar lowered Ibrahim's rifle on a rock and aimed between the whitewoman's shoulders as she ran, smiling to think she was even too stupid to cut back and forth evasively – even the gazelle knows that. The thought of her stupidity made his body want her and he did not fire – there was no reason to, really; with the camel he would catch her easily. He slung his rifle over his back, descended to the spring, glanced at MacAdam's body and the wide dark pool it made, inspected the two rifles. He turned and kicked MacAdam. 'Assassin of Rashid, trickster who made it seem there were two of you when there was but one! God has punished you!'

He loved this time the best, when daylight lifted from the land. In the distance the whitewoman's pale form shifted and diminished in day's last rising heat; he glanced at the empty canteens by the spring. Fools. He crossed to the camel, untied the canteen from the saddle and drank it down, feeling its bitterness soak into his cells. God's greatest gift to man is water. He untied the camel then suddenly sat still holding the camel's sisal reins. For a moment now he would rest before he chased her down, here in the soft chanting of the palm leaves.

Dark's silk curtain fell across the land. She walked steadily and fast. In the nothingness was no one. The boy-killer did not come; the stars moved slowly on their appointed rounds. Whatever truths the universe held were of no significance to men.

There was no sound but the crunch of her feet against the desert floor. Ahead of her the Great Bear wheeled slowly in a circle, his tail caught in the trap of the north star.

By midmorning she could see a distant plume of golden dust move from west to east across the land: the Addis road, Faille. She glanced back at Gamud sombre in the sunlight; no one followed. She beat down a fierce exuberance. It did not matter if she lived or died, but if she lived she would live it to the bone.

\* \* \*

Baring his teeth at the distant smell of soldiers and camels coming northwards, the old lion swerved east as he crossed the invisible line the white men had drawn, one day a century ago in London, between the places they called 'Ethiopia' and 'Kenya'. With the long steady lope of a great cat he shifted uphill among the deeper stones then south across the eroded, empty plains, where in his youth the tall grass had waved and the antelope had filled the land to its horizons, and countless lion prides had sung to one another from the hilltops.

# A selection of bestsellers
# from Headline

**FICTION**

| | | |
|---|---|---|
| GASLIGHT IN PAGE STREET | Harry Bowling | £4.99 □ |
| LOVE SONG | Katherine Stone | £4.99 □ |
| WULF | Steve Harris | £4.99 □ |
| COLD FIRE | Dean R Koontz | £4.99 □ |
| ROSE'S GIRLS | Merle Jones | £4.99 □ |
| LIVES OF VALUE | Sharleen Cooper Cohen | £4.99 □ |
| THE STEEL ALBATROSS | Scott Carpenter | £4.99 □ |
| THE OLD FOX DECEIV'D | Martha Grimes | £4.50 □ |

**NON-FICTION**

| | | |
|---|---|---|
| THE SUNDAY TIMES SLIM PLAN | Prue Leith | £5.99 □ |
| MICHAEL JACKSON The Magic and the Madness | J Randy Taraborrelli | £5.99 □ |

**SCIENCE FICTION AND FANTASY**

| | | |
|---|---|---|
| SORCERY IN SHAD | Brian Lumley | £4.50 □ |
| THE EDGE OF VENGEANCE | Jenny Jones | £5.99 □ |
| ENCHANTMENTS END Wells of Ythan 4 | Marc Alexander | £4.99 □ |

*All Headline books are available at your local bookshop or newsagent, or can be ordered direct from the publisher. Just tick the titles you want and fill in the form below. Prices and availability subject to change without notice.*

Headline Book Publishing PLC, Cash Sales Department, PO Box 11, Falmouth, Cornwall, TR10 9EN, England.

Please enclose a cheque or postal order to the value of the cover price and allow the following for postage and packing:
UK & BFPO: £1.00 for the first book, 50p for the second book and 30p for each additional book ordered up to a maximum charge of £3.00.
OVERSEAS & EIRE: £2.00 for the first book, £1.00 for the second book and 50p for each additional book.

Name .................................................................................

Address ..............................................................................

.............................................................................................

.............................................................................................